MW01701739

Potion Master

Fate Cycle Book 1

Sam Fairburn

SAM FAIRBURN PUBLISHING

Sam Fairburn Publishing

Website: www.samfairburn.com

ISBN : 978-1-998204-00-7 (Paperback)

ISBN : 978-1-998204-01-4 (eBook)

Legal Deposit

Library and Archives Canada 2023

Edited by Corinne DeMaagd at CMD Writing and Editing

Proofread by Samantha Gove at Raven's Wing Editing Services

Cover art by Eric Robillard at Kinos

Content Notes

Some content in this novel may be disturbing or triggering for some readers. Reader discretion is advised. Your mental health matters.

Subjects include but are not limited to: light power play/BDSM, mention of bullying, stalking, kidnapping, loss/death of family, scenes of trauma, instances of violence on page, and instances of death on page. This book contains graphic sexual scenes and strong language. This book should not be used as a reference or guide for safe power play/BDSM practices.

This book is not intended for anyone under the age of legal adulthood.

This book ends on a cliff-hanger.

If you have any questions pertaining to these warnings, please contact the author, Sam Fairburn.

www.samfairburn.com

Prologue

RILEY (20 years ago...)

The soft stone of the pendant was cold and heavy in Riley's small hand. She focused her attention on its weight in an attempt to calm her racing heart.

Orange morning light filtered across the space, bathing the small cottage kitchen in warm, golden hues. Dust, like snow, was floating through the rays. By all accounts, it should have been a peaceful sight, but the fiery brightness only bolstered the girl's unease.

"Stop fiddling with that necklace. It won't do the work for you, child," Diane said. The woman moved through the kitchen with quiet efficiency, her brows drawn in concentration.

Dry herbs and wicker baskets hung from the ceiling in an unruly array of shapes and forms. The hearth was playing twin to the heat of the bright summer day. Many different bottles and jars were aligned on the enormous wooden table, ready to be filled with small miracles, little healing concoctions that would go on to help skeptical clients.

Nobody wanted to believe in witches, but when desperation hit and options withered, the minds of the villagers turned to the back road leading to *la ramancheuse's* vast gardens. *The fixer*—that's what they called Diane, and that's what they would call Riley one day, or so she hoped.

Every witch had an affinity for at least one magical discipline. Early on, Diane determined that Riley was, first and foremost, a healer. Riley still didn't understand why the universe kept laughing at her in that way. She was convinced the energy coursing through her veins was more diaphanous smoke than rays of sunshine.

Riley drew her hands to her lap once again, like she usually did when she was caught fidgeting. She needed to be brave. She didn't want to disappoint her teacher, but she didn't *feel* brave at all. "I'm sorry," Riley whispered. "I don't think I'm ready yet."

Warm, brown eyes landed on her. Diane wiped her hands on her apron before crouching beside the corner chair Riley was sitting in. She motioned Riley to do the same as her. And so, they both put their palms onto the earth of the potted plant Riley had been staring at for the last hour.

Riley knew what was coming. Even though she was only ten, her knowledge of the healing mixtures' chemistry, as well as the body's biology, was extensive. Now was the time to train herself to use her own mystical abilities to strengthen the results. Her tutor seemed so sure of her talent, but Riley couldn't help the concern rising in anticipation.

"Concentrate. Do as I've taught you. Close your eyes. Breathe in through your nose and out through your mouth slowly," Diane said.

Riley did as instructed.

"Now, visualize a soft greenish-white light coming from your heart, flowing through your upper limbs and into the dirt."

This part was a little more challenging. The light twirling behind Riley's eyes was rebellious and disorganized. Calling it to heel would be a feat in and of itself.

"That's good, Riley. You're doing great. All you have left to do is move that healing energy into the thyme's root system so we can harvest it with the plant later."

After a few minutes of focused silence, curiosity got the best of Riley. She cracked open her eyes. Diane had withdrawn her hands from the dirt. A warm glow was coming from the plant as if a small sun had grown at its center. Eyes wide, she looked at the thyme, mesmerized—awe her only companion. Of course, she had seen Diane do this before, but she was achieving it all by herself this time. In that fateful moment, the fullness of her heart was almost painful.

Thump. Thump. Thump. Th-Thump.

Her heart skipped a beat.

No.

It was all she had time to think before a cascade of goosebumps started from the top of her head and went right down her body to her feet and into the ground. She closed her eyes and creased her forehead in concentration in an attempt to control the disturbing sensation. The backs of her eyelids were now painted in shadows.

Tendrils of black fog soon replaced the peaceful healing light that had previously crowded her veins.

Then, everything went still like it usually did when something important was about to happen.

That's when it started—the pain—it was everywhere. In every breath she took, in every part of her body, in every tremor, in every heartbeat.

Riley's muscles locked up in a losing battle to keep her in place. The carpeted ground welcomed her fall. A powerful ringing reverberated in an endless loop through her eardrums. Time lost all meaning. The intense throbbing torture became the backdrop of her existence. She couldn't get away from it all. She was well and truly locked into herself.

Riley was dying; she was certain of it.

In that moment, lost between agony and anguish, strong hands seized her shoulders, triggering a fresh flare of pain.

It started with a whisper. Then the distant voice grew stronger until it was right there, close enough to touch, to hold on to. A lifeline.

"Riley! Riley! Come back to the light, child! I cannot help you with this. You need to fight this! Push against it! *Push!*" Diane roared.

Riley's mouth opened, but only a pitiful groan of pain escaped. She wanted to tell her mentor that she had made a mistake—that Riley wasn't good or courageous or even deserving enough of Diane's teachings. Diane should just let her float away before Riley's darkness engulfed the whole world.

An image of her adoptive parents broke through the tempest of her mind.

Her light.

She latched onto it with all the strength she had left. The progress was slow. Her whole body was made of plasticine and needles. The sound of blood pumping through her veins was her only indication she was still in the world of the living.

When her gaze was finally able to focus on reality, she noted that the kitchen space had stayed the same throughout the whole ordeal. That knowledge comforted Riley. At least, she hadn't destroyed anything, or so she thought.

Diane was sitting on the floor beside her, looking at Riley's face and at something beside her in turn. Riley's body was slowly awakening back to itself, and pressure was steadily building on the right palm of her hand. When she was finally able to lift it to her face, she realized the wrongness of what had just happened.

The thyme was dead. Its once beautiful purple flowers were brown and gelatinous, showing an advanced state of decomposition. It was hanging limp from her shaking fingers.

Riley felt tears dripping from the corner of her eyes and gathering at her hairline. Shame invaded every part of her small body as grief for this once beautiful little plant life engulfed her. Diane moved to help her up, but Riley jerked away, scared that she would hurt her teacher in turn.

"You cannot hurt me, girl. Let me help you. It's fine."

But Riley didn't believe her. It would never be fine again.

Chapter 1

RILEY

The blue liquid is shimmering like its magic is trying to get out. One of my better cocktail recipes, I would say. *The Siren,* I call it, in honor of Evie. Even though she is not one of those long-extinct creatures, her voice bewitches her crowd all the same. Her tales captivate the audience with their rhythm and poesy.

"Hey! Will you give me my drink or not?" the patron shouts over the buzz of the crowded room.

Keeping hold of the glass, I swiftly glide it over the wooden bar toward him. "I don't know, Carl. Maybe a little more respect and a smile now and then could do miracles for your shitty personality and help you get what you want." I look the bastard straight in the eye, drink the shot myself, and take the money he had put on the bar top to pay for it. The liquid goes down like the charm that it is, giving me a boost of strength and energy in its wake.

Carl seizes my gloved forearm, "Listen, girl, I know that you're new here, but when I ask—"

His touch is gone in an instant. A big, burly man hauls Carl by the collar of his shirt toward the pub's door. Albert's gray-brown ponytail sways in time with Carl's feet off the ground as he carries Carl out the door. If I didn't hate being manhandled by drunk pieces of shit so much, I would be laughing at the sight.

Albert grunts as he throws Carl on his ass out in the street. "Take the rest of the night to cool off," Albert says, his voice deceptively calm. "The next time you touch one of my employees, you will lose your hand. Is that understood?"

Carl has the good sense to shut his mouth and skitter off. The patrons all shout in triumph and merrily raise their glasses to Albert. When he turns from the door, Albert's green eyes find me. His face is all red under his thick beard. I nod my head once to show him that I am okay and can handle myself. It's not my first rodeo, after all.

I don't have much time to dwell on what happened, though. The Drunken Sailor is packed tonight. Every sticky table and disparate chair is in use. A small crowd has already gathered before the small stage in the corner where my best friend will perform tonight, sipping their drinks. The decor is no different than any other Irish pub in Québec City. The only noticeable distinction really is the customers themselves—the vast majority of them have magical abilities or ties to the magical world.

My long black hair annoys me tonight, so I quickly tie it up in a messy bun before filling another pint of my first batch of beer to give to Albert as he passes behind me in the bar area. Then I go back to the steady flow of orders coming in. I am very proud of my first brew. It's a white ale with faint notes of lavender and rosemary. The balanced taste of the herbs makes for a bittersweet lightness that, contrary to popular belief, doesn't taste like perfume.

Being potion master and lead brewer are both my pride and my passion in life. It also allows me to work anywhere, in any magical establishment I want, since there are a lot of people that seem to either want to get drunk or out of a hangover—or another predicament—at some point. My healing balms and potions are particularly good if I do say so myself.

Healing is my specialty, after all, and I was well taught. *Diane.* A sharp pang of grief makes my eyes water at the reminder of my mentor's passing. They say that home is where the heart is. Well, it feels like my home vanished with her last breath. Throughout the years, she'd always been there for me—be it to kick me in the butt for acting stupid or to help me regain my footing after yet another failed attempt at making something of my life. Her passing is too fresh for me to be able to recall the good memories of her with fondness or a smile. I am still at the anger stage, where every fiber of my being wants to cry hysterically and punch a wall about it, hating death, hating myself for not being able to heal her. I wipe furiously at my eyes and wrestle my mind into a better headspace.

I was lucky to get this job. The Drunken Sailor is one of the best breweries in the province, and its owner is allowing me carte blanche to do with the product creation as I please. All the equipment is state of the art despite the pub's building being more than a century old—and looking it.

Perfect work arrangements, awesome new apartment, my best friend nearby—it's all I need, really. This time, I will plant roots. This time, I won't bolt at the very first mild inconvenience—I can't. I have no one left to catch me from a fall. I am here to stay, and I mean it.

At the table by the door, four casters are playing at levitating objects in the air while arm wrestling. The first to either lose the strength contest or lose their concentration and drop their object pays for the next round of alcohol. A stupid game if you ask me, but still fun to watch and good for the tip.

Evie pokes her head out from the kitchen door with a mouthful of I don't even want to know what. "Hey, Ry! I'm on in a couple of minutes," she says while finishing chewing. "Do you need anything before I get up there?" She motions toward the stage with her head. The movement makes her silver dress sparkle in the dim light, contrasting nicely with the soft coffee of her skin. She recently buzzed her hair close to her head, which accentuates the graceful curve of her neck.

Her hazel eyes drift to the liquid I am currently mixing. She looks fascinated and with good reason. As soon as I sprinkle my last ingredient into the potion—dried hibiscus flowers—red fire seems to emanate from it, although it's not hot to the touch. Passion is a difficult thing to capture, and it's always mesmerizing when it's encapsulated successfully. It's easily the most expensive thing we sell here. Only one swig is needed to fuel your inspirations and fantasies, allowing you to create at will. Although it cannot put ideas into your head, it will allow you to birth your ideas into the world. Well, until it wears off, that is. I pour the liquid into a small vial and hand it over to the young woman who ordered it.

"I'm fine," I tell Evie over my shoulder. "I don't need you mothering me." I wink at my best friend and turn back to the clientele at the bar. I hear her huff and puff before letting the kitchen door swing behind her. Not a minute later, she swaggers onto the stage, her generous hips swaying as she walks. The usual auditory chaos of the pub falls to whispers.

We've always been complete opposites, Evie and I. Where my best friend shines bright on stage, I prefer the darkness at the back of the room. She is all heat and sensuality, while I am all frost and contrast. My moonlight skin, she calls it. Which is a nice way of saying that I am ghostly pale.

As soon as Evie opens her mouth to sing, the crowd starts to sway in time with the rhythm of her voice. The ones closest to the stage are completely enthralled by her story of epic love. They smile and huddle closer together, not aware that they are moving. The casters abandon their game to stare in fascination. As far away as I am, I only feel a small wave of fullness and happiness, but it's still very nice. I have not experienced the brush of love for a very long time.

I pour the next beer directly onto my gloved hand, which then splashes onto my black tank top and jeans. I curse and shake my head slightly. I must have been more affected by her singing than I thought. Taking off my gloves and wiping them on a dish towel, I smile to myself. I have not been exposed to her kind of powers for some time now. I've lost part of the endurance I had built for it.

When I finally succeed at mostly drying my clothes, I throw the rag in the sink and lift my head to take the next order, but most of the patrons have now moved from the bar to the tables closer to the stage, listening quietly.

Most, but not all.

A tall man ambles toward me with purpose. I haven't seen him here before. Rogue strands of his black mane are falling over his pale gray eyes, his mid-length hair too short to tie back. The combination of light and dark gives him an almost otherworldly look. He seems to be about my age, thirty or so. The black T-shirt and cargo pants he's wearing emphasize the strong form of his body. Even though he is probably one of the most nice-looking men I've ever seen with his sharp features and lush red lips, his warm smile makes me shiver in something akin to unease...or maybe anticipation. It's hard to tell. His friendly demeanor feels fake, practiced. Warning bells ring at the back of my mind.

The muscles of his arms are coiling as he motions for me to lean in closer to better hear his order. "Two pints of whatever you brewed last and one of your favorite drinks."

His voice is gravely, resonating through my body as surely as if he had shouted his request. Goosebumps pepper my arms at the sound. A weird mix of lust from my friend's song and irrational fear twists my insides, awakening my body. His smell seems everywhere, assaulting my senses. It is a surprisingly pleasant mix of cypress and smoke, like an evergreen forest on fire.

I hastily retreat from my position leaning over the counter and turn to the back of the bar. Now face-to-face with the mirror covering the wall behind the colorful bottles of alcohol, I notice his reflection smirking at me. I glare back at him before I lower my head. He doesn't need to see the heat slowly rising in my cheeks to boost his ego. But even then, I can feel his gaze still fixed on my back while I busy myself preparing two drinks instead of one. I really need to get a grip on my lack of sex life. It's getting embarrassing.

I turn back toward him, bounty in hand. His smile disappears as he looks at the shot glasses I'm holding. I put them down on the bar and proceed to fill two pints of ale before dropping them onto a tray so he can bring everything with him.

"You didn't specify if it was my favorite to make or to drink, so I gave you both of them."

He observes the glasses as if they were time bombs waiting to explode in his face. "What are these?"

"If you don't want them, just say it," I huff, crossing my arms over my chest.

"I asked you a question, didn't I?" he says sternly, unease now tainting his tone. He takes the drinks and lifts them to his eyes to inspect the mixtures further.

What an ass.

I grapple with the short straws of patience the gods gave me and take a deep breath. "I realize I've only been here for a week, but I know what I'm doing. No need to look like I'm trying to poison you. That wouldn't be good for business." I snicker, which he answers with a deeper scowl. I point to each of the drinks in turn. "The purple one is my favorite to make. It's part of a set of healing draughts that I developed. It helps to promote good health, a tonic, if you will. The other one is my favorite to drink. It's straight-up Canadian whisky."

The tension building between us releases at once, and a chuckle escapes his lips. "I'll leave you the whisky then."

He slides the amber liquid in my direction while taking hold of the healing potion. The stranger taps his shot on the bar two times—I do the same—and without taking our eyes off each other, we drink.

I can see the effect in him instantly. A dusting of pink appears on his cheeks, and his bronzed skin seems to glow with health under the dim lights. His brows reach his hairline in surprise.

It baffles me how people can still be shocked at the quality of my potions. I mean, it says it in my title, *Potion Master*.

"How much do I owe you, including the whisky?" he asks.

I pick up the glasses and throw them in the plastic container, already full to the brim with dirty dishes. "That'll be twenty-one-twenty for the two beers and the draught. I can pay for my own stuff, thanks."

He hands me the exact count with an arrogant smirk—no tip—and turns around, his two beers in hand, too fast for me to retort to the snide behavior. He disappears straight through the front door. We don't have patio tables, so I don't even know where he's going with his bounty. None of my concern anyway.

I turn around to pick up a rag to clean the counter and come face-to-face with a big chest. My hands fly to my heart. "Gods, Albert, announce yourself or something!"

For this hulking piece of a man, I've found that he is awfully quiet. He laughs from deep in his belly, his whole body shaking with the effort. When he does that, he reminds me of the human's Santa Claus.

"You'll get used to it, Riley," he says as he starts to help me with the patrons' orders. We work in companionable silence for a while.

Albert is the first to break the flow. "I'm sorry for that shithead, Carl," he says. "He's just sour because his boyfriend dumped him, and he needs to feel in control of something in his life again."

"How pop psychology of you," I say, bumping his shoulder with mine. Well, his arm, really. He towers over my five-feet six-inches.

"Seriously, I know you're new, but I don't joke with the safety of my employees. He will lose his hand if he pulls that stunt again. I never make empty threats." His statement is followed by a grunt. "I'm going to go see the guys in the back. Are you okay here?"

"You're the second one to ask me that tonight. My answer hasn't changed. Yes, Dad, I'm fine."

He narrows his eyes at me. "Very funny. Dad comment aside, if you need any help, just yell." Then he disappears through the kitchen doors.

After Evie's show is over, the remainder of the evening is boring and uneventful. On my last round of the night, all patrons are either too drunk to order anymore or downright sleeping in a puddle of their own retch on the ground. I've come to learn that it's like this every night. The Drunken Sailor didn't get its name from nowhere.

At three, I finally dismiss the last clients, lock the front door on an empty pub, and pick up the mop. I really hate cleaning vomit; it's the worst. I then go task by task until I am back behind the bar again. This flow of work is as natural to me as my own breathing. Some find it creepy to be alone in a big, empty space at night, even more so since the building is old and creaky, but I've always loved this part of my job. The calm of going about at my own pace grounds me after a busy night. I don't meditate, but I feel that it's as close to meditating as I've ever been.

I am drying the clean pint glasses when I hear something like a door slamming in the back. Taking the last of the dirty dishes with me, I carefully open the kitchen door. I'm doing the close tonight, so no one should be here except Albert and me, although I don't see him at the moment.

The kitchen is eerily silent. I walk over to the industrial dishwasher. Halfway there, I jump out of my skin when I hear the banging noise again. It's louder this time around. It's a miracle I didn't drop the tray of glasses on the floor. What on earth can make that much noise at this hour? The more I strain to hear anything, the more deafening the silence is. Then I can make out a muffled laugh, followed by the bang again. More muffled voices.

I set the tray on the nearest table and try to find the origin of the sounds. I end up in front of a big, metal door marked *Security*. I've never paid attention to it until now. I just assumed it was a service entrance of some sort. There are no tenants under us. There is not even one window that leads to the old basement.

I try the handle, but it won't budge. That's when I spot a small black square piece of metal situated beside the door. After further inspection, it seems to have hinges at the top to be able to open it. When I lift it carefully, it reveals a glass pane with a green light behind it. I've seen something similar to this once before at a rich client's home. What is down there that needs to be secured by retina scanner access? All the over stock of alcohol and food is kept in the kitchen, so that's evidently not it.

Then I hear footsteps becoming louder and louder, coming closer to the door. My thoughts immediately spiral into a whirlwind of shady scenarios about that basement, and my reflexes take the lead. I sprint to the nearest stainless-steel table and hide behind it just as the door creaks on its hinges. From my position on the floor, I can hardly see anything other than footwear, but it's enough for me to know who it is. I'd recognize my boss's ugly steel-toe boots anywhere. His hefty gait moves in the direction of the liquor stash. Then comes the familiar clink of bottles and glasses being picked up. Albert walks back to the Security entrance, and a loud beep pierces the silence before he steps through to wherever that door leads.

I try to get to it before it closes, but I am not fast enough, and it shuts in my face. That's when I hear another voice on the other side of the door, louder this time. And it's a voice that I've heard before. One that is hard to forget.

Chapter 2

RILEY

MY MIND IS RACING a hundred miles per hour while I finish placing the bottles with all their labels toward me. It wouldn't be the first time that questionable activities are run under legitimate businesses. I didn't have the guts to knock on that door, just in case. I mean, I'm alone here in the middle of the night... It wouldn't be wise. I intend to get answers, though—in broad daylight and when I have more time to think about all of this, that is. Nobody will put my shiny new *simple* life in jeopardy.

It's likely nothing, and I'm making a big deal out of it. But now that my interest is piqued, I can't let it go. Diane was of the opinion that this particular trait of mine—chronic curiosity, as she called it—would kill me someday. Well, I'm still alive, so it's probably fine.

I walk back one last time into the kitchen to tell my boss I'm leaving. "Albert?" I shout. "I'm done. I'm on my way out. Do you need anything else?" My query remains unanswered. I go to the mysterious door and put my ear to it.

Still nothing. *Sigh.*

I fish my keys from my purse and make my way out of the pub, locking it behind me. I have half a mind to check for another outside door to the bar's basement, but dwelling in dark alleys at this time of night is asking for trouble.

The night air is uncommonly hot, even for July. The starless sky and rumbling thunder in the distance only add to the stuffiness. I am comforted by the familiar sight of the street that greets me. All the buildings in the historic district of Québec City look similar: French Romantic-inspired stone rowhouses with flower beds under almost every window. The faint aromas of geranium and carnation tease my nose as I take a deep breath.

As I turn the corner of the building, I see a form in the shadow, illuminated only by the red tip of some sort of cigar. My entire body tenses. It's not the first time, and it won't be the last, I'm sure, that a customer either waits for me at the end of the night or tries to follow me home. I make a show of putting my keys back into my purse while discreetly seizing my pepper spray can.

"Hey! What are you doing here?" I yell at the stranger. "The pub's closed for the night." My voice is strong and clear despite the knots in my stomach. The stranger drags another puff and with his exhale, perfect circles of smoke come out of the shadows.

A now familiar, gruff voice answers me. "A man cannot smoke in peace in the cover of the night without being disturbed by you, I see." He uncoils his whole body from the side of the building. As he pushes from the wall and his features come to light, laughing eyes meet mine. Since the cobblestone road is going uphill from where I am standing, the stranger looks even taller than earlier—maybe he is.

"Do you make a habit of dwelling in dark alleys at four in the morning?" I ask.

He looks at my hand, still wedged in my purse, then back at me. "I wasn't waiting for you, if that's what you think. I have a strong no-harassing-the-barmaids policy."

"Potion Master," I correct him.

His lips twitch as if he is trying not to smile, which prompts me to take out my pepper spray in full view just to spite him. "Potion Master," he agrees with a nod.

I turn from him and start walking down Rue Saint-Jean as I speak. "If it's all the same to you, I'll get going." I take a few normal steps before I pick up my pace. I don't know if what he is saying is true, and I don't want to find out.

A moment later, I hear heavy footsteps behind me. I swiftly turn around and see the stranger throwing his cigarette butt in an ashbin situated outside of a closed restaurant a couple of yards away. Though he is still at a healthy distance from me, the hair is standing on end at the nape of my neck. I continue to move, walking backward to keep the potential threat in my line of sight. "What are you doing?" I ask him.

He continues to advance toward me. "I'm going to my shop. Why? What are *you* doing?"

"None of your business, and I'm not that naïve to take what you say as gospel. Why are you following me?"

He stops six feet away and lifts his hands in the air. He has the nerve to smirk at me—again. "Like I just told you, I'm going to work."

I narrow my eyes at him as I tighten my fist around the cayenne spray. "To work," I deadpan. "At this time of night? Seriously, how stupid do you think I am?"

"Well, more than I thought, apparently, because I'm telling you the truth. Follow me, and you'll see." He gives me a wide berth as he walks past me.

I mentally stomp my foot and curse, but I still follow suit. I have to get home eventually, and he is going in that exact direction. It's either I follow him in the well-lit path of Rue Saint-Jean or take the small dark alleyways where anything can be lurking. Plus, at this hour, calling a taxi is a coin toss. They don't show up half of the time, and who knows what can happen while I'm waiting for the cab?

This evening keeps on giving. *Great.*

I trail after him at a careful distance, fishing my phone from my jeans pocket. I open Evie's contact in my speed dial just in case he attempts anything unsavory.

"If you're going to prowl behind me, we could at least make conversation," he shouts back at me, putting his hands in his pockets.

"Okay then, what's your name?" I have to raise my voice to make sure it carries to him, which prompts the stranger to slow his pace for me to catch up a little.

He lifts his head to the sky and sighs loudly. "Erick. My name's Erick. It's only fair that you know, *Riley Lapointe.*"

I know my full name is not a secret, but it is still unnerving that he went to the trouble of asking for it— Wait a minute. Who did he ask to get it? "Why do you know my full name, and who gave it to you?" I can't control the higher pitch my voice has taken.

"Albert mentioned he hired a new lead brewer, and I was curious."

At that, I stop walking altogether. "It was you, wasn't it?"

He turns around, his eyebrows furrowed in confusion. “Me what?”

“The voice I heard coming from the pub’s basement. Well, I heard many voices, but I could only make out two—yours and Albert’s.”

His eyes widen slightly, and his eyebrows shoot up in surprise. A pleased smile tugs at his full lips. “Inquisitive little thing, aren’t you?”

“Don’t patronize me. What’s happening in that basement?” I close the distance between us with biting steps, too irritated by him to care. It’s his turn to take a step back. My own lips quirk upward in a wolfish smile, my body finally starting to loosen up a little. Before I can continue my interrogation, he stops and inclines his head toward the sidewalk.

“We’re here,” he says.

My gaze follows his. I take the time to study the small space he is talking about, nestled between the health food store and a little café. The entrance to his shop, if I am to believe him, looks more like a door to a storage space than a store. That is probably why I never paid it any attention. Looking at it properly now, I can see the logo in the door window, and a sheet of paper stuck to the other side of the glass, telling people to duck their heads when going down the stairs.

I huff a laugh. “The Underground Castle,” I read aloud. “A medieval shop? You’re kidding me.”

He takes a key from his back pocket and unlocks the door. “I never kid about chainmail. Care to visit?”

“That’s got to be a front for something.”

His face closes at my comment, going emotionless. “My father and I started this shop when I was nineteen,” he states matter-of-factly.

I am not in the habit of feeling bad for speaking my mind, but I still want to clarify. "I was only teasing you. Is your father still working with you?"

"No, not directly." He opens the door and steps into the darkness before turning his body at the waist and looking back at me from under his curtain of raven hair. "I believe I didn't tip you properly tonight." He fishes out a coin from his pocket and tosses it out at me. The piece of metal glints in the streetlight before I easily catch it.

I turn the coin between my fingers. The hunk of metal is ancient, its faces depicting the faded portrait of a man and an old ship in turn. It looks to be made of bronze or brass. It is really heavy, a lot heavier than a coin this size should be, but it's probably because of the metal it's made of.

"What's—?" The door clicks shut behind him before I can even finish my sentence.

When I turn around, I know I am in trouble. My apartment door is staring at me from across the road. His boutique is situated directly in front of my home.

After the events of the night, I decide to make a detour before coming back home, making sure, to the best of my ability, that Erick wouldn't see where I live. I'm uneasy just remembering the total darkness of The Underground Castle's stairwell looming behind him. Who knows what could've happened to me if I had accepted his invitation? The whole interaction with him leaves a bad taste in my mouth. I hopped in the shower as soon as I arrived, just wanting to wash away the night's events.

I thought the water would help clear my head, but I'm still restless. As I comb my hair, it leaves water streaks on the midnight blue of my dressing gown. I chose this specific satin robe to match the bathroom it usually lives in. The vanity wall is painted the exact same shade of blue, which is reflected in the gold-veined blue tiles of the floor.

When they renovated the apartment, the owners decided to take out space from the bedroom and give it to the bathroom, so the bathroom is actually a good size. Enough to have a small shower and, the love of my life, a clawfoot bathtub. They also decided to keep all the original brass fixtures, including the giant mirror above the vanity.

I pick up a new towel and busy myself drying my hair. As I walk from the ensuite to the bedroom, I hear a faint sound. I close my eyes and listen more intently, letting my body guide me to the origin of the noise. It comes from my purse. I rummage through my stuff but then end up dumping the bag's contents on the bed.

I place my phone to my ear first since it's the item most susceptible to making weird and unexpected sounds.

Nothing.

My gaze drifts over the spilled contents, and I spot the coin Erick gave me. I really hope this is not what I think it is. I take it in my hand, and it is a little hot to the touch, which I couldn't feel through my gloves earlier.

Opening all my senses, I start to scan the thing to find something amiss. The light sound coming off it reminds me of the white noise one would expect from a police radio.

A tracking spell. *Shit!*

How could I be so stupid?

My heart is racing. A ton of questions are bouncing around in my head. Is Erick a caster, or was the item already spelled when he found it? It wouldn't be the first time in history that a spelled object found its way into the hands of an unaware witch or human. Or maybe it was given to him, and he gave it to me to throw whoever is after him off his trail? But if he really gave it to me on purpose, why would somebody I've never seen in my life want to bug me specifically? Or does he do this with certain females? A shudder runs through my entire body. I don't let myself finish that thought.

I need to put up wards on this apartment. It should have been the first thing I did when I arrived ten days ago.

Chapter 3

RILEY

I AM STILL RILED up about last night, lost in thought when a twisted kitchen towel stings my backside.

"Ouch! Evelyn Bouchard, that hurt!" I rub my behind, trying to avoid Evie's next blow. She has a mean whip. I am grateful for choosing sweatpants instead of shorts this morning because it would have surely bruised.

She chuckles, her weapon ready for another round. Her red maxi dress is swaying in time with her movements. "I've been talking to you for, like, twenty minutes, but you're not listening to a word I'm saying. I'm here to help you unbox everything. The least you could do is be mentally present. Where were you at?"

Of course, she's right. The kitchen is the only room left to unbox. I've been eating takeout for the last week, and I am over it. I put down the glass I am cleaning and pinch the bridge of my nose. I feel like the faded orange of the small galley kitchen will stay printed on my retinas forever. The landlord promised it would be repainted the same off-white as the living room before I moved in, but it still looks like a '70s den in here.

I haven't told Evie yet about last night, and I'm not sure I should. I don't want to alarm her. If she knew something was wrong about the pub's basement, or Erick for that matter, she would have told me. She already warned me about many of the regular clients' characters. She's been working at The Drunken Sailor for the last year; she would know.

"I'm sorry." I wince. "I'm a crappy friend today. It's just that this move is a lot, you know." My smile falters a little, and I try to hide it with a yawn.

My best friend is not duped by any of it. She gets up from her seat on the bench of the small breakfast nook.

Before she can drill me with questions, I hastily try a change of subject. "How about you? Any juicy gossip for me? Have you finally found the love of your life?"

She gives me a knowing look that tells me she'll circle back to my secrets later. "Okay, I'll bite. Between last night and today, you mean? No, not yet, and you?"

A loud snort escapes me.

Evie puts her hands on her hips, pinning me with a glare. She looks just like her mother used to when she was scolding us for borrowing her fancy clothes. "You know, if you continue like that," she warns, "you'll end up alone with a small army of cats and probably a crooked nose with your cauldron."

I guffaw. “Very funny. How do you know that’s not exactly what I want? I’m done with investing time, energy, and emotions into relationships that go nowhere. I was six years—*six years*—with Oliver before he up and left with someone else.” My tone turns bitter. “I naively thought our relationship was solid. I have no intention of repeating the same mistake twice. I won’t ever let anyone bury their claws this deep into my heart again, only to rip it to shreds when they feel like it. You were the one to spend the first week after the breakup with me. You saw how hard it was to pick myself back up.” Not to mention that if you’re not close to anybody, you cannot lose anybody—be it life taking them away from you or them leaving willingly. But I keep that last part to myself.

I take a sip from my orange juice. “I’m also allergic to cats, and you know that.”

Evie rolls her eyes. “Seriously, I feel like I’ve been telling you the same thing for the last four years. If you never put yourself out there again, how can you know you’re not missing out on *your* person? You learned from your experience with Oliver. You’ve grown wiser. As much as you want to make sure nothing like that ever happens to you again, vulnerability and trust are part of the relationship equation.”

“Um-hum.”

“Oh, stop it. We’re not all eighty-four-year-old cynics devoid of dreams. Sue me if I still believe in true love and actively search for it.”

I throw my towel at her and walk through the narrow kitchen doorway to the main area of the apartment. The large open space holds the remaining boxes. They are scattered about. The book boxes are close to the kitchen table in the dining room, soon to become my office. What's left of the kitchen boxes rests on the far wall of the living room.

The goal for today is to unpack all the remaining boxes except for the ones full of books, which are the majority of the boxes, really. Evie refuses to indulge my "addiction," as she puts it. For a person that moves as often as I do, I shouldn't lug around that number of books, but I can't help it. A lot of them are my own grimoires, and test notes that I have kept over the years. I also love to collect rare editions of my favorite herbarium. Most of it is nonfiction. It is useful—that's my excuse.

When I go back into the kitchen with another box to unpack, Evie is perched on the bay window bench, absently drying an already clean dish, looking out at something. "Who's the hot guy staring at your apartment door?"

The rowhouse where I live is divided into two apartments. To get to the second floor, I need to enter the building on the first floor and ascend an interior staircase to my door. The other tenant has a direct exterior entrance to their home on the first floor. I walk to her side and lean forward. Sure enough, I can see Erick leaning on the gray stones of his own building with his gaze fixed on my door.

He is wearing the same kind of attire I saw him in before—T-shirt, cargo pants, and an attitude to go with it. He's holding a sketchpad in one hand and a charcoal stick in the other.

I take a quick step back, fast enough to make Evie startle.

She tries to hit me another time with her dish towel. "What's the matter with you?" she says, the suspicion in her eyes only increasing with my weird behavior. She won't let it go this time.

I decide to tell her the Erick part of my evening. Hopefully, I can make it sound benign enough that she doesn't want to throttle him. "Something odd might have happened last night?" I try.

She stops her workflow abruptly, letting the plate fall back into an open box, almost breaking it. "Wait, what happened last night?"

"It's nothing, really," I hurry to say. I drop my box to take her hands, willing her to calm down. "If I tell you, you promise not to freak out?"

She pulls out of my grip and starts to play with one of her perfectly manicured nails. Her face is hard as stone. "I cannot promise you that. You're my best friend. More than that, you're my family, and I protect my family. What haven't you told me?"

Okay then. It's too late to back out now. I take a deep breath and tell her what happened with Erick the night before, skimming over some of the details, like how scary hot I found him, emphasis on the word *scary*. I know he's sketchy as fuck, but what can I say? The screwed-up behavior doesn't take away his charisma.

"That's nothing that hasn't already happened to me before." I wince. "Well, except the tracking spell part, that is."

"The asshole!" Evie yells. She makes for the door, but I put myself in her path.

"No! That's exactly the kind of reaction I didn't want you to have. We need to think this through before we do something rash, okay? Best case scenario, he's not even aware the coin was spelled."

Evie is one big, coiled spring. Her hands are closed in tight fists at her sides. Her eyes bore into me like she could vaporize me to get out of her way. "*Step aside.*"

The command resonates through my body, her power trying to make its way into my legs. I imagine my own will, like a physical thing made of the strongest diamond, surrounding me, deflecting her command. My shield works wonders, and I stay right where I am. Even out of practice, when I pay attention, I am stronger than her—a lot stronger.

Once she regains hold of herself, her eyes go wide and well with tears. All the tension in her body leaves at once. "Oh, gods!" she exclaims. "What have I done? I never meant to use my powers on you. I'm so sorry. I'm just... It's just... I'm the one who got you that job and the apartment. I don't want you to be in danger because of something I—"

"Shhh, shhh, shhh. It's fine." I wrap my arms around her. I can already feel her tears through the fabric of my old Guns N' Roses T-shirt. "It's fine, I know. Remember when your father showed you your first songs, and you accidentally bewitched the neighbor's boy with your voice?" I tell her in an attempt to make her smile.

She sniffles and laughs. "He deserved it," she says as she steps back and wipes at her eyes. "Sometimes, being a bard sucks."

I make a face at her. "You love the attention."

"I said *sometimes*, didn't I?" She moves to the fridge, grabs a bottle of water, and pours herself a glass. "Can you show me the coin?"

It takes me only a minute to retrieve it from my nightstand. I put it down carefully on the kitchen counter.

Evie raises an eyebrow. "It just looks like an old coin, nothing special."

"Pick it up and listen."

She carefully lifts it to her ear. Then she shakes her hand up and down with the coin in her fist. "You're right. I can hear the buzz. It's heavy, too, and I don't think it's the metal itself that has this weight." She gives me back the coin. "What are you going to do?"

"I was thinking of doing research on the spell. If I can learn more about it, maybe it'll give me clues as to why it was given to me in the first place and if Erick is really the one who cast it."

I am a lot better at herbology than spellwork—I am no caster. Most of my experience with the discipline is with rudimentary protection spells, and those usually don't require any special incantations or supplies. For anything more than that, I need to do some investigation.

Evie looks at me like I just spoke another language.

"What?" I ask.

She shrugs. "I don't get it. Why don't you just toss the coin into the Fleuve Saint-Laurent? I mean, problem solved, no?"

I start to pace in uneasiness. "Well, no, actually. Ignoring this would be like ignoring the first symptom of a disease. It may heal on its own, or it might get a lot worse. The coin already did its job in identifying where my home is. Keeping it cannot do any more damage than it already has at this point. But if I dispose of it now, I have no lead. I can never know who's behind this and for what motive. I'll be in the dark while waiting for the other shoe to possibly drop. And this other shoe might hurt more than the first one. Plus, I can't just go to the authorities without proof of a crime or the intent of committing one."

I stop and slump against the counter. "I don't know. I just don't want to feel unsafe in my own home. I need to get to the bottom of this."

"You can crash at my place for a while if you want."

I smirk. "And get in the way of you finding true love? I don't think so."

She shakes her head and sighs. "You know you can always count on me, right? Besides, I might know where you can start your research. There is a bookstore not far from here that is well renowned for the vast collection of magical texts it carries. I'll send you the link."

We both look back to the window. Erick is still drawing, but then a tall woman wearing a medieval dress that causes her bosom to defy gravity walks out of his shop.

When she spots him, she doesn't seem very happy. Correction, she looks pissed. I cannot read her lips, but her posture radiates frustration. Every so often, Erick looks from her to my apartment and back again. She punctuates one of her sentences with a smack on his arm that almost makes him lose his balance. She is not a small woman by any means, but to be able to move a guy of Erick's stature—about six feet tall with defined muscles—she must be stronger than she looks.

By the end of the conversation, she storms back inside the medieval shop. Erick just takes a deep breath, as evidenced by his shoulders going up and down, and follows her inside.

My jaw hangs open. I am at a loss for words. "What on earth?"

Evie howls enough to bring her back to tears. She almost rolls out of her seat as she slaps her hands on her thighs. "Well, someone is in trouble. Karma is a bitch." She has another fit of giggles before she is calm enough to form full sentences again. "Do you know his adorable...friend? Girlfriend? Sister? Employee?"

"No, but I should very much like to talk to her. Maybe she can tell us more."

"Please don't do that. I'll ask Albert about your mysterious neighbor, and we'll see what he says. In the meantime, be careful."

I smile warmly at her and open the box I just brought from the living room. I have some questions of my own for Albert about his basement. That should be an interesting conversation.

Chapter 4

ERICK

I CAN'T BELIEVE RILEY kept the coin.

I just needed some air, but I can't seem to muster the will to go back inside. My shop doesn't have air conditioning, and it's stuffy as fuck in there. The gentle breeze ruffles the paper of my pad. I don't have as much time as I want to sketch these days, but I love it. When I was a teenager, I could spend hours in front of a piece, my hands stained with charcoal as they are now.

I can still picture her in my head, her features so at odds with each other in a way that makes her look unique, precious. Her irises are so dark they swallow her pupils. Her long, black hair accentuates the milk-white of her skin. She is perfect for charcoal.

The only feature I cannot do justice to with this medium is her rich pink lips. I suspect her lithe body is a reflection of her strong character. She's feisty and has a mouth on her. Both of which I do enjoy immensely. I wish I could capture everything on paper, but alas, the complexity of her runs deeper than I can make out at the moment.

If I were to ever do this piece with oils, I would place my model as I saw her first—surrounded by bottles of every shape and form and filled with different colors of liquid. She would be the calm, the anchor, in a world of chaos. Maybe that will be the name of the finished work. It's been a long time since I've felt the unending waves of inspiration that consume me and swallow me whole.

When I come back to reality, I realize I've been fixated on Riley's door while I was lost in my thoughts. I chastise myself mentally for the stupid behavior and lower my gaze to my drawing once more. I don't know what this new witch is thinking, but showing off that kind of power and skill in potion-making in this city is asking to get into trouble. The fact she didn't even question the coin in the first place just proves my point.

I don't know if I should laugh or cry at her effort to conceal where she lives. I mean, really? Taking a small detour before coming back to unlock her door was just pathetic. She could've at least taken a cab to a hotel for the night to throw me off her scent.

I am attempting to capture the life in the gaze of my subject from memory when determined footsteps take me out of my creative flow. I reflexively close my sketchpad with the charcoal piece still inside, bend it, and put it in my back pocket.

"What, pray tell, are you still doing outside?" Eleanor puts her hands on her generous waist. Her long blond hair flows in time with her costume. The medieval dress is not even a job requirement, and I've told her that many times, but she seems to enjoy wearing it.

I turn from her and set my sights back on Riley's door. "I told you I am only getting some air. I know you don't care about the heat, but I sure do."

"Look at me when I talk to you."

My head whips in her direction. Her blue eyes are cold and unyielding. "What's your problem?" I ask her.

"You know full well what my problem is. You've been obsessed with that woman since you got back last night. Her fate is not your responsibility." Eleanor pulls at her lace-up vest to loosen it and takes a deep breath.

I huff. "I'm not obsessed with her. I'm merely curious. I don't see how any of it concerns you anyway. I am in no danger from her."

She moves so fast that I don't have time to anticipate the punch, and I almost lose my footing.

"Erick, listen to me. You're not in danger for now, but if the boss needs her assets, you'll be in his way."

"He won't hurt me, and you know it," I say, rubbing my throbbing shoulder.

She snarls, turns around, and slams the door behind her. At war with my temper, I take a deep breath before I follow her inside. The door opens with a ding, and I duck my head to go down the stairs.

The Underground Castle is a very literal name for my shop. From the cement floor to the exposed beams of the ceiling to the gray color of the walls, it really does look like the interior of a castle. I even kept one of the exposed stone walls. A big chandelier hangs over the overflowing racks of stuff situated in the middle of the space.

I sell everything medieval, from chainmail to LARP costumes and handmade leather items. The glass counter is chock-full of jewelry and expensive replicas.

By the time I reach the foot of the stairs, Eleanor is sitting on a stool at the cash register in the far-right corner of the shop. She takes a pile of receipts and starts to sort them, purposely not looking at me. Her hair falls on her lap, and she tosses it back over her shoulder as if it offended her by daring to disturb her task.

I walk around the display of RPG books and pick up the rag I left there earlier when I was cleaning. I wipe the charcoal off my hands before leaning on my forearms on the front of the counter beside her.

She still refuses to look at me. I've worked with Eleanor for the better part of seven years. Once she makes up her mind on something, she can be pigheaded. After five minutes of her silent treatment, I push off the checkout counter and reach for the pack of playing cards in my pocket. While I shuffle the cards, I start wearing a path on the wooden floor in front of the cash register just to annoy her. I prefer her peeved and talking to me than worried and silent.

Not even a minute passes before she lifts her head. "Would you stop that? Don't you see I'm trying to work?"

I stop and face her. "What would you like me to say? I won't engage with her more than I already did?"

She guffaws. "I would really appreciate it if you would stop lying to me. I'm not an idiot. I know what you intend to do, and I'm telling you it's a very bad idea."

I resume shuffling my cards. "I just want to test a theory. It's completely harmless."

Eleanor holds my gaze. "Harmless, my ass. There are already enough witches disappearing without a trace as it is. I just don't want you to be one of them." Her left hand closes into a fist around the receipts she is holding, which creates a sizeable paper cut on one of her fingers. Not a drop of blood gathers on her skin. She doesn't even notice the wound. It heals almost as quickly as it appeared.

I go around the counter and pick at imaginary lint on one of the fourteenth-century replica dresses hanging on the wall there. "Any movement in the back while I was out?"

She sighs, her shoulders drooping in surrender. She knows I won't let it go—I can't. "No, I didn't hear that gods-awful, high-pitched screech you have for a bell."

I put my hand on her shoulder, squeezing a little. I doubt it's any comfort to her at the moment, but I never said I was the good guy. I know I don't deserve her friendship. "Don't worry, Lenny. I won't get myself into a situation I can't handle. You know 'careful' is my middle name."

This brings the smile back to her face. "'Trouble' is your middle name, more like it." She pats my hand. "You should go back to it. If you get behind on your contracted work, it's on you."

She's right. The fresh trade I made yesterday needs cataloging and tending to before I can make money on it. The entryway to the back of the store wavers a little as I pass through.

Chapter 5

RILEY

I SPENT THE NEXT morning sorting through my books and arranging them on the shelves. I hate having to search for something, so I prefer having them codified by subject matter and then by the author's last name. Some would say it's a little much for a home library, and that's exactly why I prefer books to people.

Evie made good on her promise and texted me the address of the bookstore she had recommended to me. It's called Arcane, which I find a little on the nose for a store that sells magical texts. I want to go there before I have to go to the pub to check on my next batch of beer. The Drunken Sailor is closed on Sundays and Mondays, which gives me a chance to do background work on my end. I also need to order some supplies for potion-making. One day, I would love to grow my own ingredients like my teacher did. I already talked to Albert about possibly renting greenhouse space for that. He didn't go for it now, but I'll wear him down. Right now, I settle for growing and transforming the plants I need for my own potion-making.

I ruffle through my small wardrobe to find something to wear that isn't sweatpants and end up going for a black sundress. Its spaghetti straps leave too much skin exposed for my comfort, so I decide to put a lightweight, long-sleeve shirt underneath it. With my pale skin, it's always better to be covered in the sun. If not, I have to reapply sunscreen over and over to make sure I don't burn. I've learned that the hard way.

I make sure I have everything I need in my bag and leave my room. The bookcases, now full to the brim with colorful book spines, are a welcoming sight. Despite the addition, the space doesn't feel crowded thanks to the white paint on the walls. The rugs were Evie's idea, and she was right. They do a good job at showing which area is the dining room and which one is the living room.

The old table beside the bookshelves was left by the previous tenants. Considering its size, they probably thought it was too much of a hassle to move it. It's a beautiful antique piece made of hardwood with intricately carved plant designs. Granted, it needs a little work, but it's nothing I can't fix. It's going to make a perfect desk where I can spread all the papers and open books I want. The thought brings a smile to my lips. The table currently holds all my plants. It's a miracle they all survived the move. I still need to hang them in the windows.

As I examine my babies closer, I see a spot of brown in the middle of the fray. My devil's claw plant's leaves hang limply, drooping. Some have even begun to shrivel and dry. It is on the brink of death.

The sight sends a pang in my heart. Not all my plants are doing well after all.

"What happened to you, little one?" I ask it while picking up the pot. I set it down in front of me. "You were fine yesterday. How did you get in that state in the span of a couple of hours?" I slide my fingers through the soil and breathe deeply. "Wait for me, my love. Stay with me a little longer." My voice is soft and soothing as I try to coax the tiny thread of life still remaining to hold on.

Then I see it in my mind's eye. The black tendrils of my power, like smoke, are curling around the little life left, holding it, grounding it. It feels fragile, like a tiny bird's wings fluttering weakly. It won't be long now. I need to act fast. Greenish healing light spreads from my fingers and into the dirt, its heat a stark contrast to the cold of looming death. Nothing happens for a couple of seconds, and I'm afraid I might be too late.

As I prepare to let the plant go, let it continue beyond where I am willing to reach, something tugs back. It struggles with my power to let it free. Relief washes over me. I delicately unclasp my dark hold and let the miracle of life make its way back to this plane. I don't dare remove my hands from the earth yet, letting the plant feed off the healing energy emanating from my body a little longer. Its brown leaves fall without a sound onto the flat surface of the table while new budding green and healthy leaves take their place. I only break contact when I am satisfied that the healing will hold and the plant can make the rest of the way on its own.

There is a damper on my senses that remains for a moment. I breathe through the familiar experience, letting it unfold as it always has. It is not a side of my power that I use too often, and for a good reason. More than this tiny display, and I would be writhing in pain on the floor. Plus, if I was ever caught...

A dog's bark from the street below brings me out of my stupor and sends me into motion. When I get to the entryway, I take a minute to check myself in the new mirror I placed on top of the console table to make sure I did not put my clothes on backward. It's been known to happen from time to time. My hair is a disaster, so I decide to tie it in a messy bun on top of my head. I give myself a last once-over.

Good enough.

I make sure I lock the door behind me and hop out onto the sidewalk. It's a beautiful sunny day, and even though it's a long walk to the bookstore, I decide to go on foot.

It takes me thirty minutes to get there. The old port market is just down the street from this bookstore. My favorite pastry shop is in that market. I'll see if I have time for the detour later.

Arcane's exterior is unassuming. The arched doorway is surrounded by two bay windows displaying a combination of new releases and old editions of books. I suppose they carry new and used books alike. The wooden sign, hanging from two chains connected to a post protruding from the building, sways quietly with a gust of wind blowing by.

There is a piece of paper stuck to the outside of the door. It's a notice from the city council for the owner. I don't know why the council didn't just mail it to them. It does feel a little like a show of contempt on their part. Oh, well. I take it down and step inside.

The space is bigger than it looks from the outside. I take a deep breath, and the smell of aged paper and leather teases my nose. I already feel at home. There are rows of bookcases in the center of the space, and almost every wall surface is occupied by wooden built-ins. So many stories and secrets in the same space. Bookstores never fail to delight my curious mind.

There is no one at the counter on my left nor in the store—as far as I can see—so I leave the notice beside the cash register. I turn around and start to peruse the shelves. Everything is labeled and orderly, which means easy to find. A shop after my own heart.

I brush my fingers along the spines of the books as I look through the hoard of written works. The front of the store is mostly new fiction releases, but the deeper I get, the older the volumes look. They have an impressive collection of used historical romance books under lock and key in a glass display situated just beside a swing door at the back.

The more I focus on the titles, the blurrier they get. The letters seem to melt and warp, reminding me of a surrealist painting. The book covers waver one last time before completely changing forms and colors. My eyebrows reach my hairline, and a small laugh escapes me. To any non-magical onlooker, nothing would look amiss with these books, but to a witch…

The romance novels are nowhere to be seen anymore. In their place stands a slew of different grimoires and magical texts. I've never seen so many of these for sale gathered in the same place before. Some are reproductions, but some look original. How in the world did the owner pull that off? I flatten my hands on the glass of the case, my nose almost touching the display as I let my gaze rake over the titles. I stop my perusing when I spot a thick grimoire about ceremonial magic written by a prominent French magus of the 19th century, which looks original.

The back door swings open, and I shriek. I was so enthralled by my discovery that I didn't hear footsteps approaching. The man walking through almost drops the huge pile of books he is carrying. We stay there, staring at each other for a moment, too stunned to move.

He looks aggrieved by my presence. His glasses, a simple but elegant black frame, are slowly slipping down his nose, leaving way to forest green eyes. His dark blond hair is half up, half down, as if he didn't have time to finish the job but needed it out of his face. The stubble on his sculpted jaw and the dust on his trousers only add to a general absentminded look. He has a muscular yet graceful build, like someone that doesn't really train but has to lift heavy items many times a day. All in all, he is breathtaking.

"Can I help you with something?" His tone tells me it's not the first time he has asked me this question.

I realize I am staring at him the way I stared at the grimoires, and I can feel the blush slowly making its way up my face. "Sorry, yes. I wonder if you have anything on tracking spells like this one." I grab the coin from my bag. When I raise my head, his gaze is fixed on my lips, but he averts his eyes quickly and scowls at the floor.

The man shifts the books to one of his hands and extends his other, palm up, for me to drop the coin in. His features bunch up in concentration as he examines the object. He turns it this way and that. Then he taps it gently on the side of one of the shelves and puts it to his ear. A flash of surprise shows in his eyes, so quick I almost don't catch it.

"Where did you get this?" he asks.

"I got it as a tip at work."

He takes one last look at the piece of metal before giving it back to me. His glasses are still slipping farther down his nose, and my fingers itch to push them up. My lips part slightly to let my tongue swipe over my dry bottom lip, which brings his attention back to my mouth again. The man takes an almost imperceptible step forward, the green of his eyes getting darker by the second. Then his brows bunch together in puzzlement, and his nostrils flare.

The book at the top of his pile slips sideways, breaking the moment. He catches it with expert hands, and I can't help but notice his long, elegant fingers as he flips the book back onto the top of the tower in his arms. He straightens up and nods to no one in particular as if to agree with his own thoughts. "Wait here," he says. "Bree will be with you in a minute." He turns around and hurries back through the door he came from, still holding his pile of books.

I just stand there, my mouth agape, not knowing what to do with myself. I don't know why this man is commanding my attention like that. The last person that provoked this type of reaction at first sight from me ended up breaking my heart—Oliver, *ugh*. I am not interested in reliving that experience. No, thank you.

Muffled voices come from what I assume is the stockroom. They talk too low for me to make out what is said. My curiosity gets the best of me, and I inch closer to peek through the small window of the swinging door. But just as I go on my tiptoes to take a look, the door swings open, and I barely have time to get out of the way.

"Oh, gods!" the employee exclaims. "I'm so sorry. Did I hit you? Finn always tells me to look if anyone is in the way before opening the door, but I'm small, you see? And the window is a touch too high, so I have to jump, and it's exhausting to do fifteen times a day. It's also humiliating since I look like a toddler trying to get to the cookies." The woman is talking so fast that I have trouble following her train of thought.

She is a tiny thing, pixie-sized, with a head full of fiery red curls. The fact that her hair is hitting below her waist only accentuates her short size. With all her freckles and round baby face, she looks to be in her early twenties, but her energy and the keen spirit lighting her eyes tell me she is probably closer to her thirties.

"I'm Bree! Where's my head? My boss is supposed to already have told you that, but hey, with Finn, you never know. He always has his nose in a book and keeps forgetting real-world stuff." Not losing any time, she turns around, picks up a handbasket, and shoves it in my arms. "Here. Take this. And you are?"

"Riley. So, he's the—"

"Owner? Yes. Books on tracking spells, right?" Bree smirks and starts moving before I can reply.

She unlocks the display and rummages through the magical texts. She finally picks up one, throws it into my basket, and closes the glass case. Still looking at the grimoires through the glass, she huffs. "That one's good, but if you want to cover all your bases, you'll need more."

She goes on talking for at least fifteen minutes straight while gathering different books. Meanwhile, I follow her through the store, trying to understand how she can breathe while talking that fast. She asks me a few questions, but every time I open my mouth to answer them, she starts on a new subject. If I didn't know better, I would say she is probably fairy kin. I am still picturing her with adorable wings when she stops all of a sudden and drops everything she holds into my basket. The sudden weight threatens to topple me forward.

"Anything else?" Bree asks. "I've taken the liberty to throw a few of our new releases in there so you can try them. On the house." Then she winks at me, which makes me wonder if they are really free or if she just made them free. Unable to hide my grin, I thank her, and we walk to the cash register.

Bree picks up my bounty as if it is no heavier than a feather and drops it on the counter.

"What's this?" she says, plucking up the piece of paper I left beside the cash register earlier. "Did you see who left it there?"

I shake my head no. "It was taped to your door. I thought you might not want other clients seeing it, so I brought it inside."

"Thanks. I really appreciate that. They've been on our back since we opened three years ago." Bree makes a dismissive gesture in the air. "Anyway, you don't want to hear about that." She is silent for a moment, and I don't feel like prying any further. It's none of my business, after all.

"I've never seen you in here before," Bree says conversationally. "This store has mostly regulars coming in, so when a new face appears, it's exciting. Well, mainly for me. Finn is more interested in books than people."

My smile grows at that statement. "I can relate to that. I probably have more books than people I know."

"I believe you are made for each other," she says, amusement shining in her big blue eyes. "You should have started the conversation with that earlier, and maybe he would have stuck around to help you longer. You're totally his type. Mysterious, loves literature, and, best of all, a great listener. I'm telling you—I should set you two up on a date. Are you available?"

A giggle escapes me. "Well, yes, but I don't think he liked me very much, judging by the speed at which he exited the room. I don't want to crush your dreams, but I don't think it's gonna happen."

She makes a show of sighing loudly and pouting profusely. Then she proceeds to scan my purchases and put the items in my reusable bag.

"Hey," she says, "since you love books so much, I have an offer for you. Every year for the last three years, we've organized a book fair, and we're always searching for volunteers to help. Let's just say that Finn is not much of a party planner."

"Your words, not mine." I snicker. "I don't know. I just moved here and have a lot of work at my new job."

She rolls her eyes at me. "Come on, it'll be fun. It's only a couple of meetings, and the two days of the fair in the fall just a little over a month and a half away. I promise we won't swamp you with tasks. Plus, you'll get to meet a ton of new people. You know, make friends? And I didn't even tell you the best part yet." She looks like the cat that ate the canary. "You can pick out any ten books you want from the vendors at the fair. On. The. House. What do you say?"

On the one hand, I don't really have time for this. No matter what Bree says, it sounds like a lot of work. But on the other hand, depending on the vendors, I may be able to snatch some rare finds for free. This could save me a ton of money and help me with my craft.

Who am I kidding? She knows she got me.

But I decide to mess a little with Bree before agreeing to the deal. "Tell me something. Why would you want me to help you? You don't even know me. I might have awful organization skills and less than stellar decorating taste."

She laughs at my statement, and I swear it sounds like little bells. "I don't tend to want to be friends with the clients, but with you, I might make an exception. I don't know, but my gut tells me you're great. And my gut is never, and I mean *never*, wrong. It might also have something to do with the fact that you've been here for half an hour, listening to me patiently without telling me to shut my big mouth." Her smile brightens at her last words.

I wait a moment longer before saying, "Ok, then. If your boss is willing to put the ten-books gift in writing, I'm in."

"Deal. I'll get him to text it to you." We exchanged numbers, and she promised to keep me updated about the different meetings for the event.

I am almost at the front door when Finn steps through the back swinging door once again. My breath catches in my throat at the sight of him. The sleeves of his shirt are now rolled up, exposing strong forearms covered with symbols tattooed in black ink. When he sees me, he stops abruptly. Our eyes lock, and, this time, he looks at me like I am a giant problem to solve. I don't even have time to feel insulted because, five seconds later, Bree clears her throat. My gaze darts to her, and I wince. I don't even want to know how red my face is. After thanking her awkwardly, I exit the store as fast as I can.

Not a minute later, I receive a text from her saying that she is totally arranging a date. I simply reply that she should be thinking about the book fair instead. My phone blips again. This time, it's only an emoji, the one sticking its tongue out. I grin at the device before putting it into my bag and making the trek back to my apartment.

Chapter 6

FINN

I STARE AFTER THE woman a beat longer, the image of her embarrassment still stirring something deep inside of me.

Then I take advantage of Bree being distracted to make my escape. I only have time to take two steps before she seemingly appears before my eyes. She shoves a piece of paper at my chest, her nose scrunching in disgust.

"What's—?"

"This? Yeah, well, the city council is going after you again."

"What? Why? What do they say I did this time?" I straighten the paper and read it. I cannot believe this. "The store is too loud? *Too loud?* We are a bookstore, for gods' sake. How can they even believe that piece of shit Gavin with this kind of complaint?"

"How'd you know it's Gavin that made the complaint?" she asks.

I give her a pointed look.

"Sorry,"—she winces—"you're right. It's obvious the complaint comes from him."

I won the bidding war on this building from him three years ago, and he cannot let it go. His flower shop is right beside my bookstore, and he needed my location to expand. Apparently, he is still holding on to that dream because he's been making my life a living nightmare for the last year.

"I should just hex him and be done with it." I tear the paper to shreds and throw it in one of the numerous bins scattered throughout the store. I hate it when customers leave their litter all over my shelves. Even with all the bins, some find a way to *not* throw their garbage in the trash.

Bree stabs a finger at my shoulder. "You know it's against the law to hex a human. Haven't you been raised in a Sennex-worshipping household? You should know."

"Ha-ha, hilarious. If you are to demean my upbringing, the least you can do is help me shelve these tomes. I'm almost done putting away Friday's delivery." I motion to a pile of books standing precariously on the edge of a shelf.

When her gaze sets on the volumes, her smile grows wide, excitement written all over her face. "My, my, you've been busy. No wonder you didn't have time to help the new girl," she says, laughter in her voice.

I throw a book at her head, and she catches it easily without even looking at me.

"Smooth transition, *Bumble-Bree.*" She hates that nickname. But instead of triggering her like I'd hoped, she just keeps focusing on the tomes to put away.

"Hold that thought," she says.

Bree surveys the pile of books and pre-sorts them. She picks up the stack and goes through the motion of placing the volumes in their correct location. Her movements are swift and precise. My head whips around to-and-fro, trying to follow her. The lines of her body sometimes blur, the motion too fast for my eyes to track. She finishes the deed in less than thirty seconds.

Then she stops right before me, her hair whipping in her face. She gathers her locks and starts to braid them. "What was I saying? Oh, yeah! The new girl. I recruited her to help us with the book fair this year."

My jaw drops. "What? No. Absolutely not! We don't need any help. We've always done it by ourselves, and this year won't be any different. Text her and call it off."

My answer is a knee-jerk reaction, and I know it. I don't want to wake; the slumber my emotions have been in for the last couple of years is safe and peaceful. Now, confusion clouds my judgment. The smell of the mysterious stranger's perfume is still in my nose—jasmine with a hint of some sort of citrus. I close my eyes, but it's no use. All I can see is her lush mouth and the part of her lips as her gaze raked over me. Her self-assured tone and the way she carried herself hint at a strong disposition, someone who wants to be in control. A shudder runs through my body at the thought.

I have focused my mind on work, and only work, for a long time now—I've had no choice. Slowing down made my heart hurt too much. It's been years since I even thought about making so much as a friend. It's the first time in a long time that my curiosity has been piqued by someone new, and it's like my body is ready to open the floodgates all at once, which I categorically won't allow.

It's completely stupid to have this reaction to someone I don't even know, but the encounter felt like the electrified moment just before lightning strikes. Or like waking up—the moment you realize there is something new to discover after all.

"I don't think so," Bree continues, oblivious to my torment. She releases her hair, the red strands coming loose, unbraiding themselves with gravity. Then she puts her right hand on her heart before bringing it forward, palm toward me. Her people's symbol for love. "You know I love you, Finn, but you need to get out more and see folk other than me."

I hate being cornered, and she knows it. "I see. You don't approve of my life choices and intend to try and force my hand. I am not a witchling that doesn't want to make friends on the playground. I can make my own decisions. I like my life as is, and it's not for you to judge." I know I sound exactly like said witchling at the moment, but I can't help it.

Her eyes soften. "That's not what I said. You know I respect you, and I would never judge you. However, I do think that you shouldn't devote yourself to an existence of loneliness. I know what being alone feels like. I mean, truly alone and not by choice. I wouldn't wish it on my worst enemy. That said, I am only pulling stunts like this because I want to see you enjoy the life you choose, and you have a bad habit of getting in your own way."

I can feel my resolve slowly dissolving at the concern in her tone, so I start toward the stockroom just to move my body, hoping it will help me think, but Bree steps in my way.

"Come on," she pleads, "give Riley a chance. She's smart and funny and loves books, just like you. My gut tells me she can become a good friend of mine. She may become one to you, too. I'm not asking you two to become best friends. It's only teamwork for the time of the project. If you don't want to see her after that, or vice-versa, you won't have to. What do you say, mister grump?" She twists her hands together and averts her eyes. "It's been three years since he broke your heart... It's time to put yourself back out there."

And, just like that, I am reminded of the main reason why I don't want to know Riley more while simultaneously being fascinated by her. The problem is that my feelings are muddled. I can't tell if I feel as I do because of her or because of what—or more accurately, who—she potentially brought back into my life with that spelled coin of hers.

I cross my arms and square my shoulders, concluding that, as much as I want to escape the pain the mere thought of him provokes, my conscience won't let me ignore this situation. "Did you have a chance to look at the coin she—"

"Riley, her name's Riley." Bree waves her hand for me to continue.

"Very well. The coin that *Riley* wants to unspell?"

She frowns and takes a step toward me. "No, why?"

"I recognized the charm. Even if she finds the counterspell, she'll need an experienced caster to take it out. Or she'll need to toss the thing. It's a rare working I've only seen once before, a long time ago. I think I know who it belongs to." My gaze wills her to understand who I mean. I'm not ready to say his name out loud yet, even after all this time. He might have left me, but my love for him has stayed as bright as the northern star on a clear winter night.

The fog behind her eyes clears out as the realization sets in. "Are you implying who I think you are?" She whirls around and starts to pace, scraping her hands down her face as she goes. "No! He has no reason to do that. You haven't so much as heard a whisper about the man since you saw him when you arrived in this city. Why now?" she says, eyes wide.

I let out a breath I wasn't aware I was holding. "I don't know. It might be nothing. But if it's really him, and he risked bringing attention to himself by tracking another witch, there's something wrong. I mean, it's a dice toss. Any weak-powered witch might not have detected that particular tracking spell since its weaving is precisely done to stay under the radar, even from witches, but a powerful witch can spot that thing a mile away."

Bree opens her mouth to interrupt my monologue, but I don't let her. "I know you don't like this, but I need to make sure he's okay. After our fight, I promised to stay out of his way, but I have to get to the bottom of this. He may not want me meddling in his life, but if he's in trouble, I will never forgive myself if I don't try to help him. Call for a first book fair meeting at Riley's earliest convenience," I say, equally apprehensive and thrilled at the prospect.

The front door opens and closes. Bree balls her hands, annoyance written all over her face, and clears her throat. "Welcome to Arcane. I'll be with you in a minute." She pins me with a look. "You will not try to fix whatever this is by yourself, you hear me?" she says as she pushes me aside and storms to the front of the shop.

Chapter 7

RILEY

I KNEW I SHOULDN'T have taken up Bree on her offer. Not even an hour after I left the bookstore, she texted me to plan our first meeting for Saturday night, and I had the weekend off. I could've lied and said no, but that's not me. I committed to this, so I intend to see it through.

After some back and forth and at least two one-hour phone calls (because Bree cannot, for the life of her, be concise), we finally agreed to have the meeting at my place to get new wards up. Actually, I asked her if she knew of a caster willing to put up quality protection spells on my home at a reasonable price. Two days later, she texted me saying that Finn agreed to do it, which means having the meeting at my apartment so he can cast them then. It turns out Finn is a sort of prodigy of his time. Bree's words, not mine.

Finn... I don't know what to think. The guy is a study in dark academia university literature teacher. Even after a few days, he leaves me perplexed. We barely spoke, but I can't shake the pull of his pleading eyes when he stepped toward me. That small step felt full of possibilities even as he did his best to act detached and cold.

Bree only has praise for Finn, although I do think she is still trying to set me up with him. I don't need or want to be interested in someone right now. I haven't dated in forever for a reason. Of course, I've had partners over the years, but nothing serious for a long time. After Oliver, I wanted to start over, so I moved away. Then I moved again, and before I knew it, moving became a habit of mine—never staying long enough to plant roots...or to fall for someone. Always coming back to Diane's in between moves to recoup and regroup. Not his time, though. This time I intend to stay right where I am and stop letting my fears wreck what I have built.

As for Evie, she was thrilled about me doing something else other than staying at home or thinking about work—or straight up working all the time, for that matter. She didn't have any luck on her side, though. All Albert was able to tell her is that Erick has never caused him any problem, and he really does run the medieval shop and has done for the last seven years without a hitch. My best friend has been working at The Drunken Sailor for the last year, and not only has she never heard Erick's name before, but she also trusts our boss implicitly. I don't know what to make of this.

The books I purchased at Arcane haven't yet yielded answers, and I am no closer to undoing that tracking spell than I was a week ago. The damn coin is testing my ego and my patience every day. Sure, I could just toss the thing, but I want to know more. I can't help it. Either way, the old piece of metal cannot do more damage than it did the night I unknowingly brought a tracking spell home.

I haven't had the opportunity to ask Albert about the basement yet. I haven't heard any more voices down there either, so I don't know if it's even worth mentioning. Anyway, since it's Friday, it's my last chance to talk to him this week.

The sky split open this morning, and it's been pouring rain nonstop since then. Armed with my rubber boots and a huge umbrella, I successfully made it to work early. I throw my umbrella on the counter and beeline for the kitchen, where I find Albert lying on his back under the industrial dishwasher. I try but fail to announce my presence without startling him.

Albert jumps and knocks his head on the metal frame, dropping the wrench he is holding on his throat. Groaning, he wiggles his bulky frame out from under the machine, sits up, and rubs the growing bump on his head.

I wince. "I'm so sorry. I thought you heard me coming."

He wipes his forehead with his arm. "I assume you're here this early because you want to talk to me?" He doesn't give me time to answer. "Go ahead and check on your beer vats while I finish this. I'll be with you in ten."

I do as instructed and go to the room at the back of the kitchen where the three huge vats sit. While the rest of the pub looks right out of 1800s Ireland, this space is ultra-modern. I open the glass door and breathe deeply. The familiar scent calms me down instantly. I do my regular checks and confirm how many beer kegs were filled today. I do a little tasting and make some adjustments.

When I turn around to leave, I can see through the glass door that Albert is walking toward me. He opens said door for me. "Wrapped up in your work, were ya? You've been in here for the last half an hour. I thought I would come to see if you didn't drown in ale."

I am not ashamed to admit that I tend to get lost in my work, but I didn't come here early to work per se. I came here to get answers. I don't want to be mixed up in some shady business by association. It could tank my career real fast. Okay, I better get to it before I lose my nerve.

"You were right," I say. "I do need to talk to you. I know I'm new here, and it's probably none of my business, but—"

"Out with it, lass. Speak your mind. I won't bite," he says as he picks up discarded cardboard boxes to break them apart for recycling.

I try to infuse more confidence into my next words. "Right. I was just wondering why your basement is protected by a high-tech security system."

He considers me for a moment. Then he bursts out laughing, his neck straining with the effort. "You should see your face," he says through fits of laughter. Albert lets go of the cardboard he's holding and takes my hand. "Come with me."

As if I had a choice. He drags me behind him like I weigh nothing. Then he stops in front of the retina scanner and puts his eye before the green light. The small piece of tech emits the now familiar beep. Albert steps aside and holds the door open for me to step through.

The staircase to the basement is faintly illuminated by sconces on the walls. The red of the wallpaper was probably already faded by the time I was born. The ornate pattern of it is interrupted here and there by rips and tears.

Images of drug dens and human trafficking go through my head, but then I catch a faint smell of premium cigars. I suppose that a drug den wouldn't smell like that. Albert motions for me to get going. He closes the door and follows behind me, his weight making the steps groan.

When I get to the bottom of the stairs, I'm in a corridor. The right side leads to what I assume is an outside door, so I decide to go left. Albert lets me look around without stopping me. I pass in front of a door with a brass sign engraved *water closet* on it. I open it, and it's simply a small room with a toilet and an old copper sink. I close it and move to the next door. This is where the cigar smell seems to be coming from.

I wasn't prepared for what was on the other side. A large room spreads out before my eyes. The back wall is covered with racks of liquor bottles. A solid oak bar runs along the front of the display. Various sheets of paper cover most of its surface—pens are scattered in the fray. There are inset circular booths against the remaining walls—simple leather benches with a round table at the center. Fancy chandeliers hang throughout the space, matching the art deco style popular in the 1920s. At the center of it all is a grand piano. The instrument shows its age; the varnish of the wood is missing in spots.

As I look around, trying to gather my wits, Albert walks past me to take place behind the bar. It must have been an ancient speakeasy. I've never seen anything like it.

"You can close your mouth now, Riley," Albert says. "What would you prefer, whisky or vodka?" He seems so proud of himself that I have half a mind to take him down a peg or two for his games but decide against it.

"This is incredible! Why don't you open it to the public?" I cannot hide the awe in my voice.

Albert proceeds to pour us drinks. "You asked me what was so valuable down here. Well, my peace of mind is. I use it as my office.

I also have to make sure my collection is safe," he says as he pats one of the alcohol bottles lovingly.

I sit at one of the five benches at the bar and take a swig of the amber liquor he put down before me. The liquid is velvet smooth going down my throat. That is no cheap whisky.

"Tell me, how much will you take off my pay for a sip of this?" I roll the liquid in the glass and then take another swallow. I motion to the display behind him. "Am I to understand that this is the real reason for all the security measures? A collection of rare spirits?"

"You know, I'm not in the habit of bringing employees down here. As I said, peace of mind and all... But you looked like you thought I had an illegal fighting ring in my basement." He snickers and rounds the bar to come to sit down beside me.

"Something like that, boss." I clap his shoulder and smile at him. "Something like that."

Silence descends between us. I lean on my forearms on the bar surface, fidgeting with my glass. I am afraid that if I don't take the opportunity to gather as much information as I can right now, it might never present itself again. "I heard Erick's voice and many others from down here last Saturday night," I say to him after a moment, studiously avoiding his gaze.

"Am I not allowed to have mates over in my own basement?" he answers, shifting uncomfortably in his seat.

I know a dodge when I hear one. "So, Erick's your friend?"

His jaw tightens. "Why are you and Evelyn so bent out of shape about him? I already answered all her questions about him. If you want to know more, I'm afraid I'm not your guy because I don't know more."

My laugh sounds fake, even to my own ears. "I'll have you know that I have never been bent out of shape over anyone in my life," I say, trying to diffuse the sudden tension in the room.

Another beat of silence passes, and I have no idea what to say next. Albert saves me the trouble. "Could you keep this between us? I have no interest in mixing what's going on upstairs with what I have down here. And before you think about it, you cannot share this with Evelyn. I know you two are close, but she cannot keep a secret to save her life."

"You would be surprised," I say under my breath.

"This is not a request, Riley. You talk about this—you'll be out of a job faster than a rabbit running for its life. Is that clear?"

I turn around in my seat and lean my elbows back against the bar. I put as much contempt in my expression as I can before looking at Albert with a smug smile. "So, what you're saying is I deserve a raise for shutting my hole?"

He doesn't need to speak for me to understand what he thinks about my suggestion. His face says it all.

I spring up from my chair. "All right, all right," I say, still holding my glass. "I'm going, but not before I finish this." Albert snatches the glass from my hand before I have time to bring it to my lips.

"What I'm saying, Riley, is that you and your extortion attempts should go back to work before anyone else comes in for their shift."

I nod to him and scamper off the way I came. I'm almost to the staircase when I hear him shout, "And, Riley, be grateful that I like you!"

Chapter 8

FINN

THE MESSENGER BAG I brought with me is heavier than I expected. The weight of knowledge, I suppose. The thought makes me laugh to myself.

I am early for the meeting with Riley, and that's why I take the scenic route on my walk over there. The old part of Québec City is alive with tourists. The many restaurants are filled with laughter and wine as the sun descends over the city. There are artists at every corner, painting and playing music.

I decide to stop by the observation post at Le Château Frontenac. The view is breathtaking from this high up. The cloudless pink sky seems to spread endlessly as the water of the Fleuve Saint-Laurent reflects the bright colors of the sunset. Children run on the wooden platform, not caring who is in their path, and I almost don't make it out of the way in time myself. The heat of the day still clings to my body, making my every movement sluggish.

As I descend from the lookout onto the cobblestone street, I wonder what tonight's meeting will yield. The book fair is important to me and my business, of course, but I have many questions that need answers, and I have no idea how to bring them up to her—Riley. She doesn't know me, nor does she have any reason to trust me, but my hope is that our goals align enough to make us allies in getting to the bottom of what's really going on with that tracking spell.

My thoughts float back to the delicate curve of her nose, her exposed neck. In any case, I refuse to let my mind wander beyond those surface observations, those desires. Because that's all it is: physical, biological needs that have gone unanswered for too long. Nothing more.

I am almost at Riley's apartment when my phone vibrates in my pocket. I fish it out and groan at the text.

I won't be able to make it. I guess you'll have to improvise. I do hope you have a nice evening.

It's followed by a winking emoji.

I curse under my breath. I am not the most easygoing person in the world, and I was counting on Bree to take the lead tonight. I am still debating if I should just postpone everything when I realize where I am.

Seriously? What are the odds that her home is directly in front of The Underground Castle?

Well, then.

I open the door to her building and go up the stairs. I am still a little early when I knock softly on her door.

No answer.

I do it again, putting a little more force behind the movement. Quick footsteps approach the door, and then the sound of the lock unlatching echoes in the stairwell.

"Hey, Bree! I—" Riley stops talking when she realizes who I am, or more accurately, who I'm not.

She stands before me, a towel in her hand, trying to dry her hair as best she can, the strands leaving dark wet stains on her deep blue bathrobe. I don't want to look, but the material clings to her wet body like a second skin, the garment stopping just above her knees.

"You're early," she says pointedly.

I rub at my neck, averting my eyes. I am so awkward sometimes that I just don't know what to do with myself. I'll be lucky if she doesn't just close the door in my face. "I'm sorry. I should've texted. Would you like me to come back in half an hour?"

"No, that's fine," she says, obviously annoyed. "Just give me a minute to get dressed." She opens the door wider for me to enter and then locks it behind me. As she walks past me, she points to the couch just beside the small entryway. "Make yourself comfortable. I won't be long." The silky material of her gown floats behind her as she turns around and makes her way to the back of the open space. I indulge in one last look, letting my gaze follow the dip of her waist and the curve of her hips before she disappears from view.

A heartbeat later, I hear drawers being opened and closed, then the feathery rustling of clothes. I turn around slowly, taking in my surroundings. To my left is a narrow archway that leads to a small, faded-orange galley kitchen. The white open space spreading before me is divided in two by huge area rugs.

To my right is the living room. A green couch leans on the wall just under a window that faces the street below. A big coffee table fills the rest of the space. No television, I note.

What I assume is the dining room makes up the other half of the area, although the papers and open books covering the kitchen table, in addition to the two massive bookcases beside it, are indications enough of the use Riley chose for that space.

"Did Bree tell you when she'll be here?" Riley shouts before reappearing through what I assume is her bedroom door. She stops by the kitchen table, her hands working efficiently at gathering her hair on top of her head in a messy bun. Both her jeans and her Bon Jovi T-shirt are sporting holes in multiple places. Her only jewelry is a red stone pendant that hangs heavily at her neck. Multiple lines are etched onto it, forming the web of Wyrd. She shifts her weight from one bare foot to the other.

I still haven't moved from my spot in the entryway. I clear my throat in embarrassment. "She texted me just as I arrived at your door. She cannot make it." Silence welcomes my statement. "I bet you'll find the same text from her on your phone, too."

She grabs her cell from her back pocket and glares at it as if its contents were offensive somehow. Then she throws it on the table. "Oh, okay." Her voice wavers on the last word. She takes hold of her pendant with one hand and rubs it between her fingers, the gesture betraying her nerves. Why wouldn't she be nervous? She doesn't know me. She and Bree texted all week and even talked a time or two, but me? I am just the grumpy guy she met once. I was really banking on Bree to be the bridge tonight.

"Like I said," I plow on, "we can reschedule. I will work by myself tonight. I don't mind. I don't want to impose."

"No, it's fine. The sooner we start, the sooner it'll be done." She winces. "I didn't mean it that way. I just meant... Well, I meant that the earlier we start, the earlier we'll be ready. I hate being last minute."

My smile is genuine when I say, "I know what you meant. Still, I just want to make sure you're okay with this since we're in your home, and you don't know me."

Her shoulders relax, and she snickers. "I do know at least one thing about you."

"Oh, yeah? What's that?"

"Customer service is not your strong suit," she teases.

It's my turn to wince. "I'm sorry about that. I have other delightful quirks, too, if you must know. All part of my charm."

"Mm-hmm," she says, light dancing in her dark eyes. "Well, don't just stand there. I don't have all night, *Finn*." She doesn't wait for an answer and starts to clear the workspace.

I approach the table and carefully place my heavy bag on its surface. "I'll do my best to be quick then, *Riley*." And that was that.

We've been working on opposite sides of the table for nearly two hours. Riley is finishing up a sketch of the floor plan for the venue while I drink what's left of my fancy water. Fancy because she served it in a crystal wine glass. She said that crystal makes any liquid taste better, water included, and I believe her.

We've covered more ground than I'd hoped in this first meeting, even with Bree's absence. To my surprise, conversation runs easily between us. Riley's ideas are thoughtful and wise. She even spoke about her work a little, although Bree had already told me about her talents with potions and healing. Turns out that, in addition to an undying love of books, we have a lot of other tastes and views in common, which fed the conversation nicely. No awkward pauses or weird silences. That is, until now.

I have exhausted all the topics I had on the agenda. The scattered papers covering the table like fallen soldiers on a battlefield are proof of Riley's enthusiasm to get this over with as quickly as possible. I want to bring up the coin, but I don't know how. And there's still the matter of the protection wards to deal with.

"Staring at me while I work won't make things go faster," she says, her gaze moving sideways toward me. "Don't you have anything left to do?"

I hadn't even noticed I was staring at her. I was only lost in thought, my eyes unfocused, not really seeing her there. The question is out of my mouth before I can stop it. "Does it make you uncomfortable, being observed?"

She drops her pen and sits back in her chair. She studies me for a moment, her gaze moving intently over my face, my shoulders, my arms, my fingers interlaced on the table, and then back up as she retraces her path. Goosebumps erupt all over my body despite the heat of the summer day still lingering. Her own face is a mask of glorious impassivity, as if she is merely looking at a painting that she hasn't yet formed an opinion about. I shouldn't find her scrutiny fascinating, but here I am, squirming in my seat.

"Does it make *you* uncomfortable?" she answers plainly, one of her brows rising in a questioning look. But it feels more like a challenge of a sort, the kind that I don't want to fight, the kind I want her to win.

"That's not the word I would use, no." The small admission is but a whisper.

A surprised laugh escapes Riley's lips. "Is that so? What word would you use then?" Her dark eyes are laughing at me. She folds her body forward and drops her forearms on the dark wood of the table. "Go on."

Suddenly desperate for a change of subject, I reach for my glass of water but drop it back down when I remember it's empty. "I'm sorry if I offended you," I tell her earnestly. "I didn't mean to be inconsiderate. Forgive me."

My apology effectively breaks whatever tension was building between us. She clicks her tongue and sighs. "I've worked in bars for the best part of my adult life, so, to answer your question, it's really hard to make me uncomfortable or offend me. I can state my limits and take care of myself. And for the record, I was just teasing you. But I do like where this conversation was going."

"Is that sarcasm?"

"Well, a little bit of that mixed with genuine curiosity."

I look at my watch. It's almost eight pm. "Did you have any plans for tonight?" I ask. "We could order some food and work on your wards. I'm starving." I'm not usually this forthcoming, but I need more time to bring up the coin...and her neighbor.

Riley gives me an incredulous look, but her body betrays her. Her stomach growls just as she opens her mouth. She laughs to herself and picks up her phone. "Mexican? If we're to order out, I want tacos."

"How did you know"—fake astonishment fills my tone—"that tacos are my favorites?"

She waves her hand dismissively in my direction, picks up our empty glasses, and walks toward the kitchen with her phone already to her ear. "I hope you like extra guac on everything," she teases before stepping through the kitchen archway.

Chapter 9

RILEY

MY HEART IS HAMMERING in my chest. Why did I agree to this? Working with him was fine; my mind could focus on the tasks at hand instead of his presence. Now…I should have just asked him to do the protection spell and get out. I didn't anticipate how smart and interesting he would be. Not when he was an icy wall made of flesh the only time we spoke. Once he thawed a little, he was even funny. I am still angry with myself for enjoying his presence so much. It's been a while since I enjoyed a date. But this isn't a date, I remind myself, nor do I want it to be.

He looks so different from the last time I saw him at his bookstore. His low-slung jeans and simple dark green T-shirt make him appear less serious, less stark. Well, the fact that he smiled a time or two also helped. I had a better look at his tattoos while we worked. The design incorporates bands and runes expertly woven into tasteful patterns that run up from both wrists and disappear under his shirt sleeves. I wonder what the entire piece looks like.

Once I finish placing my food order, I gather my courage and, from the kitchen, ask Finn if he would like to have actual wine in his wine glass.

"White or red?" he answers from the living room with a mocking tone.

I roll my eyes to myself. He's picky. How charming. "Don't look a gift horse in the mouth," I tell him, still holding my fridge door open. "I could be serving you moonshine for all you know."

He chuckles then—a rich, deep sound that makes my toes curl. "Should I be worried for my life?" comes the answer.

"Bree told me you studied poisons throughout history, which is a very creepy hobby, might I add, so you should be fine. Maybe it's me who should be worried." No answer. He's got nothing to say about that, I see.

I always have a few good bottles of wine available. I like having choices. I open a bottle of Italian pinot grigio and fill our two crystal glasses that I bring carefully to the living room. I stop short when I spot Finn sitting on my couch, his brows knitted in concentration, reading my notes on growing patterns of different plant families.

"Enjoying your reading material?"

He jerks backward, turning those big green eyes to me, guilt written all over his face. Then he puts the journal back gently on the coffee table. "I know I shouldn't be nosy, but that book was already open and—"

I interrupt Finn's spiel with a chuckle which earns me a deep frown from him. "I really don't care," I say, still grinning, "don't fret about it. The real important stuff and secret recipes are very well hidden away." I put both wine glasses on the coffee table and sit facing him on the couch.

"You do have a lot of secrets, don't you?" Finn asks, his eyes fixed on mine. He's too damn perceptive, and I'm not sure I like it.

The question isn't an accusation, neither is it to make me feel uncomfortable. Like with his inquiry about being observed, he looks genuinely intrigued. A few minutes pass before either of us moves or speaks again. He keeps his gaze firmly on my face as he bends down to pick up his glass of wine from the coffee table. He then brings it to his lips and takes a couple of healthy sips.

My eyes drift to his neck, where his Adam's apple goes up and down with each swallow. When he puts his wine back down, his tongue brushes against his upper lip, and the simple gesture causes all kinds of fluttery feelings low in my belly. Then his mouth cracks in a wry half-grin, telling me he paid close attention to my reaction. Too damn perceptive indeed.

"According to the Mexican restaurant, we have a good forty-five minutes before us. What do you want to do while we wait for the food?" I ask, needing to do something to distract me from those disturbing, unwanted feelings.

I recognized my mistake only once the words had already left my mouth. His grin goes up a notch at my request. I think I will probably die from high blood pressure. But instead of making an unwarranted comment, he digs up a small black stone from his pocket.

"What's that?"

His expression sobers. "To be able to do my work properly and put up solid protective wards on your apartment, I will need you to take down all your protection work, including your personal shield so that nothing interferes."

Okay… That is not what I was expecting him to say. My heart kicks in my chest at the request. "Excuse me?" I say, panic seeping into my voice.

The spell woven around me is not one of protection, and I am not going to willingly strip it down. I wasn't the one to put it on me in the first place, and I don't even know if I would be able to put it back into place afterward.

"That's why I brought this black tourmaline with me," he says. "It's a talisman I made to protect you while I do this. You can—"

I spring up. "No! It's out of the question! I don't mind lifting my half-assed apartment wards for you to put new ones in place. I assumed that would be the case, but my personal shield stays." My tone brooks no argument. "Why can't I simply go outside while you do this?"

Finn looks at me like I said the stupidest thing he's ever heard, and, just like that, I am back to loathing his manners. "I need you here to tie the spell to you, Riley." He taps his hand on the cushion of the couch, and I reluctantly sit back down.

"Very well," he says. "It will take me longer to work without triggering your own shield, but I can do it. Would you please place both of your hands up, palms toward me?"

It's my turn to look incredulous. "Don't casters usually need some sort of material to cast strong wards? Candles, salt, anything?"

The arrogant bastard snickers. "I haven't needed to use props to cast these kinds of spells since I was a teenager. Give me some credit."

I can't decide whether he's truly a strong caster or if it's only his unparalleled ego talking.

"Now," he continues, "face me and put your hands in position like you want to high-five me with both your hands."

I roll my eyes so hard I think I can see the back of my head. "Or smack you," I cough under my breath.

Finn ignores my childish comment. He faces me, our knees and hands almost touching, and closes his eyes in concentration. Then he takes a deep breath and becomes all business. The moment I feel his power stir to the surface, it's like time slows down. Static fills the air.

His lips part slightly. "Lower your wards," he commands. His voice is deeper, rough with unshed energy.

The look on his face is mid-way between pain and longing. I've never seen him like this before, and I am so captivated by the sight that I forget what my simple task is. He opens his eyes, his gaze full of vulnerability.

"Do you trust me?" he asks. The green of his eyes seems to stir like his irises are made of oil and water battling for space.

The question is spoken with such intensity that it takes my breath away. I think he misinterprets my inaction as me having doubts because his shoulders slump ever so slightly in disappointment.

"In this, I do," I hurry to say. The moment the words leave me, I feel the truth in them. But how can I trust someone I've known for only three hours? Logic says I can't, but my gut is convinced I can. Anyway, what other choices do I have? I couldn't find anybody else who was willing to do the work for me in a pinch. I need to feel safe in my own home, and my rickety wards are not enough.

At once, I release the subpar protecting spell I cast on my apartment last week. I'm not even sure it was working properly in the first place. My specialty is definitely not spellcasting...

I don't want to speak, too scared to break both of our focuses, so I nod, telling him it's done.

Finn's eyes close once more, and I feel a rush of energy exploding from him. The walls around us vibrate and groan as if their very molecular structure is undergoing inexorable changes. The air is thick with power, but I am not scared. It feels like a sultry caress all over my body. The smell of him surrounds me—leather and something grounding, earthy, like rich, warm spices. Finn's breathing is labored, and a lonely bead of sweat rolls down his temple.

All of a sudden, the pressure leaves the room. The absence of it wrenches a whimper out of me. I then hear a series of three clicking sounds as if latches were snapped into place. When Finn opens his eyes again, they shine like emeralds under the sun.

He laces his fingers through mine, and I can feel the moment he lets go of the spell to tie it to me, so I have the control over it now. The small tether of magic buries deep inside me. He just quite literally gifted me some of his own energy to protect me. I don't know how I feel about that. I am not well versed in spell crafting and never thought about it that way before.

"You're now surrounded by three levels of protective magic," he states matter-of-factly. "Nothing is getting into this apartment without you allowing it."

I probably look awestruck, like a fish, mouth open but no sound. The power of his magic working is still raising the thin hair at the nape of my neck. I run my own energy all over his creation to check for flaws, but it's intricate, strong, perfect.

We all have our strengths. Mine are healing and potion-making. His is creating and weaving spells. Bree told me about Finn's abilities, but I thought she was exaggerating as friends usually do. However, seeing him at work and being able to touch and manipulate his creation afterward is... I have no words. I've never encountered a witch this powerful in my thirty years on this earth, well, maybe apart from Diane, but her powers laid elsewhere. It's as frightening as it is humbling to know that the corner bookseller could probably reduce this whole neighborhood to ashes if he set his mind to it.

I wonder if any other caster would have put so much effort into their work. After a moment, my gaze refocuses on Finn. He is waiting patiently for me to check his spell. His smug smile of success never comes. Finn's features remain serious, his lips in a hard line. I am breathing as hard as he is, trying to come down from the high created by the amount of power he tied to me. Our hands are still joined, and the sensation slowly makes its way back to my brain.

"Is it always like this for you?" I ask with a shaky voice. "Casting a spell, I mean."

"A thought for a thought?" is his only answer.

That's when the doorbell rings, stirring us away from our altered state. It must be the restaurant's delivery person. We get up at the same time. I hurry to my wallet for money, but he just shakes his head no. He throws a sheepish grin my way and rubs at his five o'clock stubble.

"It's on me," he says. "You already gave me wine and water. That's more than a man can ask for." He doesn't give me a chance to fire back a snarky comment before he turns to open the door.

But while he's not looking, I can't contain the stupid grin pulling at my lips.

We didn't talk much while eating. We had dinner at the coffee table, sitting like kings among the throw pillows on the floor. I haven't used my dining room table to actually eat on since I moved in, and I didn't feel like clearing it off now. The majority of my utensils live in the tiny drawer of my coffee table anyway.

I contemplate the amount of food left on the table and sigh. I'll be eating takeout for the next week, but if I ingest another bite of my tacos now, I won't ever be able to get up off the floor.

Finn turns his gaze to me and then to the empty glass of wine in my lap. He gets up without saying a word, picks up both our glasses, and heads to the kitchen. The silence is pregnant with unshed words. I don't know what he is holding in, and I'm not sure I want to hear it.

While he is filling our glasses, I busy myself with the leftovers, placing them back into their containers. When I enter the kitchen with my hands full of packed-up food, Finn is just closing the fridge door. One glance at me prompts him to open it back up. He takes the stack of containers from me.

While he is taking care of the food containers, placing them in a neat line in the fridge, I pick up the wine glasses and return to the couch. Finn emerges from the kitchen a few seconds later.

He stretches his hands over his head, making his T-shirt ride up and expose defined abs that my body responds to with a wave of heat going up my spine. I close my eyes and shiver. I don't know what it is about him that gets me in this state. The couch dips, and when I open my eyes again, he is seated comfortably beside me.

"Did you have any luck getting rid of your tracking spell?" he asks. The sudden change of pace takes me by surprise, but I answer honestly.

"I did find promising leads, but nothing concrete. I'm in over my head with this." My pride takes a hit at the admission.

"I thought you might have trouble removing it when I recognized its weaving," he says as nonchalantly as if he was talking about the weather.

I frown. "If you knew how to get rid of it when I came to your shop, why didn't you just tell me then? Why send Bree?" My body tenses as my temper flares.

He doesn't answer me right away. His gaze wanders to the street outside. Then his breath catches on an inhale. I lean over the couch to look at what has him wide-eyed.

Erick is standing there, his keys hanging listlessly from his fist, forgotten. His face is contorted in an expression I can't quite place because of the shadows cast by the lampposts. His attention is firmly fixed on Finn, who hastily averts his eyes. Erick's attention doesn't waver from his target until a passerby clips him in the shoulder as he walks by. That's when Erick sees me, too. He pins me in place with a stare a moment longer, then turns abruptly and starts walking away from his shop.

"What the fuck? Why is he still monitoring me?" I bristle, whipping my head in Finn's direction. "But more importantly, why did he look at you like he *knows* you?"

"Because he does," Finn breathes, his gaze unfocused, shell-shocked. I don't think he meant to answer my question so freely. He sounds hollow, haunted. Finn's words keep bouncing around in my head.

"What do you mean?" I say through clenched teeth.

He refuses to meet my stare. "I told you...I recognized that tracking spell. I had only seen it one time before, many years ago."

I cross my arms over my chest—a futile attempt to protect myself from the situation. "So, you knew the spell and how to take it off. You knew it was him. You *knew,* and you didn't tell me in the first place? It's a fucking tracking spell! Didn't you think I could've been in danger or that I was freaking out about being tracked? So your plan was, what? Let me stew while you pass for the hero once you undoubtedly succeeded at getting rid of the spell? What was your end goal with this? Why? To impress me? To go out with me? Are you in league with Erick, tracking women and slithering your way into their lives? What the heck, man?"

How stupid could I have been? People always lie and manipulate, acting in their own best interest, and I fell for it yet again. I had many "friends" over the years that ended up only wanting to take advantage of my powers, my skills, my connections, or even my love. I was naïve and always wanted to see the best in people, which I thought I grew out of, but apparently not.

"I couldn't be sure it really was Erick. I wasn't sure about any of it until now," he pleads.

"Do you know why he wants to track me?" The coldness of my tone is twin to the ice in my veins.

"I don't know, Riley. I swear to you, I don't know. That's what I wanted to find out."

"So, this whole book fair scheme was just so you could investigate while keeping me in the dark?"

"No! It's not—"

"Get out," I speak the words with such finality that Finn recoils as if from a physical blow.

"I just wanted to help. Please let me at least remove the tracking for you."

I'm done. I'm so done with this shitty deceitful behavior. "That won't be necessary. I'll go straight to the source myself, as I should've done in the first place. Now, I said get out."

Chapter 10

ERICK

I KNEW SHE WENT to Arcane. Of course, I knew. She took the damn coin with her. But even then, I couldn't anticipate that outcome. I can still see his wild eyes, those lips of his parting slightly as recognition slammed into him.

Finn. Fucking. Clark.

I told him. I told him to stay out of my way. I tighten my fist around my keys. I can barely feel the pinprick of pain through my stormy thoughts. He used to obey my orders so prettily back then. My mind runs to the edge of a chasm of memories so deep that I can't fathom what I'll find at the bottom of it.

No.

I can't be distracted tonight, so I do what I do best and put everything that is not swagger and confidence under lock and key deep into my gut. A heartbeat later, I can finally inhale deeply again. That's better. I'll deal with this mess later.

I really need to pick up my pace. I don't want to be late. The night is hot and humid, but I still throw on my hoodie and tuck my head deep into the hood. Anonymity is a precious currency. The cobblestone roads of old Québec City are full of tourists, even at this hour. Restaurant terraces are in full swing, and nobody is paying attention to me as I walk through the crowd.

It takes me about ten more minutes of brisk walking to reach my destination. The Drunken Sailor is an Irish pub through and through, down to the kegs of dry stout. Fortunately for me, I love the black stuff, although Riley's creations are quickly becoming the staple of the bar. The last potion master Albert hired couldn't recognize his left hand from his right lest it was written on them. Competence is hard to find these days. Let's just say that the overall quality of products increased dramatically in the short period of time she has worked here.

The establishment is already full of patrons. As I turn the corner to go around the pub to the back entrance, my path is blocked by a big man hugging the side of the building, retching all over his shoes. I slow my pace and make to go around him when he turns abruptly. The fellow doesn't even register my presence. He wipes his mouth with his shirt, smiles to himself, and stumbles toward the pub's door, babbling gods know what. But he doesn't even have time to touch the handle before the doorman blocks his way.

Well, that's going to be a long night for him. I'm still laughing to myself when I reach the back alley. I rap my knuckle on the metal door. The sliding slot opens and closes too fast for me to see who's behind it. Then the heavy lock unfastens, and the door opens on someone I don't know. I can't decide if it's good or bad. The new bouncer stops me in my tracks before I can cross the threshold.

Bad it is, then.

"Where do you think you're going?" he asks. The guy looks like he might do a little too much chest and arms and not enough legs at the gym.

I take a step back and put my hands in my pockets. "To the poker game. Where's Tommy?"

He rakes a hand through his dirty blond hair before saying, "Do you really think that by mentioning the name of a guy who works here, I will let you pass without checking with the croupier?"

I take out the deck of playing cards from my pocket and start shuffling them. "First, that was a genuine question," I say honestly. "I like Tommy, which means I am also concerned for his welfare. Second, I don't have time for this shit. I'm already late." I flip the three of hearts into the air, where it hangs in suspension, emitting a soft blue glow. Thor, here, is mesmerized by the spell. His entire focus is on the small card. For the next sixty seconds, I could jig while juggling fiery keels, and he would not remember. I pat his shoulder and make my way through the back door.

I follow the narrow corridor past the stairs and enter the vast expense of an old, repurposed speakeasy. The space is completely deserted. I look at the time. Shit! I hurry to one of the alcoves along the wall and run my hand under the table. I find the button I was looking for and press it. The booth swivels, leading to a hidden room. I have to jump out of it while it's still in motion since it doesn't stop its rotation until it's back in its initial position.

This space is a lot smaller. It's bare except for the green-carpeted poker table and the mismatched leather chairs around it. The only light comes from several oil lamps affixed to the walls. It is totally off-grid. I would never call it a dungeon in front of the owner, but it totally looks like one, and not the fun kind.

Everyone is already seated, including the owner, Albert, who is also the croupier. He motions for me to approach. Albert is in his mid-fifties but keeps in good shape. His jovial disposition and round red face make him look like a fit version of Santa.

His establishment is this city's neutral ground. It's not uncommon to see rival groups drink peacefully, their tables side by side. But once they get outside, the feud picks up where it left off. Nobody really knows who (or what) Albert is or why his pub became a neutral zone in the city. There are only rumors. It's part of the legend that people created around him, I suppose.

His warm voice booms through the enclosed space. "I'm happy to see you, boy. We were starting to think that you wouldn't show."

I take a seat at the table and return his smile. "I would have been on time if it wasn't for your new guy in the back." On cue, the bouncer makes his entry, the booth creaking softly as it turns.

"I'm sorry, boss," he says through clenched teeth. "This one got past me, although I have no idea how."

Albert looks at me knowingly. "That's fine, Stephen. You can go back to your position."

Then to me, he says, "Tommy didn't show up tonight, and I couldn't get a hold of him, so I had to improvise. The lad has never missed a day of work since he started here." Albert takes a swig of his beer. He is worried; it's plain to see. "I sent Jenny to check on him, but he wasn't home. I don't know what to make of it with all the disappearances lately." He shakes his head, and a strand of mostly gray hair escapes the leather cord he uses to tie it back. "It's probably nothing."

Unease slithers through my body as I bury myself deeper in my chair.

I take in the players around the table in turn, trying to gauge if one of them knows anything about the situation. I recognize them all. Every single one of them, apart from Albert, works for the boss—"the Berserker," as they call him. Although it doesn't matter in this place tonight.

There is Njal with his giant size, unkept red beard, and head tattoos. The constellation of freckles on his pale skin is the only thing that doesn't look frightening about him. Also, there is Clarence, one of the most trusted handymen of the Berserker. They both rose through the ranks because of their ability to carry out any odd job under the sun. Gods know, there are many of those in their line of work.

Patrick looks like an accountant, which I suppose they are. In a way... Their glasses are constantly falling down their nose. With their salary, I don't even know why they don't just buy new ones.

The last player is a young Latina woman who appears to be in her early twenties. She is looking straight at me with eyes of the palest blue. I haven't met her yet, but I heard about this new addition. She is, apparently, very skilled with poisons. I eye suspiciously the pint of beer that was already present at my seat when I arrived.

I sigh. No beer tonight, I suppose.

As for me, they all think that I am simply a pawn on the board and that my shop is only one of the many insignificant cash cows under the boss's thumb. To them, I'm just the cunning gambler that can't help but get under everybody's skin. I am happy to oblige and play the part.

Njal relaxes in his seat and looks at his cards with a stoic face. I, however, look at what destiny dealt me and grin.

Clarence glances my way and groans. "You son of a bitch," he says, his voice carrying no heat. "You'll steal the shirt right from my cold, dead body again."

The evening is quickly coming to an end, and I'm not closer to getting any answers, or any piece of useful information, for that matter. Frustration gnaws at my insides. I decide to pick up my winnings and call it a night.

The dim lights of the speakeasy's corridor remind me of the soft glow coming from Riley's apartment window. The events of earlier that night intrude, unwanted, into my thoughts. My steps become heavy with exasperation. When I reach the back door, the bouncer is nowhere to be seen. I shrug to myself and step outside. As I turn the corner of the next alleyway, I spot him, his back to me, relieving himself against the adjacent building on the other side of the road.

My nostrils flair in annoyance. "You know, there's a perfectly functional bathroom inside. You don't have to litter your filth all over."

Stephen zips himself back up and turns around, wiping his hands on his jeans.

Classy.

His glare burns a hole through my skull, yet I can't help but pour lighter fluid on the kindling fire. "Come on, you can answer me. Use your words like a big boy."

"I'll do you one better, asshole, and knock that smug smile from your pretty face." Without any other warning, he charges me.

I knew he had a grudge against me for the stunt I pulled earlier, but I didn't think he was that hot-tempered. Oh, well.

He is big, but I am a lot faster, not to mention extensively trained. I dodge him easily, and he almost loses his balance when he hits the empty space where flesh should have been. He doesn't even stop to think before he comes at me again, faster than last time, but his side is wide open. I feint to the right. He takes the bait, and I only have to give a little push on the side of his rib cage. His own momentum throws him face-first on the asphalt. He doesn't get up right away.

"You think I'm pretty?" I say, batting my lashes heavily. "I'm flattered. You know, if you wanted to go out with me, you could've just asked. Come to think of it, your manners are disappointing. You'll have to work on them if you're to woo me."

Stephen shakes the gravel from his shirt and bares his teeth at me, snarling. Even though only half of his face is illuminated by the lamppost beside him, I can still see an angry red vein pulsing at his temple. I should just go. My state of mind is not the best. Despite his disgusting habits, I have no intention of seriously injuring the guy. I am just pissy, and my mouth ran away with my thoughts again.

His next movements are more precise and calculated. But even then, he doesn't stand a chance. As we exchange punches and kicks, I ensure he doesn't wound me or himself in the process. I make sure he'll only wake up with a bruised ego and a headache in the morning, nothing worse.

I finally get a chance to tread far enough, and I lift both hands in the air, taking another step back for good measure. "Look, man, I'm tired. Can we just start over on the right foot?" I incline my chin at the pub that is now almost fifty feet away. "I have no intention of getting on Albert's bad side."

Stephen's breathing is ragged. His body is as tight as a bowstring. "I don't think so."

"Need any help?" Paul says, appearing out of nowhere, making Stephen startle briefly. Paul's police uniform is perfectly ironed, not a crease in sight. He is leaning on the side of one of the buildings, holding a Batman to-go coffee mug. He always gets his refill at the twenty-four-hour convenience store down the street. He must have heard the noise.

"Oh! Hey, Paul!" My statement is followed by a *humph* as I let Stephen tackle me to the ground, which gets him exactly where I want him—unbalanced and on top of me. As soon as he cocks his fist to strike, putting him even more out of balance, I take hold of his weight-bearing arm with both hands. I swipe my leg under his and bring his weight-bearing arm between us and up, which effectively flips him, his back to me. This maneuver enables me to put him in a headlock while both my legs trap his. No matter how strong he is, he struggles in the wrong way, only showing his lack of training.

"No, thanks. I got it," I answer Paul, a little breathless. Stephen continues to try to wrestle out of my grip, but it's no use. Even if my muscles scream at me from the effort, I won't relent. This kind of pain is as familiar to me as my own face. I welcome it like an old friend. "By the way," I carry on through gritted teeth, "I received the necklace you ordered for your wife. Just come by when you can. It's already gift-wrapped." I wink at him. "On the house."

I feel Stephen's body slump against me. Finally. I keep my hold a little longer to make sure he is not faking before pushing him off and getting up.

I. Am. Filthy. *Ugh.*

I crouch and put my palm in front of his nose to make sure his breathing is strong and even.

"I knew there was a reason why you were my favorite," Paul says without a care in the world. He takes a sip of his coffee. "Well, I gather you'll look after the angry lad, if I'm not mistaken?"

"You got it, Paul." Satisfied with my answer, he pushes off the wall and walks to his police car down the street. You can never have too many allies, whether they have powers or not. Paul might not have magic, but he is a very valuable friend to have when you get in trouble with the human justice system.

I can't really leave Stephen alone and unconscious in the dark. So, I pick up my phone and call Albert for help to get his hotheaded bouncer back to the pub. I know Albert will understand the situation, plus the fight wasn't on his premises, but I hate disappointing the man. As I wait for Albert to answer, I pinch the bridge of my nose and sigh, anticipating the bawl-out that's coming.

Chapter 11

RILEY

If Erick wanted to hurt me, he had plenty of chances to do it over the last week. I need answers, and since nobody seems inclined to give me any, I'll need to take matters into my own hands. Perched on the back of my couch, I wait patiently for the woman working with him at the shop to leave. I did my own snooping over the last week, and she has a habit of going for coffee around the same time every day.

Last night with Finn reminded me why I usually keep to myself. I just thought that, since I was starting over, I could do things differently. I figured it would be good for me to "participate" in new activities and meet new people since I've been more of a loner over the last couple of years.

Evidently not.

I am more frustrated with myself than anything else because I really like Bree and Finn already. There must be something wrong with me. It's like I only attract people who like to play games.

The woman bangs the door closed behind her. *Finally*. I can't decide if she's really that strong or just pissed off all the time.

I check for the hundredth time if I have everything. My pepper spray is in my jean's back pocket, and my keys can make a nice brass knuckle replacement if need be. I don't think I am in any real danger in an open shop in the middle of the day, but you can never be too careful.

I put on my biker gloves and steel-toe boots and make my way to The Underground Castle.

Before going in, I check through the door to see if there are any other clients in the shop. I can't make out any from where I stand. Good. I take a deep breath and push open the door. A light ding announces my presence. I carefully tread down the narrow stairs and arrive at a shop that, indeed, looks like an underground castle.

How very literal.

A raspy male voice welcomes me. "Hail, friend, well met. If you need anything, just ask," Erick says from behind the counter, keeping his eyes glued to his phone in the meantime.

I can't help the chuckle that escapes me at the formal medieval greeting, which draws his attention to me. I caught him off guard. Shock is written all over his beautiful face for a split second before he wrestles his features back into a mask of bored indifference.

"If it isn't Riley, the mighty potion master," he croons.

"Cut the crap." My steps are assured as I move through the displays to unceremoniously drop the coin onto the glass counter in front of him. "Why are you tracking me?"

"Not able to remove my little spell, I see." He doesn't even bother to deny it.

"Answer me. Why would a back-alley caster spell my tip?" I bristle.

The insult falls flat. I can see the gears turning behind his eyes as he looks for a way out. Then the side of his mouth lifts in an arrogant grin. "If I say that I'm sorry and promise not to do it again, would it be enough to make you leave?"

Cocky prick!

Fine. If that's how he wants to play this. "Finn says 'hi,' by the way."

Silence meets my comment. He frowns and gets up from his stool. "This conversation is over," he says as he looks at me one more time before crossing the threshold to his stockroom.

"Oh, no, you don't." I round the counter and hurry after him, but when I step inside, he is nowhere to be seen. Puzzled, I take a step back. Nothing is amiss. I go through the motion a couple more times until I pick up on a light warping that happens when I move over the threshold.

A roar of frustration rumbles from my throat. "Take down that extension charm or illusion spell or whatever the crap this is, and talk to me!"

Nothing happens.

"I am a very patient woman," I lie, "and I will wait here until you answer my questions." I cross my arms and wait. And wait.

Like a curtain has been lifted, in the space between one blink and the next, I see what's really behind door number one. Erick stands right in front of me with what I assume is the trigger for the charm—a playing card—flat against the doorframe. There's only an inch between our bodies, and even through my anger, his smell of cypress and smoke reaches me and roots me in place. My body has a mind of its own, and my lips part slightly on a shivering exhale.

His face lights up at the sight. "What are you waiting for, *Darkness*?" he drawls, reaching for a lock of my black hair. "You wanted to talk to me, then talk."

"I am not your *dark* anything." I duck under his outstretched arm before he can make contact and stalk into the room. As soon as I am completely through, he pockets the king of spades, and the illusion returns.

At first glance, I don't understand what I'm looking at. The space is arranged as a mirror image of the front of the store, which means that I find myself behind a counter once again. Well, it does look more like a giant hunk of driftwood than a counter, and there is an opening on my right to a real storage space this time.

The middle of the floor is occupied by a hand-carved wood display containing all sorts of trinkets beneath its glass top. All the walls are covered with staffs, swords, and even a painting or two. As I'm standing there, I find it hard to breathe. The atmosphere feels stuffy, as if I am walking through a thick fog. That's when understanding dawns on me.

I whirl around and spot Erick lounging against the doorframe with his hands in his pockets, waiting for me to say something. "You run an underground magical artifact operation? Why on earth would you let me see this?" Dread pricks at the back of my mind. "Oh, gods, you'll make sure I can't talk." I take a step back while I reach into my back pocket for the pepper spray.

Erick breaks into laughter. "I only let you see this, as you say, because if Eleanor catches you threatening me, she'll pancake you. And believe it or not, I'm trying to protect you, Riley."

I throw my hands into the air in utter disbelief. "I'll need more than—" A high-pitched screech cuts me off.

Erick mutters a string of expletives, raking his hands through his hair. "I was sure I had locked that damn portal." I didn't notice the unassuming door that leads to the back alley until this very moment. Its surface is rapidly dissolving now, and taking its place is a substance that looks suspiciously like glittery water. The horrible sound must be the portal bell warning of someone's arrival.

"Fuck! Fuck! Fuck! I don't know when Eleanor will be back. I can't send you on the other side alone, just in case." I am about to ask why his employee would be a problem when he points to the storage space. "Quick, hide! If you value your life, you'll stay hidden and quiet."

The adrenaline flooding my system stops me from arguing, and my survival instincts take over. I scramble past him and lay my back flat on the other side of the wall inside the real stockroom.

The nasty sound recedes and is replaced by heavy footsteps. "The boss needs his truth-mining talismans. Now. He says you have them ready," the stranger declares.

"Hello to you too, Clarence," Erick deadpans.

Truth-mining? Those must be rare artifacts, indeed. To dredge up unfiltered, pure truth from someone is no easy feat. Only a couple of objects throughout history were known to be able to do such a thing, and the spells used to enchant them were cast over multiple generations and are now lost to the world. People will pay a pretty penny for a fraction of that kind of power. To have one of those in your possession is extremely rare, but to have more than one is unheard of.

There is a small round mirror in the storage space placed in such a way that someone working in here can make out the counter area, but not the other way around. I can see the man. His brown hair is cropped close to his scalp like a soldier's. Frown lines are permanently etched on his forehead. His posture speaks of quiet danger.

But Erick doesn't seem to care. "You know as well as I do that the delivery was supposed to be tomorrow. Tell him I'll have them ready by then." Not a hint of fear or unsteadiness filters into his tone. He is all haughtiness and charismatic smile, hands flat on the wooden surface, a king in his kingdom.

"The boss knew you would say that, and he told me that if you argued, he would come down himself to get them."

They both stare at each other for a beat longer, but Erick decides to go with it. I don't know what's at stake here, but it seems like the idea of "the boss," whoever he is, coming over is enough to make Erick fold.

"Of course," Erick drawls. "Give me just a minute. They're in the back. I'll put them in a bag for you."

He walks through the storage room entrance without looking at me. He lifts a couple of boxes before he finds what he's searching for. Then he comes back to the small table on the other side of me and lays down what looks like ten pieces of rubbish. There are five old coins, four worn-out dice, and a pearl necklace that has seen better days.

"No funny business," Clarence says sternly. "If I die here, he'll know, and it'll be your turn next."

Erick doesn't pay him any attention.

Die here? Like Erick would kill him? I discreetly scoot as far away from him as possible. It's laughably useless, but it makes me feel safer somehow. I know Erick has seen me move, but he doesn't acknowledge it.

He steps to the back of the small room and pushes one of the stones on the wall, which prompts two bigger stones to move back and away from each other, revealing a safe. He retrieves a glass orb from it. The sphere fits perfectly in the palm of his hand and emits a faint blue light.

It cannot be what I think it is. It's supposed to have been lost for centuries, never to be recovered. The eye of Sannaleika should be shining bright as an evening star. But this orb is only a ghost, a fraction of what should be a vast power. It was said that the mere proximity of it could reduce a god's will to ashes and make them confess their darkest secrets. But as Erick approaches with it, I don't feel a thing except for a deep unease.

Once he reaches the table, Erick's whole demeanor changes. He exhales loudly, and his shoulders droop. Then, with pleading eyes, he gestures for me to stay quiet.

He closes his fist over the orb and covers the small trinkets with his other hand. The soft glow of the orb starts to pulse and sputter in his fist like a dying star. Then the blue light enters Erick's body, creating thin lines that crawl over his forearm and disappear under his shirt to reappear down his other arm. The energy exits his body through his other palm and enters the now new talismans. The process is almost instantaneous, but I am in such disbelief over what I am seeing and the implication of it all that I experience everything as if it were in slow motion.

With a heavy heart, I come to the realization that the eye of Sannaleika is no more.

However, this sadness is mixed with an overwhelming feeling of wonderment. I was so captivated by the process that I moved closer to the table without meaning to. He is not a caster, after all. I lift my gaze to Erick's, and my lips form the soundless word—*syphon*.

From what I can remember of my history books, syphon witches were the Sennex's—our witch government's—darlings. They were a faction of void-born witches—as opposed to power-born witches—with a rich culture of combat training and battle strategy.

Given their dispositions and skills, most of them worked for the army alongside power-born witches. There is not a whole lot we know about them since they were very secretive when they were still around. The worst tragedy in recent witch history caused their extinction about two hundred years ago.

Although they could not produce their own magical energy, their gift allowed them to withdraw what they needed. A simple brush of their skin on their target's surface or skin allowed them to syphon magic from inanimate objects and magical beings alike. They then became masters of that energy until it was spent. I remember pictures. They used to always have a brass disc with them that was utilized as a receptacle to hold the energy they didn't want to wield right away. It has been said that they could syphon curses and hexes without being affected and then redirect them onto their opponent. I know there's more, but my scrambled mind cannot recall.

I am in awe. These kinds of abilities have not been witnessed in two centuries. Why doesn't this guy report to the Sennex? He would be worshiped as the gift that he is.

Then I remember another detail—syphons can feel and differentiate the distinct types and strengths of powers with only a touch of skin on skin. I stiffen at the thought and abruptly take a step back. This is not happening—he cannot touch me. Nobody can know. Erick's features fall when he sees my hasty retreat. I want to tell him that I am not afraid of his power but rather afraid of my own, but I can't speak unless I want to be discovered.

Erick picks up the talismans and puts them into a leather pouch. I am practically trying to fuse with the wall as he goes around me and back into the clandestine shop.

"Took you long enough," Clarence says.

"Tell him these are the last ones he's going to get. I couldn't find more. And remind him that, once activated, each talisman is only good for one truth." I can't hear the rest of their conversation through my astonishment.

The sound of the portal reopening makes me lunge into action. I still don't know if Erick is a friend or a foe. With the man's comment about dying, I can't be sure of anything right now. I am scrambling around the small storage space to find something to defend myself with when I remember the pepper spray. Holding it out in front of me, I step carefully back into the main room.

Erick is on the other side of the space with his hands still in his pockets. His teeth worry his lower lip. He looks so young then, uncertain, so at odds with his usual self-assurance.

I take measured steps toward the back door, which is now completely solid.

"It's unlocked," he whispers. "You are free to leave whenever you want, but please hear me out before you go." Something in his tone, his posture, in the general feel of him, makes me pause with my fingers gripping the handle.

"Why was that guy worried he would get killed here today?" I know it's not the most gracious thing to say, but it's the only one that comes to mind at the moment.

Erick clears his throat but still doesn't move a finger. "I know you don't have any reason to believe me, but I am not a danger to you, Riley." He rakes his hand through his hair, something like sorrow twisting his mouth. "Ask Finn. You'll see. Please, just give me a chance to explain before outing me to the Sennex. But not here. In a more secure location."

I guffaw. "You really think that I will go anywhere alone with you?"

“Not alone, no. With Finn,” he says, his voice breaking on Finn’s name. My heart sinks at the deepening anguish rolling off him in waves.

It’s enough to make the logical part of my brain work again. Ever since I first saw him, Erick never did much more than annoy me to tears. Also, I feel like, even if Finn didn’t tell me about his true intentions in the first place, he would have warned me if I was in any danger from Erick. And there’s the matter of Albert vouching for him.

I have a feeling that in the wondrous world I just stumbled upon, what you don’t know can indeed kill you.

“What you saw here is as much a danger to you as it is to me,” he continues, giving me confirmation.

“How will I know where to find you?”

“Follow the invitation.”

“When?”

“Tonight.”

Without hesitation, I step through the door and into the midday sun.

Chapter 12

FINN

THE PICTURE PAINTED FOR me when I arrive at Riley's doorstep just amplifies the sense of foreboding that grows in the pit of my stomach. She's sitting on the interior stairs leading up to her apartment, her head in her hands. She wouldn't tell me why she needed to see me over the phone, but after last night, the least I can do is be here. She was right. I should have told her my suspicions right away and worked with her instead of around her.

The evening sun casts a menacing shadow over her body. I stop before her slumped figure, but she doesn't move, doesn't look at me. "Is he dangerous? Please be honest," she breathes.

I don't have to ask to know whom she's talking about. I want to tell her that, yes, he is dangerous. I want to tell her that even though my body was his to cherish, his to punish, the worst wound he gave me was not a physical one. But I don't say any of this because I am a coward. "I don't believe he is a threat to your safety."

She laughs a shriveled, dry sound. "That's a very political answer." She still refuses to look at me. "Were you aware that he operates an underground magical artifact business?"

"What? No. He owns a medieval shop." My mind is racing, trying to find a way to reconcile the young man I knew with the person she's talking about. Why would he put himself in danger like that? It doesn't make sense.

"I saw it with my own eyes, Finn. The least you can do is be honest with me."

"I swear to you, I had no idea. Yesterday was the first time I'd seen him in three years."

She finally lifts her head. Her irises are but two pools of black ink, and the angles of her face are sharper in the dim light. She looks like a queen ready to pass sentence, a vengeful goddess.

Erick would paint her like that.

My fingers itch to cradle her face, to reassure her, but she's not mine to treasure, and the look on her face tells me she never will be. Whatever seedling of pull that had been growing between us, I screwed it up before it even had a chance to grow.

I can't wait any longer. I have to know. "What happened, Riley? Did he hurt you?"

She frowns. "No more than you did."

Ouch. I deserved that, but it still sucks to hear.

A muffled notification sound beeps in the staircase. She pulls out her phone from her pocket and reads whatever it is. Then she turns the phone around to show it to me.

You've got mail.

That's all it says, and it comes from a private number.

I don't understand.

Without preamble, she gets up and walks outside to unlock her mailbox. She pulls out one of those cheap convenience store maps of Québec City. When she unfolds it, I can see her name written in red Sharpie beside a dot on the map. On closer inspection, I notice the dot is moving with Riley's name following beside it. Then it stops completely.

"Erick said that I should give him a chance to explain himself before I make up my mind and get him arrested by the Sennex's task force. He said to follow the invitation. And you're coming with me."

Our destination is a seemingly abandoned building. The red brick exterior is falling to dust. There is graffiti all over, but one, in particular, captures my attention. It's a rune, the same one I have tattooed in the middle of my chest—*thurisaz*. My thorn, my destruction, my salvation.

I rub at the rune on my chest as I walk over to the one sprayed on the wall, Riley in tow. I trace over the graffiti with my index finger, and as soon as my hand leaves the surface, the door to the underground cellar beside us unseals with a *pop*.

When we walk in, it locks immediately behind us. We find ourselves in an antechamber with two cameras in opposite corners of the ceiling. There is only one place to go from here, and the door leading there is already cracked open. It's just three steps, but it feels like I'm about to throw myself off a cliff. My pulse hammers erratically in my ears.

I take a moment to gather my courage before I carefully pull the handle and find myself in an empty command center. To my right is a wall full of screens with different views of the building. Military-grade monitoring and security equipment are scattered under them on a long desk against the wall. The rest of the space is a common room with a couch, chairs, a TV, and different game consoles. A reinforced steel bunker door lays open at the back.

I'm about to walk to it when Erick steps through and leans on the doorframe, flicking a coin in the air with his thumb—Riley's coin. He pockets it and crosses his arms. His ethereal gaze moves from me to Riley, and something shatters a little in his demeanor. When he looks back at me, I can see, for a fleeting moment, the storm raging—anger and pain and loneliness and regret and everything that makes his heart beat so strongly.

"Thanks for agreeing to meet with me," Erick says, his deep voice strong and assured despite everything. I haven't heard his gravelly tone for so long. I had almost forgotten the effect he can have on my body with words alone. My legs loosen, and I almost drop to my knees, but I don't. Instead, I force myself to seem as unaffected as humanly possible.

He motions for us to take a seat. Riley keeps her eyes on him and chooses the chair closest to the door. I want to tell her that it doesn't make any difference because no one is getting out of this place unless Erick disables the lock on the exterior door, but I don't. I don't want to freak her out even more. For my part, I choose to sit before the security console.

Old habits die hard.

We are both still silent when Erick nods to himself, coming to a decision only he is privy to. "Want any water?" This he directs to Riley.

"What I want is for you to get on with the explanation you wanted me—us—to hear."

"Okay... Okay..." He rubs at his day-old stubble like he's trying to find the right words. "I am a syphon." The breath he lets out is all self-loathing, and I just want to rip it away. As I sit there, all I can do is hate everything, all of this, with every fiber of my being. I hate the distance, the things left unsaid between us, and the alienness of it all.

"I didn't plan on broadcasting it, but my hand was forced."

"The order from the boss?" she asks.

"The boss," he confirms.

"I didn't plan on lying to you either," he continues. "It's just that it's always been safer that way. All my life, I've been told to stay under the radar because, although there are monuments erected in honor of the fallen syphons, my parents weren't sure how my talents would be received now. Sadly, people are often scared of differences. For a long time, the only people aware of my void were my parents. They used old training textbooks saved from The Great Extinction to show me how to syphon magic from small objects that I would keep in my pockets. So, if I was asked to perform magic by a friend, I would be able to do it and not arise any suspicion."

He reaches for a pack of playing cards in his pocket and selects the five of spades, turning it around between his fingers. "These are my magic. They are all single-use spells. Nobody thinks twice about them because casters can enchant objects as much as they like with their own energy. They usually don't go through the trouble of doing it because they can manifest and create those spells on the spot, but still, people just aren't that perceptive or inquisitive." As he finishes his sentence, he throws the card up, and it detonates, producing a small explosion. I am not easily startled, but Riley squeals in surprise.

I try to hide my smile as best I can. The amount of energy he was able to put into that simple vessel while keeping it stable is truly impressive. Normally, casters have to use much sturdier receptacles than a piece of cardboard to hold a combat spell. The scholar in me itches to ask him how he did it, but I don't want to interrupt, afraid he will just stop talking altogether.

When I look back at him, he already has another card fisted in one of his hands. "It's also my fail-safe. If I ever was in a situation where I needed a lot of magic in one go, I could just syphon the deck all at once and use it."

Although I've known that he is a syphon for over three years, I've never seen him use his abilities before, and it's breathtaking. I only notice the pulse of energy he absorbs because I'm attentive. To anybody else, nothing would look amiss. A moment later, flames dance in his other palm until the magic sputters and dies, spent.

He looks at me then, his sad smile magnified by the ghosts behind his eyes. "Apart from my parents and Eleanor, the woman working with me, you're the only ones who know about my void now. And, after my explanation, I hope you'll want to keep it that way, too."

Just as Erick heads back to his position against the doorframe, Riley waves for him to sit. Despite his obvious hesitation, he steps forward and sits down on the couch.

"I don't get it," she says. "You are a syphon, Erick. The Sennex would welcome you as a hero. The earthquake that caused the landslide that destroyed the syphon settlements was the most painful tragedy in recent witch history. No one ever thought we'd see your line rise from the ashes of that disaster. It's a miracle. You represent hope, Erick. You do."

He snorts. "I don't think the Sennex would agree with you." He glances in my direction. "For some political shit I won't get into right now, my father and I had to flee where I grew up when I was eighteen. We're still on the run from the Sennex. I think they might know what I am. I'm not sure, though, since I never used my void in front of other witches back in the day. Even so, it would be stupid for me to use my void in the open now. The Sennex would get wind of a syphon's presence here, and when they inevitably figure out who I am, I would be taken into custody."

I still remember the night he and his father had to flee like it was yesterday. I felt so powerless, so lost, so full of rage for him.

But, later on, I added resentment to the list. Resentment that he deemed me unworthy of his secret for all these years. We were best friends our entire lives until it became more, and even then, he didn't say a word about his void to me. I had to learn about it three years ago when I finally tracked him down. Let's just say that the reunion didn't go as I had planned it in my head.

"My father and I started both businesses when we landed here," Erick says. "He left everything to me when I turned twenty-one."

His father, Victor, is also a syphon. To my knowledge, they are the last two. Victor's secret was revealed when Erick's family estate was raided by the Sennex for suspected treason. Victor had to act and protect his wife and son, which resulted in him using his void in plain sight. But where *is* Victor? Was he captured by the Sennex? The question is on the tip of my tongue, but I don't ask it. It's not my place to decide what Erick wants to share with us.

"I know it's not ideal," he continues, "but now, I have clients in high places all over this city and obligations I can't shy away from."

"Who's the boss?" Riley asks, steel in her voice.

"The Berserker. He is the leader of an organized crime syndicate. Magical mafia, if you will. Let's just say he didn't get his name because of his soft temper."

"And you have business with him?"

"Well, I don't really have a choice, but yes, I supply him with different artifacts that are hard to find. He has a posse of skilled magic wielders at his disposal, but, sometimes, even they run out of solutions."

"So, he pays for all of this?" She waves her hand around the space to indicate the bunker and its contents.

"Fuck no! Nobody apart from you two and Eleanor know about this place. It's my own, paid with untraceable money. I have a decoy loft in the middle of the city where I sleep most nights. *That* is paid by the Berserker for my services, but I know it's only a gilded prison to keep me under his thumb. If I've learned anything being on the run, it's that you always need a contingency plan."

Riley's frown deepens, and she crosses her arms over her chest. "Why let me see this side of your business at all? And what's Eleanor got to do with it?"

As soon as Eleanor's name is mentioned, Erick smiles to himself. A pang of jealousy that I have no business feeling hits me. "When my father left everything to me, I needed help to manage things. Eleanor runs the front, while I run the back, usually. She knows the ins and outs of both businesses. At this point, she's more family than friend. But Riley, I wasn't lying. She's very...protective. I let you see my operation in part because if she had arrived in the middle of our argument, she would've come to the rescue, and she can quickly get...physical where I'm concerned.

"The other reason is obvious. You were onto me, asking questions to Albert and not being subtle in your research at all. I needed to make you understand that asking questions so openly could land you in hot water. And I had a feeling you wouldn't leave it at that unless you were shown proof." I can clearly see that he is not telling us everything, but I can't fathom what more he could be hiding.

"And the tracking coin?" Riley asks.

Erick rubs his neck, no doubt thinking of a way to say what he has to say without making her bolt. "Witches have been disappearing without a trace over the past six months. Some of them I knew very well, and nobody was doing anything about it, so I decided to take matters into my own hands. There seems to be no rhyme or reason, no pattern that I'm aware of, for the ones that get picked off. They were all from different walks of life, different jobs, different powers, and so on. Most of them were above-average powerful, though. So, when I heard of you, Riley—new in town and a very skilled potion master and powerful healer—I figured you could be a target. So, I decided to track your movements. That way, I could at least have a lead if you disappeared, assuming you kept the coin. I could have a slim chance to maybe find the others, too."

"Come on," Riley says, disbelief coloring her tone. "Don't you think it could be your Berserker crime leader pouring cement shoes behind all of this? It looks obvious to me, at least."

"I don't know," Erick answers, perplexed. "Of course, I thought about it. But why now? Why those witches? Why risk exposing his operations to the Sennex by attracting too much attention? It just doesn't make sense to me. Before taking action against the most dangerous man in this city, I want proof that he's involved, at least. I just... Please stay away from all of this, both of you. From what I gather, you could both be possible targets. I was—I *am*—trying to help."

Riley huffs a bitter laugh and gets up. It's as if she's completely forgotten that I even exist. Her razor-sharp focus is solely on Erick when she says, "All I'm hearing is that you thought you knew better, and you decided to take those choices away from me. Turns out, without the necessary information, yes, I would have probably done something incredibly stupid. I don't want to be a pawn in your investigation. You will *never* use me like that again. Understood?"

Without another word, she storms out of the room. I swivel on my chair and spot the screens with the antechamber feed. She stops short at the outside door, places her hand on the doorknob, and looks directly at the camera. I don't hear Erick approach, and I almost jump out of my skin when he bends down beside me to press the lock release.

Just like that, she may be out of both of our lives for good.

I am still staring at the screen when Erick turns around and sits on the desk beside my chair. I don't know what to say. My mind is racing. This is the most I've seen of him in three years. The situation is fucked up, and I agree with Riley. He should have told her the information she needed to protect herself instead of using her as a pawn.

I don't look at him. I can't look at him. "Why didn't you call me when things got rough?" I ask. "You knew full well where I was. I could have helped." The man is the only reason I'm still on this side of the Atlantic. I refuse to believe he doesn't think I would help him, no matter how things ended between us.

"I wasn't your problem anymore," he answers.

I don't know what to say to that. We're silent for what feels like hours after that, just breathing side by side. Then I get up and do the only thing I can think of that will make me feel better in that moment.

I punch him in the gut.

Chapter 13

RILEY

"YOU'LL RUN A PATH in your new rug. Stop. You're making me dizzy," Evie says from her seat on the couch. Then she calmly takes a sip of her glass of wine, her bloodred nails blending with the color of the Merlot. She's so chill with all of this. It's annoying.

I called my best friend as soon as I got home. When she heard the panic as well as the overflowing anger in my voice, she hung up on me, ditched her date, and came straight over. Apparently, she wasn't impressed by his choice of restaurant. Her words, not mine. I've spent the last hour telling her every single piece of convoluted info I learned earlier in the evening.

"Tell me there's a way out of this that I didn't think of," I tell her. "I mean, yes, the easy way out would be to report Erick to the Sennex. But if everything he said is true, the Sennex is not even investigating those witches' disappearances. What if he's getting close to saving them, and I get in the way? What if 'the boss' learns that I'm the one who snitched on his operations to the Sennex? No, if I involve the authorities, I'm dead. *Argh*! I'm so..." I trail off, bringing my clenching fingers forward as if I was trying to strangle the air between them. Anger feels too tame of a word.

I know I'm rambling, but my mind feels like mush. If I could, I would just up and leave.

I hate this.

This place was supposed to be a new beginning. No drama, no complicated situations, just freedom and fun. I just want to finally build a life for myself in peace. All the savings that I had went into this move, which means I am financially tied down for the time being. Also, I finally landed a job that allows me the independence to create whatever the fuck I want as long as it sells. It's not something to give up lightly.

In moments like these, I miss my parents even more. Although the car crash happened almost ten years ago, I still have days when I forget they are no longer on this earth and dial their old phone number to talk to my mom. But when the error message comes over the line, I remember the death and pain all over again. If she was alive right now, my mom would tell me to come back home in a heartbeat. At least until I figured out what I wanted to do next. And my dad would make everything better like he used to do.

Okay, Riley. Take deep breaths. In. Out. In. Out. Now, push all those yucky emotions down and think clearly again.

Evie captures my hand as I pass for the thousandth time in front of her and tugs me down to the couch. "Breathe, Riley. Do you believe that either Finn or Erick wants to hurt you? Do you think your immediate safety is threatened by them?"

The fact of the matter is I don't know. How can I trust those men when all they've done since I met them is dodge the truth and manipulate me in some way? They haven't done anything directly to hurt me, but collateral damage is still damage.

Breathe and push down, I remind myself. My life is a long calm river. *Argh*! Fuck this!

I'm already freaking out that there's organized crime and witches disappearing in my own neighborhood. Add to that, I am now in the know with information that could be worth something to dangerous people—it's a lot.

And then there's the matter of Erick being able to feel my powers. I haven't spent all this time hiding that part of myself for it to be outed now. "He's a syphon, Evie. He's a miracle, yes, but one that can feel my powers with only a brush of his skin against mine."

Her growing smile becomes feline. "Well, well, well. You plan on touching him skin to skin in the near future?"

I hit her knee with mine. "Of course not! I don't plan on touching either of them," I say pointedly.

"Okay, okay." She rearranges herself on the couch, sitting straighter. "I get it, Ry. But don't you think someone who had to hide what he is for his entire life would understand? And wouldn't you say that the other someone who accepted the first someone without disclosing his secrets all these years would also understand?" She pauses and lifts an eyebrow. "Because it seems to me like if they agree to be honest in the future, and if you want to make sure you're not a target for those disappearances since it's evident you're freaking out about that...."

I roll my eyes at her, still irritated she doesn't seem to think it's a big deal,

She continues, "It would be better to work with those two and have them in your corner to get all this shit under wraps as soon as possible than stay in the dark on your own. Necromancy is a part of who you are as much as the color of your eyes or your knobby knees." Evie snickers, and I throw my pillow at her. She barely has time to lift her arm to save her wine.

I scowl at her. "Yes, but you know as well as I do that witches with my kind of necromancy as a primary gift have been shunned and ostracized unless they were Sennex employed. If it were to get out... Diane never wanted me to use this part of my powers for a reason. I know it feels disingenuous of me, but just because Erick told me his secrets doesn't mean I need to share mine. Like I said, I don't know either of them, not really."

I pinch the bridge of my nose in an attempt to squelch my growing headache. "I do agree with you, though," I carry on. "I am pissed, but I don't feel in any danger from them directly. And I do think I would be better with them in my corner. I'll just have to be careful." I drain what's left of my wine and get up to refill our glasses. Evie follows, not far behind.

There are still so many other things that bother me, though. I can feel there is a lot more that I don't know, and I can't be sure they will tell me. From what I've seen of Finn, he's not the chatty type. He didn't say one word during the meeting. Not one. Would he be honest with me if I were to ask him direct questions?

More than that, Finn and Erick. There's obvious history there. I just can't put my finger on what might have happened to drive them apart. Were they friends? Were they more?

Evie nudges my shoulder. "Hey, where did you just go? You've been staring at that bottle for, like, two minutes straight." She wriggles her delicate eyebrows. "And you were blushing."

My hand goes reflexively to my cheeks to feel the warmth there. I busy myself filling up the glasses. "I was just thinking about what more they could be hiding and if they would answer straight up if I asked them direct questions."

"Mm-hmm." She picks up our drinks and goes to sit at the breakfast nook. "You were definitely not thinking about how fine both of them look. Or how their backhanded protective behaviors annoy the crap out of you but excite you at the same—"

Giggling, I put both my hands over her mouth. "Stop. Stop. You made your point. You want me to spell it out? Yes, I find them attractive. But no, I don't want to pursue that attraction because, without trust, nothing can happen."

She pulls my hands from her mouth, her eyes full of mischief. "Yes, but with a little thrust, a lot can happen."

"Shut up!"

Evie's smile almost reaches her ears as she tries not to laugh at me.

After a moment, we sober up. "Seriously though, I want the truth," I continue. "I want to make sure I'm safe. And the only way I know to make sure I get the truth, and nothing but the truth is to unearth it myself. Since I don't know where to start and the guys have more info than I do on the situation, I'll take advantage of that. If I'm to work with them, though, I'll do it on my own terms."

"What do you mean?"

"You'll see soon enough."

Chapter 14

RILEY

NEITHER OF THE MEN tried to contact me after Erick spilled the tea yesterday. It's just as well. The closer I get to Arcane, the faster my heart beats and the stronger my resolve becomes.

Breathe in. Breathe out. Push the nasty feelings down. My life is my own, and nobody but me will take charge of my future.

When I open the door, I come face to face with Bree. I haven't talked to her in a couple of days. She steps aside to let me pass and whirls around to face me.

"Riley, I'm so sorry." As she says this, she balls her right hand into a fist and rubs it in a circular motion on her chest. "I had no idea of the rabbit hole you would step into. I was only trying to get Finn to make new friends, and it all got out of hand so quickly. I didn't know where the tracking spell came from when I asked you to help with the fair. I swear it wasn't a ploy to get Erick and Finn to reconnect through you. I'm truly sorry. If there's anything I can do, please just ask. I'll be happy to help as much as I can."

I don't know what to say to this. I confess I didn't even have the brain power this weekend to think about Bree and her side of things in all of this. Can I assume she knows everything Finn knows? Or is she only an employee? Is she even telling me the truth now? My face must show my bafflement because, the next thing I know, she's hugging me while mumbling more apologies. I stiffen and don't return the gesture, which doesn't deter her from squeezing me half to death. I don't think she's familiar with the concept of personal space.

She pulls away at the sound of the swing door in the back. Finn steps into the space with assured strides that falter slightly when he catches sight of me.

"Will you be okay?" Bree asks him. "Do you need me to stay?"

Finn rakes a hand through his sandy hair. It's the first time I've seen him with his hair loose. The wavy strands reach his shoulders. It suits him. Infuriating. "No, it's fine, Bree. I'm closing early anyway. I've already put up the sign in the window," Finn answers.

Worry is etched on her forehead at the idea of leaving her boss to fend for himself, but she still does as asked. Her piercing gaze lingers on him a moment longer in case he changes his mind, but then she goes.

Finn watches me intently as he says, "I've reached out to Erick as per your request, but I don't know if he'll show. It was short notice, and, considering what we learned yesterday, I had to improvise to get the message to him undetected. I don't know if he'll remember our old codes."

I'm about to ask him about said code and how he and Erick know each other when someone swiftly enters the shop and locks the door behind them. Their breathing is ragged as if they'd just run.

"I'm sorry, the store is—" Finn stops talking when the stranger removes his cap and glasses and turns to face us.

Erick is here. He came. He's wearing black trousers and a gray button-up shirt with a loosened tie. The look would be more at home on Finn than him, but I suppose it was on purpose.

He pulls on the tie and puts it in his pocket, then shifts from one foot to the other in discomfort, which brings my attention to the dress shoes he has on. I can't help the small smile pulling at my lips.

"I came as soon as I could," Erick says. "I had to take a detour to change clothes and make sure I wasn't followed, just in case."

"You remembered the code," Finn declares.

"Would you prefer I had forgotten it?" Erick asks.

Finn ponders the question, but I'll never know the bottom of his thoughts on the matter because, instead of continuing with the conversation, he turns around and walks to the back of the store. His steps are too measured, his movements too calculated, to appear casual. I wonder what goes through that big head of his. Erick doesn't need more encouragement to start walking. He gives me a wide berth as he goes around me.

I guess that's all the invitation I'll get, so I follow suit. When I get to the stockroom, Finn and Erick are waiting in front of a big storage shelf full of books. Erick's frown deepens when Finn reaches for one of the books. Finn pulls it down, opens a small latch on the side of it, and puts his thumb inside.

There is a click and the sound of metal on metal as the shelf swings slowly outward, revealing a spiral staircase. Seriously, I don't know what it is with these two and the cloak-and-dagger stuff.

A light buzzing sound comes from the entrance. Finn presses one of his hands on the wall just beside the doorway. After a few seconds, crackling electricity starts to dance throughout the opening. Then the energy fizzles down and grounds itself. I didn't even see the magical barrier before he took it down. If anyone had tried to get through before the security was disabled, they would have been fried in place.

Finn snickers. "Go ahead. It's not a torture dungeon, I promise," he says.

Erick shrugs and starts his descent.

"You can make jokes? That's new," I mock Finn before stepping through the doorway myself.

The metal steps are small and shaky. Each one creaks and groans under my weight. The only light illuminating our descent comes from the foot of the stairs. The door closes after Finn and makes everything vibrate, which prompts me to take hold of the rusty railing.

These two are going to get me killed.

The first thing I see as I step into the space at the bottom of the stairs is Erick. He has already walked into the middle of the room and is slowly turning around. His hands hang limply at his side, and his eyes are wide. His stubbled jaw opens and closes as if he wants to say something but doesn't know where to begin.

I suck in a surprised breath of my own when I finally focus on the huge library behind Erick. Stone floors, similar to the cobblestone outside, complement the multiple wooden tables arranged neatly in two rows in the middle of the space. On each side of the tables are bookshelves after bookshelves full of dusty old tomes. On every table, there are bankers' lights—small, ornate desk lamps with stained glass shades. The rest of the underground space is illuminated by hanging tiffany lamps. I can't see any windows from where I stand. I don't know how Finn managed to do this, but this library is even bigger than his own bookshop.

"You finally found it," Erick breathes in awe. His features are all disbelief and shock.

"You found what, exactly?" I ask, puzzled.

Finn approaches one of the tables and gently glides his fingers over it. "Many witch families gather knowledge over generations but generally focus on one or two aspects of the craft, the magic their bloodline is most skilled at. It's rare to find anyone interested in knowledge that is not readily useful to them.

"However," Finn continues, "there is an old tale that speaks of a talented French caster that used to take payment for his work in books and hidden knowledge instead of money. He succeeded in building the biggest privately owned collection of magical tomes in recent memory. He didn't have any heir, so, before his death, he hid and sealed the collection away, designing a complex set of clues and tests so that only the worthy could find it."

He throws his hands out to show off the library. "Well, I found part of it."

"That's only part of it?" Now, I am openly gawking.

Erick plops into one of the many chairs and puts his feet up on a desk. His nonchalance rubs me the wrong way, and I glare at him. I can't fathom how he can remain so chill around us with everything we know about him and how easily we could have him arrested.

"Don't wait for an invitation or anything," Finn tells Erick. I suddenly like Finn a little more. He chooses to lean on the table on the other side of me. I can't sit right now—I'm too wired, so I stay right where I am.

"So, Darkness..." Erick drawls in an echo of how he addressed me in his shop yesterday. "Have you come to a decision? Will you deliver me on a silver platter to our good government?" The last part of his sentence drips with sarcasm.

"You know my name. It's Riley. You're not the sharpest tool in the shed, are you? Taunting one of the few people that could ruin you is not a wise game, boy."

Erick guffaws while balancing his chair precariously on two legs. "Boy? Do I look like a boy to you?"

No, he doesn't. I did the calculations, and if he hired his employee seven years ago when his father gave him his shop at twenty-one, he's now twenty-eight. So no, not a boy, but still younger than me by two years.

"Not to pile it on, but, children, let's get on with the reason for this meeting. Which is...?" Finn looks expectantly at me. I was purposefully vague when I contacted him to set up a meeting.

I take a deep breath and try not to fidget or pace, even if the nervous energy in my body demands I do. "I am still pissed that both of you chose to lie to me by a shitload of omission," I tell them, putting my hands on my hips. "But I won't involve the Sennex...for now, at least. Snitching on your underground operation"—I point my chin at Erick—"would just make me a target for your Berserker crime boss."

Erick does his best to look stoic, but I can clearly see his shoulders relax in relief.

"As for the disappearances," I continue, "if what you said is true, Erick, it—"

"It's true," Finn interrupts. "I checked. A lot of them didn't make the news, and the Sennex's task force does virtually nothing to move these cases forward."

I put all the iron I can in my voice when I say, "Here's my proposal. I want us to work together to get to the bottom of the evident safety issue we have on our hands. I refuse to feel unsafe in my own neighborhood. To be clear, I don't trust either of you, but I don't know where to start to make sure I'm not in any immediate danger, at least. So, teamwork seems the most sensible option at this point since you obviously have more information than me."

"No." Erick's tone is final. "Like I said yesterday, I'm already on the other side of the law, so I'm not in any more danger by continuing to do what I do. You"—he points at Finn and me in turn—"are not. I can't babysit while—"

"Babysit is exactly what you're trying to do!" Finn explodes, surprising me. He starts to pace, his angry steps biting at the stone floor. "We are not witchlings, and you don't get to make our decisions for us, in case Riley didn't already make it abundantly clear yesterday. This situation concerns all of us. At least, that's what you insinuated when you said we could both be possible targets because we're powerful and skilled." Finn removes his glasses and scrubs his hand down his face. The way his body has tensed reminds me of a predator about to pounce. It's the first time I've seen him loosen the tight grip he usually holds on his composure.

Even though he is leaner than Erick, at this moment, I truly don't know which one I would bet on if a fight was to break out. Finn has his back on us when he growls, "Don't repeat old mistakes and take the fucking help."

"What makes you think I made a mistake?" Erick croons arrogantly.

That's all Erick has time to say before Finn whirls around and rushes toward him. I just have time to get into Finn's path. "Stop! Stop the pissing contest this instant! You"—I point to Finn—"get a grip on whatever has your underwear in a bunch. And you!"

I turn on Erick, who hasn't even lifted a finger throughout the whole ordeal. "You either agree to my terms, or you'll find that I can be a real pain in the ass when I want to be. You're not the only one that knows how to play this game."

My statement wipes the smug smile from Erick's mouth, and he turns his face away from me, jaw clenched. I can hear Finn walking back to his seat behind me.

"Now, that's better, isn't it?" I ask. Both men refuse to look at each other. I pinch the bridge of my nose. "Divide and conquer is the name of the game here. I'm all ears. Does anyone have any idea where to begin?"

Crickets.

"Do I have to bring Bree into this to make you two talk?"

Finn straightens at the mention of her name. "I think the first step would be to find a pattern for the kidnappings, if any. Perhaps this will allow us to find a reason for why the disappearances happened, which, in turn, may narrow down the list of possible perps."

"Perfect!" I try and fail to sound enthusiastic.

Erick drops the legs of his chair down and leans on the table before him. "That's a lot of conditional."

"Do you have a better idea?" I say drily.

"I don't like this."

"Tell me something I don't know," I fire back.

"Very well, then. If you want to be stubborn and put your lives in the line of fire, you'll damn well follow my instructions. I don't want your blood on my hands."

Finn sneers. "Yes, sir."

Erick tenses at the comment. He grips the top of the table so hard that his knuckles are almost white.

"Okay..." I cut in, my gaze bouncing from one man to the other. "What are your *requests*? No orders, just reasonable requests. We'll follow them if we judge they are justified."

"You don't—"

"Understand?" I finish for him. "Oh, I think I do. Go ahead, talk."

Erick doesn't surrender exactly but has the decency to not argue further. "I have a vast contact network. I can shake the web and see what it yields. It's a little more out there than I would like, but I've exhausted all other subtle options. As soon as I get more intel, I will feed it to you. You are not to engage in any shape or form with any of the Berserker's people." I'm about to interrupt him, but he doesn't let me. "No, that is not an order. It is a reasonable request. You don't know them like I do. I know he's your prime suspect, but it would be more than stupid to risk a move on him for nothing. In the meantime, I will make sure that you both get access to everything I've already found so far. I've rounded up a handful of persons of interest that might have a hand in this, so it's not clear-cut at all."

Erick looks at Finn then. Their gazes are at war, even if their words are civilized. Erick asks him, "Can you set up a secure line of communication for the three of us other than code appearing and disappearing randomly on my skin? I'm not used to the tickle anymore." He says it so casually. It's like he is talking about the weather.

"Excuse me? That's how you communicated with him?" I say to Finn in disbelief. "But you'd need to have access to a piece of him that he willingly gave you to do that." Finn doesn't refute my observation, so I ask, "What is it?"

"Oh, Finn! Our Darkness is curious. How cute," Erick fires back mockingly.

If I wasn't trying to avoid disclosing my abilities, I would have punched him in the face right then and there. But something else snagged my attention—he said *our*.

Finn gets up abruptly and scowls. "I will get us a secure way of communicating, but, for the love of the gods, drop the act."

Erick seems caught off guard, not able to find a good retort.

"Good," Finn says. "Now, one last thing. In case we're, in fact, targets, everything needs to look as normal as possible. Whoever kidnapped those witches must not know we're onto it. Riley and I have already started to work on the book fair together, so it would not arise further suspicions if we were to meet regularly between now and the fair. We'd obviously need to keep the fair on track as planned, but it would allow us a pretext to work on the gathered data."

Erick nods his assent.

I take one step back toward one of the bookshelves and pick up a grimoire. "These might also come in handy to research the different powers and how useful they could be to a third party. It might also be useful to check if something similar has already happened in this city..." I trail off while browsing the volume I hold.

Finn walks over and takes the book from me. He is close enough that I have to raise my chin to look into his green eyes. "You'll have to work your way up to access my private collection, *Darkness*," he says, picking up on Erick's nickname for me.

Kill me now.

Chapter 15

ERICK

I'VE BEEN AT IT for a week, and it's getting more and more irritating. Trying to dig up information on all the witch disappearances feels like punching the air and hoping it'll get hurt. At least Tommy wasn't among the headcount. He finally showed up the day after the poker game. His mother fainted, and he had to take her to the hospital. In the frenzy, he just forgot to call in sick. From what I gather, she's his only family. I'll have to ask him how she is the next time I see him.

I've sent everything I had on the actual disappearances to Riley and Finn through an untraceable online communication board. I'm not ashamed to say that Finn has always been the best of both of us for security matters, and for good reason. He spent all his youth, books in hand, in the guards' surveillance quarters of his parent's upscale residence in the Faroe Islands—the Sennex's stronghold. I knew he would come through with the secure line.

I've been lucky none of my sources questioned my inquiries. I had to call in a couple of favors and trade a few more, but other than that, my contacts were none the wiser. I'm still waiting to hear from one of the most promising leads. In the meantime, another caster disappeared last night, and I wasn't even close to guessing that a witch of his profile would have been a target. There was nothing special about him that I could find, no great powers I'm aware of, no link to crime families or any shady operations.

People are disappearing in my neighborhood, some of the missing witches I have known for years, and I cannot do a damn thing about it. How am I supposed to live with that? I still don't get why the Sennex doesn't get involved. I mean, I'm happy they're out of my hair, but isn't it the job of the Sennex's task force to make sure witches are protected, just as it is the job of the human police to make sure humans are secure? This is just more proof of what I have been thinking for years. Unless the crimes impede directly on their reign, or unless it concerns prominent, powerful witches that could be useful to them, the Sennex doesn't give a shit. They're no better than the organized crime they let thrive in this city by closing their eyes.

I understand that Riley and Finn want the clues to easily point to the Berserker and be done with it, but it's not that simple. With all the information I have been feeding them via the secure online board this week, even they have to agree that there are other plausible suspects and explanations that we have to investigate first. If we move against the boss in haste and are wrong, the whole organization will fall on us.

I won't strike before I know for sure who's responsible. I will punish the guilty once I know for certain they are guilty, whoever they are. Maybe that makes me weak in Riley's eyes, but I refuse to become a monster because of my fears. There is already enough darkness in me, enough void. I don't need to add to it.

Eleanor sighs exaggeratedly from her seat behind the counter when she sees me enter The Underground Castle. The doily she's crocheting is almost done now, a delicate mint green table centerpiece.

"You were out pulling strings again, weren't you?"

I don't even bother arguing with her. She's made it perfectly clear she doesn't agree with me asking questions and risking exposing myself to get more answers. She knows the plan. I didn't really have a choice whether to tell her or not since she's the one managing the place for me while I'm out fishing.

"You know," she says, "I would really be more comfortable with all of this if I could be there to protect you. I can be discreet. I don't even need to breathe. Plus, they can't hurt me, not really, anyway."

"I know that, Lenny, and I appreciate your concern more than you know." I throw a weak smile in her direction. "But I have to do this. I need to. Because if it's *him*...I need to get ahead of this. You know he's been acting increasingly erratic. I have a bad feeling."

"I don't want you to get hurt. You're my duty to protect and, more than that…." She whispers the last part. "You're my friend."

The comment propels me forward. I put my hand on her forearm, and the familiar pulse of her grounded energy flows under my fingers. "You won't lose me. Besides"—I point to where her hands deftly move the crochet hooks through the yarn—"you have other hobbies now than babysitting me."

My attempt at joking to disperse the growing tension is wildly unsuccessful.

"How are Riley and Finn doing?" she asks. "Did they find anything interesting?"

I turn around and gather my hands behind my head. My back cracks and pops in the process. "Last I heard, there were still no new developments."

Riley's been working with Finn on every piece of intel I collected, but nothing jumps out of their analysis besides what I already knew. A big portion of the missing witches were powerful enough, but many of them were specks of dust in the great scheme of things. I know we're missing something, and it drives me crazy. I feel lost. I'm so used to being in control. It's messing with my head to be so powerless. Well, there are other things messing with my head, too.

I haven't seen Riley and Finn in the flesh at all since last week. Being close to Finn again after all these years is excruciating. To witness how thoroughly I have burned that bridge... But I won't apologize for it. It was the right decision. I couldn't let him throw away his life, his freedom, his safety.

As for Riley, the fact that she got under my skin so quickly is even more unnerving to me. Her spirit, her feistiness, her will to bite back. Those are all things that tug at my guts, and I can't help but want to draw them out of her, to poke and prod to get her to react.

At this point, I can no longer decide if our working together is more of a danger to them or to me. I am a seeker of thrills—I had to be to survive—yet this feels different somehow. Recollecting the last time I saw them together, him getting a book from her, their proximity, and the mischievous smile he threw in my direction to nag me creates a visceral shiver that runs through my body.

I have never been a great sleeper, but they both haunt my nights in different ways now. I have no right to the attractions I feel, but

I can't help it. I am like a moth drawn to an alluring flame. They captivate me. She's the fire to his water. They balance each other beautifully.

A real work of art.

But those are useless thoughts anyway. Finn won't ever forgive me, and Riley's reaction to my revelations was clear enough; she has no intention of getting remotely close to me. I take comfort in knowing that they both hate me and if push comes to shove, they will hopefully save each other and throw me under the bus.

They are not mine to keep, and they never will be. The farther away from this fucked up crime world they are, the safer I can keep them.

The shop's door dings, and I'm about to issue my standard welcome when I take stock of who's coming down the stairs.

"Berserker" is all that Eleanor dares to utter.

The man doesn't even pay her attention. He walks straight up to me with a half-smile that shows rows of straight, white teeth. His salt and pepper hair are the only indication of his age. The smoothness of his skin reminds me of those marble statues you find in Greek gardens. His tailored suit does nothing to cover the brute strength lying beneath it. He's a warrior through and through—with his words as much as his body. His gray eyes, twin to mine only in color, are cold and unyielding.

"Hello, son."

Chapter 16

ERICK

I DON'T LET THE wave of surprise that hits me show in any way, shape, or form. I force my breathing to remain steady, my gaze fixed on his. I wrap my whole demeanor in a disguise of boredom and disinterest.

"Father." My voice is steady and strong. Dignified. "What are you doing here?"

Victor spins around slowly, inspecting the state of the shop while tugging at his gold cufflinks. "'Hello, Father,'" he says, exasperation rolling off him. "'Long time no see. I'm happy to see you. How've you been?'"

"Hello, Father," I repeat monotonously. "Long time no see. I'm happy to see you. How've you been?"

When his gaze lands back on me, his smile now reaches his eyes. If I was one of his goons, I would turn and flee at the sight, but I'm not, so I just smile back. It's a shame. Those gray eyes of his used to be so full of warmth, but not anymore.

When he speaks next, it's not to me, although his piercing gaze doesn't leave my face while he talks. "I wouldn't do that if I were you. I made you as you are and can unmake you as I wish. You have only one purpose to me, and the day that purpose expires, you will be of no use to me anymore. Is that clear?"

I step back, hitting a cold arm in the process, and realize that Eleanor has moved from behind the counter to presumably do her "purpose," as Victor so aptly put it, and protect me. Fuck this. I don't have time for a dick-measuring contest. Anyway, everything here belongs to him. The only money I can truly call my own is my gambling winnings.

"Enough," I say firmly. "Lenny, please, would you sit back down behind the counter?" Eleanor stays behind me for a moment longer but finally moves back to her initial position.

I address Victor again. "I've already sent you the report of last month's earnings, and you have no delivery pending. What more could you possibly need? Why are you here?" I ask him.

My father cracks his neck and shrugs. "Clarence told me you acted strangely with him the other day. I wanted to check how my precious son was doing," he drawls in a way so similar to my own, it's eerie.

"You wanted to check if I was doing stuff behind your back, more like."

He inhales sharply and puts a hand before his mouth, feigning indignation. "You wound me. Am I not allowed to care about my own flesh and blood? My only son?"

Then, for a split second, his mind leaves the room. I can see it in his vacant stare, in the way he loses his focus. He's been a daydreamer for a long time, but he's getting caught up in his head more and more frequently nowadays. His mental state worries me a great deal. Even though he is the head of the most profitable crime syndicate in this city, he's still my father. What's more, if he's losing it, it will suck for everyone. The power struggle over his territory that would ensue would hurt crooked witches and innocent people alike.

One of the first things I checked when I started investigating the disappearances was if his micro absences and the kidnappings began around the same time, but no. The witches started vanishing into thin air weeks before his weird behavior increased in frequency.

I tried to talk to him about his absences, but he completely shut me out. The only thing I can do is to continue monitoring whatever this is in every way I can.

My dad shakes himself, remembering where he is, and walks over to a display of leather belts. Then he drags his index finger over the metal surface and rubs it with his thumb, sporting an expression of disgust at the dust he finds there. Hopefully, it will make him leave sooner rather than later.

"I heard that your favorite"—he stops, searching for the right word—"alehouse acquired quite the new potion master."

My heart skips a beat at his mention of Riley. Why the fuck is he interested in her? He barely pays attention to anything I do or anywhere I go. His goons wouldn't mention me unless it was about his artifact orders. No one knows I am the son of the Berserker apart from Eleanor, so they usually don't bother even bringing me up in conversations. In everybody else's eyes, I'm just another pawn on the board. The worst that could happen at this point is that he wants to bring her talents into the fold.

Over my dead body.

"I wouldn't know. I'm not one to drink anything more than tap beer. Limited budget and all," I say, trying to steer the conversation away from Riley.

His beautiful features scrunch into a deep scowl. "If you would use the generous salary that I pay you to its fullest instead of taking only breadcrumbs from the pot, you could live like a king," he rebukes.

I turn my hand to look at my nails. "Well, you know. Children need their independence and blah-blah-blah," I mock.

He breaks into a big belly laugh. This is not good. "You always had my wit and my talent to slither your way out of conversations you don't want to have."

Shit.

"They say she's also easy on the eye, this glorified bartender. In your artist's opinion, is that true?" It's his turn to deride me.

If I show a hint of interest, he's going to dive for it like a bird of prey. On the other hand, if I display no interest at all or try to change the subject again, he'll know something is up. There's just no good answer, so I decide to go with a half-truth. "She's pretty enough."

He gives me a knowing smile. "Don't worry, son. I won't deprive you of your entertainment. Albert and I have an understanding. I don't poach his employees."

That's the first I hear of this deal. "And what does he give you in exchange, oh, dear Father?"

Without missing a beat, he resumes his fake hurt. "It's never appropriate to kiss and tell. You should know that at your age."

He straightens his jacket and removes imaginary lint from his shoulder. He doesn't even look at me when he says, "You will buy her most expensive potion for me. I will have Clarence pick it up with my next order. I'm curious to see for myself if the rumors of her skills are true."

I want to tell him to shove it, I'm not his errand boy, but I do none of that. This gives me the opportunity to control the narrative. Not only can I reduce the contact Riley has with my dad's thugs by doing it myself, but I can also ask her to trip up the drink so that her talents appear completely average—good but average. In reality, I would never in a million years be okay with doing his shopping for him, and he knows it. So, I'll have to improvise.

"Fine," I answer through clenched teeth. I hope he buys the frustration I carefully let into my body language. Again, true feeling, but not for the reason he thinks. A grain of truth is always necessary to weave a believable lie.

"Well, well. You really do want to get me out of here, agreeing with what you're told for once."

"Don't push it," I snap back for good measure.

I can see he's trying to find my end game here, but I don't let him think about it for too long. "Is that all, *Dad*?"

He mulls over his answer, but it never comes. He chooses to leave instead. Just before climbing the staircase, he turns back. "I love you, son. I'll see you around."

The words are a punch to the gut, leaving me breathless. I haven't got the faintest idea if he even knows what love is anymore.

I'm not stupid enough to let my guard down before he's been out of the shop for several minutes. Then the tension leaves me all at once, and I have to catch myself on a rack of shirts to help my legs bear the weight of my body.

"What are you gonna do?" Eleanor asks.

I had completely forgotten that Lenny was in the shop with me, but I don't have any energy left to startle at the sound of her voice. Her brows are drawn in concern, concern she must see reflected in my own face.

"I don't know," I whisper.

"You have to tell Riley and Finn about Victor."

"I *said* I don't know."

Chapter 17

FINN

SINCE THE PUB IS closed on Sundays and no vendors deliver on that day either, Riley is here with me, doing research. I mean, we've spent the week bouncing ideas back and forth on the online board, but nothing seemed to stick. It feels like the more we think about it, the more questions without answers we unearth.

Erick has been M.I.A. since yesterday. He usually checks in every day with new intel, but nothing for the last twenty-four hours. I know he can take care of himself, and it's probably nothing, but the overwhelming need to make sure he is okay suffocates me. I fire up the private board on my computer and write a quick message.

Anything new?

I don't expect to hear from him right away. Still, the small action makes me feel productive, like I'm moving forward instead of back.

Riley is currently sitting beside me at one of the center tables of my personal library. Her long raven hair pools around her on the wooden surface like a curtain. It's almost nine pm, and I've seen her frown getting deeper and deeper every hour since she's been here this morning. I can't say that I blame her. We're trying to put together a puzzle with missing pieces, and nothing fits.

The alarm on my watch goes off, indicating there is activity in the back alley of my shop. I pull up the camera feed and see a hunched-over figure banging frantically at the door, though we can't hear any of it from this deep into the basement. They're wearing an oversized black hoodie that covers most of their features. I can't see anything else from this vantage point. It looks like they know where the camera is and are purposefully dodging the revealing angles.

I close the screen and use the book beside me to knock on the one Riley's reading. "Hey, I need to check something up top. I'll be back in a minute."

She's so absorbed in her reading that she only mumbles something that sounds like "okay."

I quickly rifle through my mental hall of knowledge to find the best option to defend myself if need be. As I run up the stairs, I quietly repeat my incantation to help me focus and build up the energy required to fire the spell.

As a statue frozen in time, your movements are now mine.

Cold spreads over my palms. The heavy sound of a fist on metal is all I can hear in the stockroom. I take down the section of my protection spell covering the back entrance and open the door to drag the stranger inside by their shirt. A second later, my wards are already back up. I take advantage of the surprise I created to pin them by the throat on the wall with my forearm, my other hand lifted, ready to detonate the charm.

Wide gray eyes meet mine, but Erick doesn't thrash or try to get away. His breathing is ragged and uneven. This close to him, I can see his pupils constricting and expanding in turn. Understanding strikes when I notice the ink of my bare forearm against his naked throat. The amount of energy I gathered to the surface for the spell is like a siren song to his syphon powers. He slowly lifts his hands and gently tugs my arm, but I don't budge. I don't want to, not yet.

Like the clean air after a thunderstorm, the atmosphere around me lightens as I ground my magic and release my focus on the spell. I drag his hood down before placing my free hand flat on the wall beside his head, essentially caging him. We're so close that we share the same air. His tongue darts out to wet his lower lip, making me shiver. I inhale deeply, and his woodsy smell stirs up memories and feelings I'd rather forget.

Then his strong fingers curl firmly around my arm, trapping me to him instead of the other way around, and I cave. Only this once, I let my forehead lean on his and close my eyes.

"You really shouldn't do stuff like that. I could've hurt you." My voice is gruff with the rough edge of long-forgotten desires.

"I didn't plan to, but your fucking protective wards are impenetrable. Why didn't you recalibrate them to allow for me?"

I thought about adapting the spell to allow for him as well as Riley, but to do that felt like giving both of them free reign to invade every corner of my life as they please. Although I miss him with every fiber of my soul, and she's quickly becoming the first person I talk to in the morning and the last I say goodnight to, they already have enough space in my thoughts. I don't intend on acting on my screaming instinct anyway. If this investigation stretches itself out, though, I will eventually have to recalibrate the wards, but for now, this small restriction does feel like the protection that it is for my shop as well as my heart.

We both push off the wall when we hear light footsteps approaching. Riley emerges from downstairs and stops short. I don't know what she sees in our demeanors, but her cheeks become a pretty shade of pink, and she refuses to look either of us in the eye.

She clears her throat. "Hi. Am I interrupting? I was just wondering where you went. I didn't even hear you leave. I wasn't aware we were having a group meeting tonight."

She is rambling. I've never heard her ramble before. Interesting. I file the information for later.

"I wasn't aware of it either," I say while looking pointedly at Erick.

"I promise you—you'll want to hear what I have to say."

"Not here." I stop him. "Let's go down."

Once in the library, we all gather around the research table. Riley and I sit on one side while Erick sits on the other.

Erick is silent for a minute before he clasps his hands together on the table. "My dad came to see me yesterday." He looks down as he says it, and although I am curious about Victor's whereabouts, I'm not sure I want to know the rest of the story. Riley is worrying her lower lip while we both wait for him to continue, but he stalls.

"What does that have to do with anything?" she asks as she crosses her arms over her chest.

"Everything."

Chapter 18

RILEY

"You've got to be shitting me!" It's all I can muster without throwing something at Erick's head. How stupid does he think we are? It's not enough to be working for the man, but he also happens to be his son? I've been pacing for a good half an hour while listening to his account of yesterday's encounter.

"Please try to understand why I didn't share this information at our first meeting," Erick pleads. "I didn't want you to think I would somehow be influenced in my investigation because of who the Berserker is to me."

"Understand? Understand? You lied to us! Again! You looked us in the eye and agreed to work *with* us, not despite us!" I whirl on Finn. "And you, did you know about this?"

In true Finn fashion, he hasn't moved nor said a word yet, waiting patiently for Erick and me to finish hashing it out. He doesn't answer right away. He gets up and walks past me toward one of the cabinets in the corner. Then he comes back with three glasses and a bottle of bourbon. Still silent, he pours the alcohol and doesn't even wait for us to pick up our glasses before draining his own.

"No," Finn finally says as he pours himself a second drink and faces me. "I didn't know where Victor was. I haven't seen him since I was eighteen. Quite frankly, I remember him as a real political mastermind, so when I think about it, it weirdly makes sense." He's silent for a moment as if pondering what to say next.

Finn casts a severe look at Erick, to which Erick answers only with a simple nod. "This changes things, though," Finn carries on, "because, like his son, Victor's a syphon. Only a much more experienced one."

"No one knows I'm his son apart from Eleanor," Erick rushes to say. He tenses at the admission as if every word has to be dragged out of him. "No one can know. My safety, and the safety of anyone who enters in contact with me, depends on it. I would be an easy target for rival gangs that want payback or territories. No one is aware of his powers, either, since it would make him an easy target for the Sennex because of the arrest warrant still pending on both of us. The Sennex is aware of my father's void, hence the hiding and underground activities."

My mouth opens and closes to ask more about this past fallout with the Sennex, but I remain speechless, unable to form the words. After a moment, I just walk away from them and collapse on a chair two tables over. "Is that all?"

I hate how empty I sound, but I have nothing else to throw. My anger is spent. All that remains is an overwhelming sense of being in over my head without knowing who to trust. I wish I had a piece of that truth orb right about now.

Erick picks up his drink but only looks at the alcohol swirling in his glass. “My last source came back this afternoon with something interesting. One of my father’s warehouses has had higher foot traffic than usual for the last couple of weeks. It might be nothing since his installations often have spikes in activity throughout the year. He frequently changes his illegal cargo, banned artifacts and the like, from place to place to throw off competition and make stuff harder to trace.”

“Have you already checked it out?” Finn asks.

“No. My source told me that the perimeter is heavily guarded, and there was construction work done to the building in the last year, so I’ll need you to pirate the new plans from the city’s urban planning department. Then I’ll go alone. It’ll be a quick in and out.”

“Not a chance,” I chime in. My pendant is cold in my hand, grounding my thoughts as I lay down the new rules of the game. “We’re coming with you. If you insist on not telling us everything, we’ll have to get the intel ourselves.”

“And I bet you’re not totally sure of every point of security in that place,” Finn cuts in before Erick can argue. “You’ll need me to circumvent whatever surprises we’ll find.”

Erick’s sigh is drawn out as he comes to a decision. “Fine. But if you want to come with me, you’ll have to be well prepared. I am not ready to risk either of you getting hurt or getting in the way because you cannot defend yourselves. We’ll start combat training this week.”

Okay, I wasn’t expecting that request. “You want us to train with you?”

Erick puts both hands on the table, a power posture if I've ever seen one. "If you're serious about this, that's my requirement."

"You have some nerve making demands when you're the one that's lied to—"

"Children," Finn mocks, "we all have to put water in our wine. I agree to train in combat, but I'll keep the plans of the building to myself until you"—he points to Erick—"absolutely need to see them to move forward with planning and operations. I'm not trusting you to not go by yourself if you get the chance."

"Fine," Erick answers. I only nod my assent.

"Now that it's settled," Finn says, "I have something to confess of my own. In addition to investigating the disappearances this week, I dug through whatever I could find on syphon witches. I'm even happier I did this now since your father is involved. I found a couple of interesting facts if you would be so kind as to confirm them for me."

Erick doesn't even look phased by that statement. It's like he anticipated Finn to do research on his powers. He only gestures for Finn to go ahead.

"Void witches can syphon the magical energy from objects as well as feel and differentiate the strength and kind of powers used. All of this is possible by the syphon's skin directly touching the object. Any part of the syphon's skin can gather magical energy. It doesn't have to be the hands, just as long as it's unobstructed contact. Syphons can't, however, syphon magic from thin air. That's why you couldn't penetrate my wards earlier."

Erick nods his agreement.

Finn carries on, "Void witches can also syphon said energy from another witch or magical creature, thus rendering the syphoned being weaker." Another nod from Erick before Finn asks, "Then why didn't you try and syphon me before when I almost hit you with the petrifying spell?"

Oh, that's what I walked in on earlier.

Erick straightens in his chair, clearing his throat. "I've never syphoned a living being," he confesses. "I've never been shown how to do it, and I won't risk hurting someone with my ignorance." His gaze goes distant. "I've also never needed the skill before."

The admissions surprise me. I can't hide the disbelief in my voice when I ask, "You're telling me that your own syphon father never showed you the ropes? What about your mother?"

"Yes, Riley, that's exactly what I'm telling you. Growing up, I didn't even know my father was a syphon. As for my mother, the last I heard, she's power born."

I can't help but wonder if he's lying to us again. "Wait up. You can *feel* powers. You never touched him? Did he not hold you as a child?"

"That's not what I'm saying. I'm *saying* that whenever I touched him, he always felt like any other witch to me. Full of power. I've spent my youth thinking I was the only one of my kind."

"What? How's that possible?"

"Glad you asked"—this from Finn—"because it's my next order of business. Syphons used convergence disks as receptacles to store the energy they didn't want to use right away—essentially using them as you use your pack of cards, Erick, only vastly stronger of a container. However, some of the more powerful syphon witches could use their own bodies for varied periods of time as a receptacle, which means they could go unnoticed for a while. They eventually had to ground that power because their body was not designed to gather, hold, or produce magical energy, but still. Some could hold it in for days and use it as any other power-born witch would."

"Can *you* do that?" I ask Erick.

"I don't know. I've never really tried." Erick moves from his place at the table to walk over to one of the bookshelves next to Finn. "Could I borrow some of those texts?" he asks.

Finn puts a hand on Erick's shoulder and squeezes—the contact lingering a little longer than necessary. "Of course. I'll gather some books for you. I left a few works on syphons that could be useful to you upstairs. I'll be right back." With that, Finn leaves us to our own devices.

I don't feel like talking anymore. My mind is full. I cannot take another twist or turn.

I purposefully ignore Erick while I pick up the list I made earlier and make my way to one of the shelves to take down new books to bring home. I see my first target. The book is situated too high for me to reach, so I grab the rolling ladder and bring it over. Erick stays in his corner, observing me.

Once I'm up on the ladder, I see other tomes that could be useful, and I busy myself getting them down. As I reach for the last one, I extend myself farther than I should and lose my balance. A small squeal escapes me as I try to regain my footing. Two strong hands land on my waist from behind and lower me down gently.

"Please try not to break your neck. It would..." Erick's teasing words die down, and he swiftly withdraws his hands from me, hands that were in direct contact with the skin of my stomach.

Panic seizes me. My heart hammers at my rib cage like a trapped bird. I cannot look at him, so I stay put, my head bent down, facing the rows of books. "Please don't say anything. Just...please."

We stay like that in the charged silence for what feels like ages, waiting. Then I find my courage and turn slowly to find Erick, eyes wide, completely stunned, with his hands twitching at his sides.

"You weren't supposed to...." I trail off, searching for the right words to make him understand. "Nobody's supposed to know. I never use that part of me anyway. It's not like you. If word gets out, I won't be seen as the mythical hero returning. My type of necromancy"—even the word is hard for me to say out loud—"is not without consequences. It's bad. It's—"

"Stunning," Erick breathes.

"No, not stunning. Awful. It's dark and twisted and terrible. I'm an abomination." Silent teardrops roll down my cheeks. Erick brings his hands up but stops his movement before making contact, asking me with his eyes for consent to touch me.

"Go ahead," I whisper.

He gently cradles my face and wipes away at my tears with his thumbs. "Is that why you were avoiding me, Darkness?"

I half-laugh, half-sob. "Well, that and the fact that you're a lying prick that always thinks he knows best. You know, I don't like you one bit."

His unrestrained smile is breathtaking. He looks so much younger, like a burden has been lifted from his shoulders. "I didn't mean to invade your privacy. I'm sorry." His apology is genuine and open. "It's not my place to judge what you want to display of yourself or not."

Erick's hands fall to the sides of my neck, and I shiver. "As for your power," he says, "I can feel the damper you've put on it. The tempering spell you're using is intricate, well done."

I know it's well done. Diane was the best.

"However, I can't agree with you. You're as far from an abomination as I've ever met. I've seen firsthand how the Sennex can spin information, and I don't believe your necromancy is terrible. Dangerous, yes, as all powers are. But not terrible. Neither are you." Erick's eyes search my own. "If you could feel your powers like I can, you would never think that way."

Our eyes are still locked, the moment stretching itself. Neither of us hears Finn approach until he clears his throat.

Chapter 19

FINN

THE SCENE FROM YESTERDAY keeps replaying in my mind. Erick with his hands on Riley's neck. Her clothing rumpled. Both enraptured in each other enough to not hear me come back. I mean, after I made myself known, she did push him away—hard—yet I don't know if the look of annoyance on her face was directed at her, me, or him. But still, it took Erick a beat longer to completely release Riley. His fingers kept twitching afterward as if he was still remembering the way her skin felt under his touch.

Everything is so tangled up in my head. Hurt. Jealousy. Envy. Desire. Well, most of all, unbridled desire, if I am to be honest with myself. They were so arresting together. Apart from Erick,

I've never felt that pull toward another person. It's messing with me in all sorts of ways.

More than that, I was under the impression that she was avoiding him, loathing him, even. Obviously, I was mistaken.

"Hey! What did those books do to *you*?"

I jump at the sound of Bree's voice as she enters the shop. I needed to exert my frustration, so I decided to move some displays around. Apparently, I didn't realize I was placing books down a little too energetically. I wince. "Sorry, how did it go?"

Bree flips her fiery locks out of her face and picks up an empty rack to place in front of the window. "Well, the city council wasn't thrilled that you weren't present for your own business' hearing to answer for the accusations. I stalled them, but we won't be able to keep that up forever, Finn. They did agree to postpone the hearing to a later date. You'll receive another convocation letter, but they asked me to tell you it's the last one. After that, you'll have fines to pay, and they'll have grounds to expel us before long."

"Shit." I rake my hands through my hair. "I don't have time to deal with this circus."

I sent Bree with a bogus reason as to why I couldn't attend. I wasn't in a state of mind to defend my honor from Gavin's false accusations this morning. My conniving neighbor be damned.

She bumps my shoulder with hers. "Hey, how are you? What happened to put you in this sour mood?"

"I'm not sour." I regret the lie as soon as it leaves my mouth. "No, you're right. I'm sour. I'm sour because...." She waits expectantly for me to continue. "I walked in on Erick and Riley having a moment."

Bree loves gossip. "A moment?" she asks eagerly.

"Yes, a moment. It looked, I don't know, serious? No, that's not the right word. Intimate, maybe? Like he was comforting her about something." I feel stupid just saying the words out loud. They're both consenting adults; they can do whatever they please.

"Seeing as it obviously bothers you," Bree says with her *mother-knows-best* voice, "did you ask them about it? Or did you just act like nothing happened, assume stuff, and move on with business as usual?"

"Second option?" My hands go out in a pleading gesture. "I'm not the keeper of them, Bree. They don't owe me an explanation for their behavior."

She cocks her head to the side and puts her hands on her hips. Now she really does look like my mother. *Ugh.* "Of course, they don't. But, if you don't use your words to communicate clearly and share with them how you feel, nothing will come of it. You'll be left out when you clearly want in."

"In? In what?"

She sniffs and lifts her head in indignation. "Don't play dumb. I've seen your face every time you look at your stupid online messages from either of them."

"I'm not entertaining this with you." I may not know exactly what I feel and even less what I want, but I will decide all of this in my own time—and that time is not now. Also, even if I had feelings for either of them, how would that even work? He hurt me more than I can say, and she doesn't even trust either of us.

In an attempt to keep Bree from questioning me any further on the matter, I go for a change of subject. "Did you find the book I asked you for?"

"No luck," she answers, clearly exasperated by my refusal to talk more about my feelings. "You should probably take your chances with Erick's side of the business in rare artifacts."

Bree has a knack, and admittedly a lot of connections, to track rare editions of magical texts. A lot of the rarest works I own, the ones that weren't already in the downstairs library when I bought the building, were found by her. She's also very good at bargaining, which doesn't hurt.

I suspect there's a lot more that we don't know about syphons. There is some information I came across in my readings that doesn't make sense, as if we're missing a big part of the puzzle. The book I asked Bree to track is an old syphon family grimoire. As far as I know, it's one of the only ones left from the Tragedy that isn't in the Sennex's possession. I lost my privileges to access their Hall of Knowledge a long time ago. Anyway, most of that information would have been in the restricted section, which only Sennex members can access.

After a moment, Bree says, "Oh, and just saying, I deserve a prize for doing most of the heavy lifting for the book fair."

"Yes, you're right. You deserve even more than a prize." I bow before her. "You have my undying gratitude, oh powerful fiery one."

She sticks out her tongue at my declaration of thanks. With the midday sun putting her constellation of freckles on full display, at this moment, she looks more like a petulant child instead of the ancient being that she is.

I laugh, and she smiles. "By the way," I inform her, "I won't be able to make it to the meeting with the new bookmark supplier as planned tomorrow afternoon. Can you call her to postpone it to next week?"

"How come?"

"I have mandatory combat training."

Bree's interest perks at that, one of her eyebrows lifting in inquiry. I proceed to tell her about the plan and how self-defense was included in the deal. For once, no client sets foot in the store to interrupt my monologue. I don't know if I should be stoked or worried at the lack of business today.

"You mean to tell me you'll spar with both of them?" Bree says with enthusiasm. "Like getting all hot and sweaty, rubbing against each other, kind of spar?" Her excitement at the prospect is irritating. Lately, it feels like she's following my life as if it were one of those TV reality shows she loves so much.

I breathe out my ire. "Nothing like that. It's all very functional. We will work to improve our ability to take care of ourselves. That's all it is."

Bree winks. "Mm-hmm. Obviously. All work. No fun."

Chapter 20

ERICK

I HOPE TO THE gods that Riley's potion won't raise my father's suspicions. She made it as per my specifications—she hated it—but the mixture needed to be powerful enough to make sense with the praise she's received and simultaneously be ordinary enough that my father wouldn't be interested in her talents for his extracurricular activities. He already has prolific potion artists and many, many healers in his employment, but he's always recruiting new talents.

As I go about the business of unrolling the mat to prepare our training ground, I can feel the anticipation stir inside of me, a harrowing mixture of excitement and dread. Touching either Riley or Finn is akin to being parched in front of an ocean, not being able to drink the salty water because you know it won't quench your thirst, and you'll just want to consume even more until you die from it.

I've been around great powers before, but never in prolonged exposure. I feel deeply my lack of practice, for I am sure there is a way to shield myself from this hunger, but the predator in me just wants to consume and consume. It wants to drink them whole, to possess them completely, to make them *mine*, or maybe it's just me and my embedded needs. Either way, it's torture.

But it's a small price to pay to make sure they are safe. If I cannot protect them from whatever we'll face, I will make sure they can protect themselves.

I thought Finn's books would help me find a solution to control that part of my power, to control the impulse to hunt and trap and feed. It didn't. All I found were small pieces of lost history and facts I already knew for the most part. Yet, it was still comforting to read about my people just the same.

It ails me to witness how Riley perceives her powers as dark, twisted, and bad, whereas I am the real monster parading in sheep's clothing. I can understand why the Sennex praised my kind for their feats in battle. War is in my blood, and I constantly fight my nature with my moral imperatives. I'm not even sure training my void would help me with that perpetual struggle.

The bunker alarm chimes, and, just like that, I am forced to put one foot in front of the other and go on with the chasm of confusion that threatens to rip me in half. I can't pinpoint exactly when Riley buried herself into the deepest part of me, but what I thought was just power lust for a beautiful woman turned out to be so, so much more. I can still feel the supple skin of her waist under my hands. I had to fight the urges her pleading eyes triggered deep into my core. All I wanted to do was trap her in the confines of my body as I kissed her tears away one by one—devouring her fear and pain one drop at a time until it belonged to me. Until she belonged to me.

As for Finn, simply breathing beside him is hard. My soul still yearns to be close to him. Even though I did my best to push him out of harm's way, out of my life, he never left me. Not really. He has taken a permanent residence in my heart. The memories of him pale in comparison to the real man, but they were a constant friend throughout the years. I know he never understood why I didn't share all of me with him, why I said 'no' three years ago, why I had to push him to let me go.

Finn thought I didn't want him, that he wasn't enough for me to hold on to. I let him believe it because he is better without me; they both are. I am a danger to them. Even the simplest things in my life have the potential to endanger them. I couldn't forgive myself if they got hurt simply by being in the line of fire, close to me. It's not just my father but many competing rivals who do business with me. I had near misses in the past, not to mention the whole reason I am hiding in this city in the first place—the government holds grudges for a long time, as proved by the arrest warrant still on my head.

No, I can do this. I will help them as much as necessary, and when I am sure they are safe, I will disappear from their life for good. I had to rebuild my life from the ground up once. I can do it again.

By the time I reach the surveillance console, I have stitched myself back together enough to wrap all the swagger I can muster around me like the comforting lie that it is. I press the entrance button, and the door buzzes. It takes only a minute for Finn and Riley to appear, both in workout gear—leggings and tank top for her and low-slung sweatpants and T-shirt for him.

Fuck. They're the textbook definition of temptation. Riley's curves and plump breasts are on full display, and I can follow the shape of Finn's pecs through his tight shirt. I have to swallow the growl building in my throat at the sight of them.

"Hey, where can I put this?" Finn gives a small tug on the mat strap dangling over his shoulder.

"No need. I already got everything set up. Right this way." My steps are smooth and even, not betraying the tempest created by the path of my earlier thoughts. They follow me, apprehension thick in the way their strides falter just before stepping through the doorway of the training room. Well, I don't really have a dedicated training area. The room is mostly open space with my bed, a small side table, and a dresser in the far corner. The connecting bathroom has barely enough space for the shower stall and utilities it contains.

Everything is efficient and discipline-oriented. Some would say military, but I hate that word. I am the master of my own drills and no one else's, certainly not an asshat instructor that does nothing but yell orders. Let's just say that I have a mild discomfort with authority. I need to be in control of my own power, to know that my mistakes, as well as my successes, are my own.

When I look back at Riley and Finn, they are perusing through the assortment of weapons I laid down for them. I didn't know which ones they would be most proficient in, and since we don't have much time to prepare, I wanted to go with the ones that felt most natural to them. Hand-to-hand combat evasion techniques will be my priority, but I still want to see where everyone stands in their abilities.

I purposefully chose not to include guns as I don't intend for any of us to kill anybody in this reconnaissance mission—a life is a life, no matter whose it is. It's a precious thing to preserve. If we need to take down people, we'll do it stealthily and without hurting anyone more than we must to defend ourselves. Finn and I can use combat spells if need be.

Riley turns her back to me to gently drag her fingers over the wooden body of a bokken, a training sword. That's when I see her own weapon strapped to her back, a long staff with a metal hook at the top that makes it look like a shepherd's herding staff. From the look of it, the hook is probably more useful to hang stuff on than to be functional in battle. Although, if wielded correctly, even random objects can hurt.

"Are you sure you're okay with us training in here?" Finn says, his eyes riveted to the bed in the back corner.

My mind turns dark, and, for a brief moment, all I can think about is what I would do to him on that bed. How I would make him beg… I clear my throat, trying to refocus on thoughts that don't send blood straight to my groin. "My home is what I need it to be. For now, I need it to be a training ground, so it is." I turn to Riley, who is studying our interaction with interest. "You brought a weapon?"

"I brought an *heirloom* that is most precious to me. It's the only weapon I've ever used, and it's as solid as your thick head, even against sharp objects like axes and swords. Its previous owner had it spelled." The mocking quirk of her mouth and the glint of mischief in her eyes are twins to Finn's. He snickers, and my fingers tense with the need to show those brats what happens when they mouth to me. But instead, I take a deep breath, reminding myself that I can't go down that road with either of them. I can, however, play a little, completely platonically, of course.

If they want to poke fun at me like that, I'll at least return the favor.

"We'll start with a warm-up," I say, sporting my most charming smile. "Thirty push-ups and fifty crunches. Any questions?"

They both look at each other. "When does it get fun?" Finn asks.

"Fun? For me? Right about now," I say as I drop to the ground on my hands and start with the push-ups.

After having Riley and Finn struggle through ten minutes of jumping jacks followed by ten minutes of burpees, I take pity on them and talk them through some self-defense basics.

"Ready to test it out? Finn, if you remember ten percent of the lessons you hated so much as a kid, it should be easy for you."

Finn gives me the evil eye before getting up and helping Riley to her feet.

"I. Hate. You," she says as she rubs her backside, which is no doubt already starting to be sore.

"Good. You can use that to fuel your technique." I wink at her, and she gives me the finger in return.

"Very mature," I taunt her, but she doesn't give in to the gibe. Instead, she moves around to spar with Finn, who looks very uncomfortable at the idea of hitting anyone.

I still remember how he loathed his mandatory combat training. He would go on about it for hours at a time, but it was a futile exercise. He couldn't get out of it even if he wanted to. Every child of a Sennex council member was required to go through it. He would flounce every test on purpose and come back home with a bloody shirt and an equally bloody smile, appalling his parents with his behavior. A grin tugs at my lips at the memory. The ever-so-quiet boy with his ever-so-hidden displays of rebellion.

"Okay then," I instruct Riley, "try to hit Finn."

I barely have time to finish my sentence before she lunges at him and takes him by surprise. She wraps her arms around his knees and pulls with all her might. Finn hits the mat with a *humph*—the air knocked out of him at once. Riley doesn't engage him further. She only retreats to her initial position, waiting for him to get up.

I help him stand and clap him on the shoulder. "Well, you might be a little rustier than I'd hoped."

Finn shoves me off him. "Fuck off."

"You don't want to play the offended damsel. It's not a good look for you," I drawl. Teasing him used to be one of the joys of my life way back when and my taste for it hasn't lessened. He's so serious and stoic all the time—*controlled*. I just want to push him to lose said control and become undone. The fire behind his eyes when he's crossed is magnificent. I can't help but fuel it.

A ripple of delight runs up my spine when Finn takes the bait. He moves swiftly to the left and succeeds in grazing my side with his fist. I jump back away from his reach. I am prepared for his next maneuver, however. I move with the kinetic energy of his kick, turning around as I take hold of his leg and lift it straight up, which effectively knocks him flat on the ground. Again.

Before I can descend on him, I receive a vigorous hit in the stomach from something harder than flesh, which makes me double over. That staff is certainly enchanted; it felt like being hit by a metal pipe in the gut. Years of training propel me into action and in a defensive stance. Riley has one knee on the ground, her staff still in the position where it hit me. She slowly gets up, heat in her eyes, and gives a hand to Finn. They both close in on me.

"Tag-teaming, I see. How is that fair?" My tone drips with sarcasm and mockery.

They look at each other, speaking silently between themselves. When Finn glances back at me, his forest green eyes are full of glee. That's when understanding hits. He was faking his lack of training; they both were.

Well, shit. In any case, I don't mind a challenge.

Riley moves first, and I duck backward to avoid another hit of her staff. She miscalculates the strength of her maneuver, and I take advantage of this to swipe my leg under her, but she anticipates this and jumps over my leg easily. Well, well, well. More fun for me then.

All the while, I keep track of Finn's movements, but he now purposefully remains in my blind spot. If he thinks this gives him an advantage, he is sorely mistaken. I was able to fight in complete darkness by the age of fourteen. I close my eyes and rely on my other senses to feel both of their presences. Finn is almost on me. I feint to the right, but he follows my movements like a shadow, a well-trained shadow at that. Riley swings her staff at my head. But, at the last second, I let myself fall flat to the ground. Finn, who was close to me, barely had time to avoid the blow himself.

She cringes in apology, and that's when I seize my chance. I use Riley's earlier technique and hit them both in the back of the knees with my forearms. Riley loses her grip, and her staff flies at the wall. A frenzy of near misses and locked limbs ensue until we end up in a three-way stronghold where none of us can move. They both pin me down as I have them pinned down. The short lull in adrenaline is followed by a tidal wave of feelings. During our training exercises, I made a point to avoid touching their skin for too long, but they apparently don't have the same mercy now.

The weight of their bodies against mine, mixed with the magic rolling off their skin, is almost too much to bear. It's like my brain cannot process the avalanche of information. Riley's powers over death and healing create ice and fire on a blanket of vivid colors coming from her skills in potion-making. It is not uncommon for a strong witch to have two primordial abilities, but to have three is rare. The rest of her energy creates a small buzzing in the background that I can feel in my bones.

Finn's powers feel completely different. My whole body erupts in gooseflesh at the contact of his magic. The crackling lightning in his veins sings of storms and reckoning.

Together, they are the embodiment of might.

The moment my attention is concentrated on their powers, I lose my focus on their combat maneuvers, which rarely happened to me before. They react swiftly and disable all my possibilities of movement at once.

We lay there, Finn and Riley holding me down, me not wanting to hurt either of them to free myself. The only sound is our labored breathing. Finn looks at me with his piercing gaze, and I know he understands what happened. He always understood too much, saw too much. I must deal with this newly discovered weakness of mine if I am to stay a faithful guardian around them. I cannot lose my focus in the middle of a dangerous situation because I am overwhelmed by their powers and the siren song it sings to mine.

At last, I have to deal with the hunger within.

Chapter 21

RILEY

As we walked side by side this afternoon, I could see the worry etched on Finn's brow. The farther from Erick's place we got, the more troubled he looked. He didn't say it, but we were both thinking it. Erick struggles with his gift. Being deprived of a teacher growing up may have been his parents' solution, but it wasn't the right one. I can imagine the young boy, all black wavy hair and charming smile, hiding his struggle away from the world. How alone he must have felt, how truly alone he must have been.

It's a slow night at The Drunken Sailor, as are most Tuesdays, and I thank the gods for it. My movements are sluggish. Everything hurts. I discovered muscles I didn't even know I had, but I am happy with my progress. By the end of the day, I was able to evade most of the guys' attacks, and I even landed a few hits, mostly on Finn. That was probably because his glasses kept slipping off his nose every time he moved too swiftly. Or it might also have been because of the obvious distraction in the room—Erick.

I gathered that Erick and Finn grew up together, and it's obvious there is history of at least friendship there, but I wasn't aware they both had to train in combat. This means they must have belonged to elite families, or at least families with ties to the Sennex. I have a feeling they must have learned the scheming and the secrecy from somewhere—politics and business require both of those attributes. I mean, it's also possible they both grew up with warrior parents that wanted to teach them, but my gut tells me that's not the case.

I'm still pissed off at Erick for all the drills, but I can't deny the training helps. I feel more in control already. The last time I exerted myself as hard was when my teacher, Diane, showed me the ropes. I had bullies to fend off, and she was proficient with her staff, so she did her best to instruct me. I fell on my ass more times than I care to admit, but she refused to pull back her punches, and I have never been one to back down. That's how I became stronger than my fears. At least the fear of being beaten up by young thugs.

I don't know how I always seem to find myself in these outlandish situations. It's one talent I would gladly give back. This is also one of the things that pushed me too many times in the past to uproot my entire life and leave. I despise complications, but complications are fond of me.

Yes, complications are fond of me, indeed. Today, when we were all tangled up on the floor together, I had the strangest impression. It was like our connection by touch unlocked something—something more than simple desire. As if we were starting to make out the inner workings of whatever weird link is slowly forming between the three of us. Everyone was so damn careful with each other after that. Polite.

The intimacy of the moment felt alien to me, but the distance afterward was even weirder. I'm like in this bizarre in-between where there is no good answer. I can't go back to the way things were yet, but I'm afraid that moving forward will only entangle me further into something I've been trying to avoid for the last couple of years—opening myself up just to be abandoned with my bleeding heart out of my chest.

As much as I want to remove myself from them to protect myself, I feel like the moon. No matter how many times I circle in my orbit, I can't get away from the pull of their gravity. My curiosity demands that I keep bruising myself—quite literally—in pursuing the truth, which I can't make out quite yet.

"You okay?" Albert asks as he rounds the corner of the bar. He is wearing his hideous leather pants tonight, and I can't even. They are so tight on him. He probably bought them back in the 90s when he was a little less imposing. My smile and laughter are genuine, and his answering smirk tells me he doesn't take himself seriously enough to be offended by my reaction. "What? You can't handle raw masculinity?"

I know he's only piling on to cheer me up, and I am grateful. "No. What I can't handle is that you can keep your baritone voice while wearing pants so tight I'm afraid they'll rip if you breathe too deep."

"It's a gift," he retorts. "Well, if you want to be precise, *I* am a gift to this world." I throw my rag at his head, and he avoids it easily. Albert has been more than understanding in the last few days. I've been preoccupied, and it shows in my mood. Even though he doesn't know what's going on with me, he tries to lift my spirits every chance he gets.

"Well, you and your pants have put me off my game. Can I go for my break?" I finish shining the last glass from the clean dish rack while he takes a customer payment.

When he looks back at me, I can see he wants to say something but hesitates. I raise a questioning eyebrow at him.

Albert comes a little closer so he can talk quietly. "I know something is going on. Evelyn is unusually tight-lipped when it comes to you these days. If you are in any... difficult situation, you can tell me. I know I'm only your boss, and you don't know me very well since you haven't been here long, but I take care of my own." He bumps my shoulder softly with his fist.

He's right. I've not been here long. But in the short time I've worked at the pub, I've seen him giving cash to a bouncer who needed it for his mother's treatments, help one of the waitresses move, and even stitch fallen sequins back onto Evie's dress once. It's safe to say that Albert does care about the people he employs.

When I return the gesture, my fist looks ridiculously small against his shoulder. "I know. Don't worry. It's nothing I can't handle." At least, I hope so.

"Go then, take ten. I'll cover the bar for you."

"Well, you'll try. I don't know anyone that is better than me at this job," I boast.

I don't give him time to reply before I leave through the kitchen door to go to the calmest place in the joint, the brewing room. When I sit in here, it feels like I am suspended in time, watching the outside world go on through the glass surrounding the room while I remain still, unbothered. All the sounds of the kitchen are muffled in here.

My thoughts wander back to this afternoon. Finn and Erick are like Russian nesting dolls. As soon as you think you've seen the last of it, there is another doll, and another, and another until you can hardly see the features of the piece of wood that you're holding in your hand.

I can't deny my attraction for Finn is more than physical. There is an easiness in our interactions like a dance the two of us know the steps to. The more I rub shoulders with him, the more... I don't know. It's in the way I don't get bored hearing him nerd out about obscure knowledge. Or his thoughtful nature, like when he brings me tea without being asked because he feels I haven't hydrated enough that day. He and Erick are so different from each other that it's hard to imagine what brought them together in the first place. Maybe being at opposite ends of the spectrum brings everything into a fragile equilibrium for them.

Meanwhile, Erick has a knack for getting under my skin that I dislike more than words can convey. That's why I don't understand the reasons I can't get enough of him. This, too, feels like a dance, only a much more primal one. One where there are teeth and claws instead of beautiful music and fancy clothing. I despise the ease with which he spins the truth around pretty lies to achieve his goals, but I suppose it's to be expected when any misstep might put you six feet under. I'm not saying it's a good way to deal. I'm just saying I can see the logic behind his choices. This doesn't mean I trust him, or even Finn, for that matter.

Perhaps the most troubling thing to happen to me lately is that I am not bothered by their proximity anymore. If I'm being honest with myself, I seek it.

Since I was a little girl, I've been somewhat of a recluse, preferring my own company to anyone else's. I was uncomfortable with physical touch and preferred observing instead of interacting. Those traits, albeit a lot less pronounced, have followed me to adulthood.

Let's just say that it takes me a moment to acclimate to new people in my life. Maybe it's the amount of time we have to spend together, but somehow, those two sneaked their way under my armor, and I am not ready to live with the downfall of it all. I have enough trouble keeping up with my own life. I can't let two beautiful liars entrance me.

No. I have to find the answers I need as soon as possible so we can part ways before my resolve melts like metal in a smithy. I refuse to let myself feel what's building between us because whatever this is, it's doomed from the start. No matter how good it gets on the way, pain is always found down that path.

Chapter 22

FINN

MY PRIVATE LIBRARY HAS been a place of rest and peace for so long it's not used to the unease it's been containing these past few days. I can feel it all around me; the air is thick with unshed restlessness. We've been planning this reconnaissance mission for the last two weeks, but Erick would still want us to gather more information to make sure of everything and to train more, even though we've already trained as much as we can with both him as an instructor and on our own. If Riley and I were to listen to him, this mission would be postponed indefinitely until *he* judges we're ready, which I bet would be never since he clearly doesn't want us to go.

I did pirate the warehouse's floorplan from the city's server, and there are gaping holes in the architectural design. Surely, Victor has somebody on the inside to ensure his installations are never completely exposed. This means we cannot totally be certain about the lay of the land.

I gave Erick access to the plans only last week. Although I was ninety percent sure he wouldn't betray Riley and me and go by himself, I still didn't want to give him too much wiggle room. He is the master of aloofness, which makes it hard sometimes to read him and anticipate his choices. One thing I know for certain is that he doesn't want us to get hurt, which worries me the most.

I am starting to gather that his drive to protect at all costs might be one of the reasons for this abyss of space that he has carefully crafted between us. I need to find a way to broach the subject with him at some point because I'm not sure how long I can keep being with him without being *with* him. I can't keep waking up every morning needing his touch but finding that I am alone in a cold bed.

I tried to hack the security cameras of the Berserker's building remotely, but he has skilled tech experts, and I was short on time. I haven't found a way to enter their system without triggering an alarm. Usually, I don't even mind setting the alarm off since I am untraceable, so I still collect as much data as I can before they find a way to bar my access. However, doing so at this stage would only prompt Victor to increase his security protocols, and that's the last thing we need. I'll have to get to the cameras directly onsite through the building's system, which won't be a problem. It just sucks we cannot get the heads-up.

Riley arrived early to the meeting, which gave us a little time to discuss alone. Like me, she's worried about what we will find. Best-case scenario, it will only be pricy merchandise, rare artifacts, and stuff like that. But the alternative is a little trickier. What if Victor really is behind the disappearances? How will Erick react to this? I know he can fend for himself, but speaking from experience, finding out your family is even worse than you thought muddies the waters. Will he be able to take the necessary steps to ensure everyone's welfare, even if it means going up against his father?

When Erick shows up, his face is drawn in concern, his steps heavy as if he doesn't want to move forward at all. "In the spirit of efficiency," he drawls without totally covering up the unease in his tone, "could I convince you to stay behind?" he says as he looks at me, then at Riley.

I don't even deign to acknowledge the question. Riley, on the other hand, gives him a murderous look. "You can try," she answers, her voice sweet and dripping with sarcasm, "but we would all be losing precious time."

Erick puts his hands up in surrender. "Well, then, we move tonight," he says as we gather around the table where all our notes are laid out. "Sundays are when the guards have the longest shifts, so they are bound to lose focus by the end."

The building is surrounded by a barbwire fence, a prison fence, which does not bode well. Erick has been doing reconnaissance around the perimeter to gather information about the guards' routines and shift changes, in addition to where the physical security cameras and possible alarm triggers are. He couldn't find any indication of magic being used outside, so I assume only the warehouse is protected with spells, but we'll only know for sure once we're onsite. That's where my specific skillset will be useful. I'm not just deft with computers. As a caster, I spent a lot of time studying protection magic, how to create it, and, above all, how to disable it.

"We'll get as close as we can via taxi," he continues.

Riley's ears perk up at the mention of our means of transportation. "Taxi? With all our gear? And a driver that will surely ask questions? Seriously?" she says.

"I called in a favor from a friend that owns a garage with a car junkyard. He lent me a taxi with a fake plate. No need for a driver, and the vehicle blends in easily." Erick would usually have commented something infuriating to get on Riley's nerves, but today, we all feel the weight of the situation. His lack of repartee is but one sign of it.

"Once we're close enough, I'll go first through the hole I found under the fence. I know some of the sentries. If our luck runs dry that early in the plan, I'll be able to sweet talk them about a special shipment their boss wanted to be delivered by me personally."

I see where Erick is going with this, and I won't let him take on all the challenging parts alone. He doesn't want us there with him, that is clear as glass, but he needs to face the music. I won't be put aside when I am qualified to help, and Riley is definitely not taking his shit anymore, so he'll just have to deal.

I clear my throat and point on the map to the location of entry we've chosen. "I will be the first to enter the building since I am the one to bypass the physical and magical protections."

Erick's shoulders tense, his hands closing into loose fists on the table.

Riley looks at him and huffs. "Get over it, Erick. We're doing this with you no matter what. You can brood as much as you want, but it won't change a fucking thing. We made our bed, now we'll lie in it. Period."

My thoughts exactly.

"I prepared the potions you asked for," she carries on, "in case we get hurt or need a boost. I put everything in shatterproof containers. It should be enough for the three of us in case of emergency without wasting too much space or weighing us down. Also, if I can reach you, I can heal you directly. It's going to cost me, but in a pinch, it's best."

"I don't like this," Erick says under his breath.

Riley throws her hands in the air in defeat.

"Don't we know it," I say, rolling my eyes.

Erick finally lets out a long sigh of resignation. He cracks his neck, looking intently at each of us in turn. "Fine. But once inside, we stay close to each other. We don't know what glorious surprises we'll encounter. And, if push comes to shove, you get out of there by any means necessary. Don't look back, and don't try to be a hero."

"What about you? You really think we would leave you there to die and go about our day as if nothing happened?" Riley says through gritted teeth, fuming. "How thick of a skull do you have? We. Are. A. Team. Stop being a douche."

"I'm not being 'a douche.'" Erick gestures air quotes around the word.

Here we go again. These two cannot spend a day without bickering like an old couple. This brings a smile to my lips.

"What are you smiling about?" Erick and Riley say in unison.

I'm not a fan of being their focus right now with all their anger redirected at me, so I sober my features real fast. "Nothing. Not a damn thing." They both go back to staring daggers at each other. In the meantime, I still have trouble keeping my stupid smile at bay, so I tuck my lips between my teeth.

"As I was saying," Erick picks up, "I'm not being dense. I'm much more valuable to them alive than dead. They will bring me to the Berserker for a sentence. They won't take the chance of eliminating on sight one of my father's cash cows without his approbation. No matter what I did or didn't do. You, on the other hand, are expendable in their eyes. They won't hesitate to eliminate you on sight."

Thick skull, indeed.

Chapter 23

RILEY

THE EQUIPMENT PROVIDED BY Finn is sleek. From the small earpiece that fits perfectly to the breathable Kevlar protection, I feel like a spy in a James Bond movie—albeit way less skilled. I don't even want to think about the cost of all of this or where that money comes from. There's no way a small bookstore owner can lay down that kind of money at the drop of a hat. But that is a mystery to unearth later. I can only focus on so much at the same time.

We left the cab on a quiet road nearby where we were sure there were no cameras or streetlamps so we could slip into the night unseen. I am grateful for the gloves since my hands are moist with anticipation. Being sandwiched between Erick, who leads our small convoy, and Finn, who closes it, feels like having two bodyguards. I would normally grumble at their obvious attempt to keep me out of harm's way—I can hold my own—however, in this instance, I welcome the gesture. I am not stupid enough to assume I know best over an adept security expert and an extensively trained warrior.

I can already see the warehouse and the patches of shadows we'll have to tread in between the light sources to stay under the radar.

We're almost at the fence when Erick lifts his left fist to signal us to stop. He waits a minute to make sure of the sentinel's pattern. Then he crawls carefully through the hole under the fence left there by scavengers. He disappears immediately into the darkness. I don't think Finn and I even breathe until we hear the small hoot of an owl in a distinctive pattern, our signal to proceed.

Finn lifts the bottom of the fence a little higher as I pass through to make sure I don't get stuck. And, as agreed, I don't wait for him to get through to make my way to the meeting point. My heart hammers in the quiet of the night as I try to make out my path through the darkness. Relief floods my system when I spot Erick's frame beside the door.

Finn's faint footfalls follow soon after, and he immediately busies himself with the security systems. He takes off his gloves and places his hands directly on the door of the building. Then he mumbles something I cannot place, but it has a rhythm like a lullaby. It's as if he is trying to coax the protection spell to let us through, to make it believe we are old friends of the original caster and allowed to be here. That's genius. If the spell stays completely in place, no alarms can be triggered.

I still cannot see or feel anything out of the ordinary when he pulls his hands back and slips on his gloves once more. Stealth is the name of the game here. He nods to indicate that the magical side of things is taken care of before moving on to the physical security system.

While Finn was reprogramming the wards, Erick had time to perforate a small hole beside the door to access the building's wiring. Where to find a point of entry to the security system's mainframe was one of the things we weren't sure about. Maybe Victor had stuff installed differently in comparison to the security industry standard. Who knows?

Finn reaches into the opening and plugs a small box with a screen on it into the building's security system. When the device brings up all the tiny camera feeds at once, we all exhale in relief—it's working. None of the images show the ghost room, the part in the building's blueprints that is blank. It's all corridors, storage rooms, and employees' quarters.

Finn loops the camera feeds for the next thirty minutes as agreed. After that, he pushes a plethora of buttons on his device until the door before us unlocks. He steps forward to lead the way into the building, but Erick doesn't stand for it. He immediately pulls Finn and me back into our original formation, placing himself in front. Finn scowls at Erick on his way to the back of our line, but Erick doesn't pay him any attention as he opens the door. Erick's head moves from side to side repeatedly, monitoring the narrow space that extends on each side of us. The dull neon lights cast a yellowish glow on the hospital-like corridor. Barely perceptible footsteps are progressively getting louder, approaching from our right. Erick motions for us to duck into an unlocked janitor closet beside the entrance we just used. The individual passes by none the wiser, continuing their path down the corridor. After that, we make our way deeper into the building.

I memorized the plan we pirated from the city's server—we all did.

Right. Left. Right. Right. Until we reach the edge of the hole in the plan. From here, we're in the dark as to what we'll find.

Erick guides us to a dead end where two locked doors stand next to each other—which also coincides with the start of the empty space on the building plan. I don't know what compels him to pause, but he makes us wait there for what feels like an eternity. Then he points to the right door and motions for us to back up the way we came from. The ninety-degree turn hides us from view of the two doors. There's a loud beep, then two male voices arguing. If they decide to go down the corridor instead of through the other door, we're done for. My heart hammers in anticipation. There's another beep, and Erick lunges silently into action. He just has time to catch the right door before it locks shut again.

Finn and I stay in place to wait for the left door to close completely after the two men. Then we follow Erick through the right door. I can't spot any cameras or motion sensors in this part of the warehouse, which is good for us, I suppose. The front of the huge open space we enter is lined with wooden crates and metal boxes. All of them are nailed or padlocked shut. I assume those are the precious artifacts of the Berserker.

That's when I hear a groan from the back of the room. We all stop dead in our tracks and crouch behind the nearest crate. The groan becomes a whimper and is followed by the rattling of metal. Dread peppers goosebumps down my spine as we resume our movements toward the back of the room.

The smell of urine and vomit hits me first. Then my own stomach churns at the sight before me—cages, metal cages like in zoos, but not even big enough for a full-grown human to stand in. I immediately recognize the face of the first person I see from the pictures of the missing witches I studied so much during our weeks of preparation. The young woman, Martha, is crouched at the back of her enclosure, eyes rimmed black from exhaustion. Her skin has the recognizable grayish tint of someone near death. Her eyes grow wide when she spots us.

I lunge forward to get to her, but Erick, now white as a sheet, puts his arm in my way and signs to the woman and the others, who slowly awaken to our presence, to stay quiet. He turns around and examines the space while Finn removes his gloves again to press his hands onto the floor. Once they are both satisfied that it's not boobytrapped, Erick signals Finn to go to the first cage. As Finn approaches, Martha shakes her head vigorously for him not to touch the bars.

He turns around and wiggles his fingers in the air to indicate that the cages are spelled. Erick moves to three more cages, and every inmate confirms that their cage is also spelled. He looks stunned, lost. We all knew it was a possibility. That's exactly why we're here. But I think he never really believed his father could be responsible for the disappearances. His routine check is quickly becoming a nightmare.

"Shit," Erick whispers-shouts under his breath.

As I look from cage to cage, my eyes well up with angry tears. Some of the witches in them weren't even in our research. Twelve in total.

Twelve.

But why torture witches? To what end? It doesn't make sense. One of the captives, a man I don't recognize, seems in better shape than the others. He must be the newest acquisition. A shudder runs through me at the thought.

He approaches the edge of his confinement as I crouch in front of him.

"What happened?" I whisper.

"I was grabbed from my parking garage. I didn't see who it was. They knocked me unconscious, and I woke up here not long ago when two men with masked faces came to take out someone from a cage." He nods toward the now empty cage. The man gulps loudly, clearly dehydrated. I wish I could give him water without triggering the spell on his enclosure. My heart breaks a little more.

He lowers his head and picks at the dust on the floor. "She wasn't responsive," he says. "She looked...dead." A silent sob shakes his thin frame.

Resolute to help them get out, I walked back to Finn and Erick, who were also quietly speaking with other prisoners. As we convene in the middle of the space, they all look at us with hope.

"We need to get them out," I plead.

Erick looks about to be sick. "I know," he whispers. "I saw a door in the back of the room, on the other side of those cages. If I remember the building plans correctly, this should be the exterior wall of this ghost room. So, the door there should lead outside. One of the prisoners told me that touching the bars is very painful and triggers an alarm. Touching the enclosure won't hurt me if I syphon the spell, but I don't have enough receptacles to keep the energy in afterward, and I'm not trained to keep it inside me. Also, I don't know if the seconds between me touching the bars and syphoning the spell from the metal will be too long and maybe trigger an alarm." He turns to Finn. "Can *you* find a way around the spell of their cages?"

The wheels are frantically turning behind Finn's eyes. "I... I know of this kind of magic, but I need more preparation to take down all twelve. Also, we don't have much time left before the cameras reboot. I can maybe take—"

That's all he has time to say before the door we used to enter the room opens once more. We scarcely have time to hide behind the nearest crate. From here, we can peek through the wooden slats and see the situation unravel. All the witches' heads that I can see swivel to the newcomers.

Three men enter the space. Two of them are dressed in security guards' uniforms—blue shirts with black pants and a gun holster at the hip. The third man stands out. His tailored suit and neatly cut hair reek of money. His polished demeanor stands in stark contrast to this makeshift dungeon. I feel more than hear Erick's sharp intake of breath.

"We put the new one over there, boss," says guard number one.

The boss. Erick's father.

"Bring him to me," Victor orders, voice as hard as steel.

The cage is too far away for me to see how they take down the spell. The familiar click of a lock follows. The man kicks and screams, but the two guards are well-trained. The closer the prisoner gets to him, the sharper Victor's features become. His posture goes from relaxed to menacing.

As soon as Victor lays his hands on the thrashing man's cheeks, the two guards let go of him. The prisoner's arms fall limply to his sides as energy passes from him to the Berserker. My muscles scream for me to take action, but the spectacle roots me in place. Victor releases the man less than a minute later, letting him fall into a heap on the ground. The man's breathing is labored. He looks a lot paler, the way someone does after having given blood.

When Victor looks back at the guards, they both take a step back.

"Not the power I need," he says. His voice is flat, completely devoid of emotion. The tone itself will haunt my nightmares for the foreseeable future.

Without warning, Victor turns around and touches the bars on Martha's cage. The spell doesn't even register to him as he swiftly syphons it away. Then he uses the magical energy he stored in himself to create a small explosion and rips the door clean off its hinges.

He moves so fast I hardly have time to see him drag Martha out by the neck. Erick grabs my hand without even looking at me. We're trapped. We cannot help the captives. We cannot escape until Victor and his goons leave. All we can do is witness whatever is going to happen next. Because witness we must if we're to do something about the situation later.

"But you," the Berserker carries on, "you have the power I need. Did you have time to replenish your shadows, love?" The term of endearment sounds wrong, terrifying. Martha is clawing at his hands, trying desperately to escape his iron grip.

Victor cocks his head to the side like dogs often do when they try to understand something. He is feeling her powers, I realize.

"Not enough, I see. I'm sorry, love, but it's been too long now," he croons as if to a baby. "Your powers are no use to me anymore, but your remaining years are."

I don't understand what Victor is doing to her at first. However, when Martha starts to scream in agony, my reflexes demand that I jump out from my hiding place to help her, but Erick keeps my hand firmly in his while Finn circles my waist with his arms, securing me in place. Her scream ends with a gurgle when a bright white light passes from her body to Victor's. Then her lifeless form slumps forward. The tears run like a torrent down my face. The anguish renders me numb. I try to draw breath, but it's no use.

She's dead. She's dead. She's dead. The words repeat themselves in my head over and over again like a macabre melody.

He syphoned the life out of her. Painfully so.

Victor takes a moment to straighten his jacket and finger-comb his hair like he didn't just murder an innocent. "You will find me the one I need, or you'll meet the same end. Is that clear?" he seethes to his two employees.

"Of course, boss," they answer in unison.

The two guards look at each other, not knowing what to do next, and their incompetence seems to make Victor's blood boil. He starts to shake slightly. Then he closes his fist, and a crate explodes on the opposite side of the room.

"Bring me my necromancer!" Victor bellows, spittle flying out of his mouth like a rabid animal.

Erick almost crushes the bones of my hand at the unhinged roar of his father because he knows. He knows I am the prized mare his dad is after. A powerful necromancer. The guards scramble to gather up Martha and the other man from the floor.

My mind is reeling, but I don't have time to give way to the panic because Finn and Erick pull me up from the floor, determined to take advantage of the general frenzy to make our escape.

Chapter 24

ERICK

We escaped that snake pit just in time to see two unmarked jeeps with tinted windows screech their tires as they left. Goons trying to be useful enough not to be my father's next victim, no doubt.

I don't know what I expected to find, but it wasn't this. Growing up, my father was always smiling and willing to help others every chance he got. He would tuck me into bed every night with stories of faraway lands and incredible feats. He was a loving partner to my mother and an adoring father to me. He would never raise his voice and consistently spoke of tolerance and compassion.

It all changed after "the betrayal," or at least that's what I call it. That fateful night when Sennex officers came to our Faroe Islands' home to arrest my father as a political traitor. The night he had to defend himself as best he could. The night I learned that he was like me. The night he looked at my mother with the eyes of a desperate man, but all she said was, "Leave with the child. I will hold them off as long as I can."

I wasn't a child anymore then, though. I was almost nineteen and head over heels in love. I followed my dad in the cover of night, my heart breaking a little more with each step I took away from *him*. No one knew how much it hurt—no one but Finn. We wanted to keep our relationship private back then because we knew that, in the political game, this beautiful link between us would be exploited in some way, tarnished. We talked about leaving all the time. I just didn't think that I would leave without him and on the run from the only home I've ever known.

We only spoke of that night once, my dad and me. He didn't answer most of my questions, but he did speak of my mother. He was certain she was the one who had reported him to the Sennex. On what grounds? For what offense? I'm still not completely sure to this day.

When we fled the Faroe Islands, the Sennex's stronghold, where most of the high political players live, we had to hide. No credit cards, no work unless it paid cash, and false identities. Although we kept our first names since they are very common, we just left the family name—Ferguson—behind.

Of course, I was aware when he took over Ovila's operation—the mobster we ended up working for after landing in Québec City. Victor was his right hand, and when Ovila was found dead in his penthouse without a named successor, my father took the burden upon himself to lead the gang. Indeed, Ovila's men were, for the most part, already loyal to Victor or downright afraid of him, which led to the same outcome of ensured loyalty. Hence, this course of action would avoid unnecessary bloodshed and provide continued stability for the territory. At least, I thought that was why he did it. Now, I'm not so sure anymore.

After that, he left me both the shops to manage. The man I grew up with slowly became someone else. Someone hard and unyielding. Someone with no warmth left. But, throughout the years, I never knew him to be unnecessarily cruel or vengeful. His men always respected him and thought him forceful but just.

Until now, I really believed he was doing only what he needed to do to survive. What *we* had to do. A lot of it I didn't agree with. I knew it was wrong—is wrong—and I tried as best I could to soften the blows and give back to the community. To atone for his sins and mine. I know my efforts will never be enough, and I will carry that burden to my grave.

But the beast I saw today wasn't my father. It's an abomination. It feels like the man I once knew has been poisoned or replaced by a vile twin. How could he do that to innocent people? No end can ever justify the means I witnessed today, no matter how fanatical you may be. He's lost it. He is not connected with reality anymore.

"Erick, talk to us," Riley implores.

I have been pacing through Finn's home for the best part of half an hour now, unable to speak, unable to feel anything past the horror burning its way through my brain.

Finn proposed his own place to lay low. He made the case that, given the circumstances, there were no guarantees that my father didn't know about my bunker. He also pointed out that even if Victor knows about his own home, it's already a fortress. He assured us that if my father's followers were to try something, he would know and be more capable of defending our position and escaping from here.

I didn't have the energy to argue. I feel the exhaustion through my bones, but I can't seem to stop moving. I'm tracking dirt and mud all over, but Finn doesn't stop me. He lets me walk the length of the big open space that is his house. I try desperately to focus on the details around me. I need to bring myself back from this state. I need to get a grip and move forward.

Finn converted an old industrial building into his home, which means the ceilings are so high that his and Riley's hushed voices echo through the space. Everything is new. The kitchen along the back wall is dominated by a huge island counter. Before it sits the biggest couch I've ever seen. Its three sides form a U-shape and could easily sleep a person on each side. Art that probably costs the entire price of my own home hangs on the wall. I stop in front of the bookshelves that separate the bedroom from the living room and attempt to read the title of the book before me. My last ten efforts were unsuccessful—my general mental state making the letters blurry. But this time, this time, I can.

My chest cavity expands on a deep, full breath for the first time in the last day. I turn around to look at the darkened sky. Windows cover the width of the front of the house. I know nobody can see us because they are spelled to make the inside look like an abandoned warehouse to any onlooker. They are also bulletproof. Finn takes safety to a whole other level. Since he's the son of a Sennex member, I suppose it's warranted.

I can't help my piss-poor attitude right now. "Finn, shade the damn windows." He doesn't say anything, nor does he move. I turn around to face Finn and Riley, seated on the couch. Their faces are serious, but no pity in sight. Thank the gods.

"You had enough money in your trust fund to pay for electric blinds," I hiss, "so push the fucking button and close them." I am shaking like a leaf now, trapped in my crash of adrenaline.

Finn gets up and walks toward me slowly, as someone would do a wounded animal, and I hate it. I hate it so much. He stops right in front of me. "You're only looking for a fight to punish yourself," he says, "and although I don't owe you an explanation, I'll have you know that I never touched a penny of that trust fund. All you see here comes from my own investments, and I won't apologize for being good with the stock market." His tone is soft and soothing. Not a trace of outrage in sight, which makes me feel even worse.

His movements are slow and measured as he covers the last of the distance between us and wraps me in his arms.

"Don't touch me. I'm a monster." The words leave me of their own accord. "At least I'm the son of one, and the apple usually doesn't fall far from the tree." I don't push Finn away, though. I can't. My whole being yearns for all the comfort it can get. I'm so numb I don't even feel his powers when I bury my nose in the crook of his neck, breathing him in.

I don't cry. I don't deserve to.

How could I have been so naïve? I should have been able to prevent this. I should have kept a better eye on my dad.

"No. Your father *acted* like a monster today, and I think I might have an idea why." I don't grasp the nature of Finn's words immediately.

"You know something?" Riley asks from her position on the couch.

Finn takes my shoulders and pushes me away to look me over and make sure I can stand on my own. Then he tugs my hand and brings me to the big, stuffed chair beside the living room windows before he takes his place back at Riley's side.

"I wasn't able to confirm it, not before today," he says. "But I read of the uncontrolled power hold of some void witches. It's not an illness, or not in the way we think of illnesses anyway." Finn opens the book sitting on the coffee table before him. "It is said here that some void witches would syphon energy and either keep too much inside themselves or keep it for too long. From what I gather, it's like with the yogis and breath practices. The most extraordinary yogis can control their breath to a great extent. Still, they, too, must come back to regular breathing after a while, or it can create damage. For syphons, not discharging the overflow of magic or keeping the energy in for longer than your strength allows can create damage, too."

I'm not sure I want to know the answer to my next question. "Can it be cured?"

Finn's brows draw together. "I read one account of a woman being successfully brought back from the edge, but no indication about how it was done."

"Did you know syphons could syphon the life out of people?" Riley asks no one in particular. She looks shell-shocked; we all are. The scream of that witch dying will stay with me forever.

I shake my head no. Absolutely not.

"I haven't seen any reference to it in my research," Finn answers. "The only thing I am certain of is that void witches cannot syphon non-magical beings, so it's safe to assume they can't syphon their life either. I obviously will try to find information to assure myself of that fact. In the meantime, this raises a lot of questions."

"No shit," I deadpan.

"Victor said that the witch's remaining years would be helpful to him," Finn carries on without missing a beat. "Can he prolong his own life? How old is he, then? His real name might not even be Victor. I mean, I know he's your father, but beyond that, who is he? He—"

Riley puts her hand over his mouth. "Stop," she says, letting it drop to her lap again. "Stop. We get it. There is a lot we don't know." She seizes her pendant and rolls it through her fingers. "Things like, why does he need a necromancer? To what end?"

I look at her then. Finn doesn't know of this side of her powers, but we all need to be on the same page if we're to move forward wisely. Riley's shoulders slump forward under my insisting stare.

"What?" Finn asks. "What is it?"

"I am a necromancer," Riley confesses.

"And a powerful one at that," I complete.

Finn looks hurt when his gaze lands on me. "How do you know that?"

"I helped Riley get down from the ladder in your library a couple of weeks ago, and I accidentally touched her skin. She didn't want me to tell anyone, and at the time, it didn't influence any of this." My hands dart forward, palms up, begging him to understand. "We already knew she was a powerful healer and potion master, and during our research, we found nothing pointing to precise powers being targeted."

Finn's lips move into a thin line. We all stay quiet for a moment, motionless, just contemplating the pile of shit we stepped into.

Finn breaks the silence first. "I think that, if we dig a little deeper, we may find that many of the less powerful witches that were taken probably had necromancy as a gift. Like Riley, they weren't using it, but it was there to syphon, nonetheless. I believe that since your father cannot find a powerful necromancer, he is trying to Frankenstein himself as much necromancy powers as he can."

Riley is getting paler and paler. "But why?" she asks. "Do you think he knows of my power? How did he find out about the other witches if we couldn't even find anything about their possible necromancy with our resources? And what about those captive witches?" Her voice cracks as fat tears start to run down her cheeks. "How do we help them? How do we get them out? I couldn't even give them water or healing tinctures through the fucking spell of those abominable cages."

Finn gathers her in his arms, and she lets him, now sobbing uncontrollably. I can't do anything about those witches now, but I can at least try to be useful and lend her the little strength I have left. I get up, sit on the coffee table before her and take her hands in mine. Both of them look at me now. I can see the hurt they sport through their open expressions. How will I fix this?

"How—how do my powers feel to you?" Riley whispers.

I don't know why she asks, but at the moment, I would give her anything if it would ease a fraction of her pain.

I close my eyes and take a deep breath, letting my void make out the nature of the powers I touch. "There is an overwhelming buzzing created by the vast strength of your magic. Even with the damper you put on part of it." I hear Finn's sharp intake of breath at this information before I continue. "Your necromancy feels cold, but it twists and twines with the waves of warmth created by your healing abilities. I don't know how to explain the rest to you. It's like I can feel, more than see, a kaleidoscope of vivid colors coming from your skills in potion-making. The rest is just background." My body relaxes a fraction at the pleasant mix of sensations.

I open my eyes then. Riley's cheeks have become a soft pink, and she shivers when her gaze meets mine. I turn to Finn, who watches the interaction avidly, having inched closer to us unconsciously. He is near enough that I can see the heartbeat at his neck. I didn't plan to say the next words out loud, but... "I never forgot how *you* felt," I tell him.

We all stay like that for a bit, staring at each other, until Riley's soft inhale breaks the weaving connection between us, or whatever it was. I shake myself and move back to my place on the chair.

I rake a hand through my hair and clear my throat. "To answer your question, I don't think my father has any idea about your necromancy or even the extent of your powers as a whole. If he did, he would have already moved to capture you. He is— I mean, it seems he was careful to take only certain individuals to not arouse the suspicions of the human police or the Sennex." Or my suspicions, I remind myself. Or mine. "But he clearly doesn't give a fuck anymore. Some of his captives have been on the six o'clock news. I don't even know if you and Finn are safe now just for being witches. I mean, he even started to throw caution to the winds and use his powers in the open in front of his minions, for fuck's sake."

I lay back in my chair and press my palms into my eye sockets until I see stars. "We need to go to the Sennex. They have the resources to stop my father. I don't care if I get arrested in the process. This needs to stop," I tell them, letting my arms fall back down in defeat.

Finn huffs. "What do you think is going to happen exactly? The Sennex's task force didn't even move a finger to help the ones that disappeared other than filling out the official paperwork. I mean, yes, if you tell them that Victor is behind all of this, they will be interested in capturing him, but only him. They won't care what happens to those prisoners during their intervention, nor will they care about the ensuing war for territory and power that will ravage this city after your father's capture. Plus, are you sure that your father doesn't have moles on the force that will alert him the very moment he is discovered? At this point, he'll only go into hiding and pick up whatever the fuck he's doing where he left off."

Riley's eyes are red-rimmed. She shudders as she whispers, "And I'll always be looking over my shoulder, not knowing if Victor found out about my necromancy."

"What's the alternative?" I ask, despair and frustration seeping into my voice.

Finn sighs and throws his hands into the air. "I don't know yet, but there's got to be a solution better than that."

My splitting headache won't go away any time soon. I need rest. We all do. "We sleep here tonight. We'll think clearer in the morning," I tell them.

Riley throws an incredulous look my way.

"We're all exhausted," I plow on, "and Finn is right." At that, Finn raises one eyebrow at me in amusement. I send him my *do not test me* look, and he squirms under the weight of it, which I enjoy way too much.

"Our places are not rigged enough yet. Plus, we'll need to decide what we're going to do about the situation first thing tomorrow. Riley, you can have the bed. We'll take the couch."

Finn's annoyance at me barking orders in his own home does not prompt him to retort with a scathing comment like I'd hoped. Instead, he looks me straight in the eyes, gets up, and kneels in front of the console table beside me to get out sheets and the like for the couch. The gesture tugs at my guts, and my fingers twitch on the arms of my chair. Once Finn gets up, he looks at my hands with a satisfied smile. The bastard wanted to get a reaction out of me.

Finn throws the bedding on the couch. "Fine," he says, "I'm going to call Bree and let her know we're okay but that she has to be careful. She'll also have to man the bookstore by herself tomorrow."

He doesn't wait for an answer before leaving for the bedroom. A few seconds later, I hear him talking quietly on the phone. When I turn back to Riley, she is looking back and forth between me and the entrance to the bedroom where Finn disappeared, her confusion evident.

"You okay?" I ask her.

"No." Silence falls between us for a couple of seconds. Then she says, "I'd better call Evie to let her in on the new development and tell her to stay away before we know more. You're lucky the pub is not open on Mondays. Otherwise, I don't take orders to stay put from a mob boss's son I barely know." She dials and sits at the kitchen island, her back to me.

Okay, I deserved that.

There's only one thing left for me to do tonight. I scrape my hand over my face, pick up my own phone, and call Eleanor.

Chapter 25

FINN

I WAKE UP AROUND six in the morning. We went to bed late last night, but my biological clock didn't get the memo. I keep my eyes closed, enjoying the warmth of the morning sun filtering through the blinds I deliberately left open the night before.

I am not ready to face the coming day yet.

It is strange how life can get so messed up so quickly. A couple of weeks ago, all I had to worry about was the next stunt Gavin, my store neighbor, would pull on me. Today, we'll have to face the horrors we witnessed and find a solution. Today, we'll have to make hard decisions and, for some, difficult sacrifices. But today, I am grateful to not be alone in facing it all. I am grateful for the new connections and the old ones rebuilt—or rebuilding, at least.

I have no idea what's to come. I just hope we can manage everything quickly with no casualties. It may be wishful thinking, but I will do everything in my power to make my hope a reality, and I'm sure Riley and Erick will, too.

When my eyes finally adjust to the bright light flooding the room, the first thing I see is Erick. He is sitting on the same chair he was in yesterday but moved it to see all the living room and the street outside from his perch. He refused to accept my offer of pajamas last night, so he's still wearing his clothes, but he lost his shirt and boots during the night. His blankets and T-shirt are neatly folded on his side of the couch.

He is twirling a playing card in one hand—the queen of hearts—while his head full of thick raven hair rests in his other hand. His gaze is fixed outside, deep in thought. A soldier guarding camp.

"Did you sleep?" My voice is rough with slumber.

"I rarely do," he answers as he pockets the card. He doesn't continue the discussion and doesn't look at me. Silence hangs between us.

I haven't seen him shirtless in a long time. In truth, I haven't seen him at all in a long time. The reminder creates a small pinch just under my sternum, but I don't rub it away. I memorize it and keep it preciously because, after this, I don't know where any of us will end up.

His chest is peppered with new scars, some wide gashes, some small pinpricks. It's like they tell his history, and I missed it all. I can't imagine what he had to go through in our years apart, let alone what he is going through right now. He looks so lost. I just want to shake him to make sure he mentally comes back to me, to us.

"You don't have the right to order me around anymore like you did yesterday," I whisper. "You gave up that right three years ago." I hope he'll take the bait. I hope his fire will ignite once again and consume me whole like it used to.

Erick tenses at the words. But when he looks back at me, his eyes are haunted. "I know," he answers quietly. As the silence stretches between us once again, his gaze leaves my face and starts its journey down my body. That's when I notice my sheets slipped to the ground during the night, leaving my naked torso exposed. My loose linen pants are askew and hang low on my hips.

Even with all the power I have, I cannot hide my body's reaction to the intense stare of that man. It's been a long time since my mind even considered intimacy at all.

Erick sees the evidence of my arousal, and his breathing picks up, but I dare not move. I want to keep burning in this man's stormy gaze as long as I can. He has the arms of his seat in a death grip, which he forces himself to release before looking back outside.

"Do you believe we can get through our kind of history?" he mumbles.

I don't even want to entertain the thought. I don't want to feel hope that he will stay—that *they* will stay. My mouth opens to answer, but we are interrupted by a sleep-mussed Riley emerging from my room.

She hasn't yet changed back into her own clothes, and the sight of her in one of my button-down shirts only sends more blood south, which she thankfully can't see from her position. Gods, she's sexy in the morning. I should be ashamed. I don't know if she's even interested in him or me or...us...that way. I would imagine my face looks like Erick's does, ravenous.

She stops walking, but she doesn't shy away. I can feel the air thicken. She looks down at her body and seems to just remember that she's still in my shirt. Her cheeks become this pretty shade of pink, and her nipples harden through the fabric. Riley's body sways slightly forward, but she stops before taking another step toward us. It feels like magnetic forces are demanding that each of our bodies move to be one unit.

She still doesn't turn away. She only bites down on her lip and looks at Erick and me in turn. Her gaze is soft as she contemplates the portrait we must make. My attention is drawn to a small movement she just did with her legs, as if rubbing them together to put pressure on—

Get out of the gutter, Finn! You're probably making her uncomfortable!

I try to sound as unaffected as possible as I say, "Morning," effectively breaking the building sexual tension.

Riley startles at the sound of my voice. Her face is now bright red, and she ducks her head. "Can't do morning without coffee," she answers.

"Sure, I'll get that for you. Feel free to use the shower while I fix us all breakfast if you want." I give her the escape on purpose, and she bolts like the living room floor is made of lava.

Congratulations, Finn, you're officially a creep.

Chapter 26

RILEY

My cheeks are burning. The racing pulse in my veins makes me feel lightheaded. I close my eyes and lay my forehead against the tiled shower stall. Well, if you can call it a stall. I could fit my whole bed in here. I thought I had dreamt this bathroom last night, but no. Finn wasn't kidding when he said that he was good with economics. This shower alone must have cost a small fortune.

The space is just off the bedroom. The first thing you see when you come in is a huge bathtub set deep into the earth, like those Roman bathhouses. With the three steps you use to get in, it feels more like a small inground pool. My imagination stirs with ideas of all the possibilities that this bathtub alone holds, and I have to turn off the hot water completely to cool my body.

Entertaining the idea of a relationship, even just a carnal one, with one of them is bad enough, but thinking of having both of them is completely ludicrous. It's just...seeing them rough from sleep and shirtless first thing in the morning is testing my willpower.

I have to remind myself I am still annoyed beyond reason with Erick's stupid information protectionism and Finn's wanting to do the most without displeasing anybody in the process, the eternal peacemaker. It's the weirdest feeling, though, being drawn to men I am cross with, unable to control my traitorous body's reaction.

And what a reaction it was. I am incapable of remembering the last time I've been so aroused without anybody touching me. I can still feel the brush of Finn's shirt on my sensitive breasts, the beat of my heart at the apex of my thighs, demanding pressure. Finn's reaction to the instinctive movement of my legs rubbing together says volumes. We were all feeling it, the urge to act, to do something, anything to relieve that deep itch at the back of our minds.

My teeth are chattering when I push from the wall to start washing myself. Even though I can see the entire bathroom through the shower's glass, my gaze is unfocused. I'm so lost in thought that it takes a minute for me to place the smell of leather and warm spices from the expensive body wash. The deep scent, Finn's scent, lathers my entire body, which makes my insides quiver. I grunt in annoyance at my own weakness and finish the shower in record time.

I take a plush towel to dry myself off and move to one of the vanities. There are two in total, one on each side of the doorway. Their light gray marble matches the marble of the floor.

I don't bother wiping the mirror as I start the task of untangling my hair with my fingers. I give up halfway through and sigh.

Good enough.

Sadly, I can't stay in here forever and avoid reality. So, I get dressed and enter the lion's den.

Both men are fully clothed when I emerge from the bedroom, and I don't know if I should feel relieved or disappointed. As promised, Finn made coffee and breakfast—eggs, bacon, and hashbrowns. The small gesture tugs at my insides, so I scowl at myself, which earns me a puzzled look from Erick, who is eating his bacon on the other side of the kitchen island.

We have breakfast in silence. The awkwardness of the moment only grows at the polite requests to pass the salt or refill the coffee. Gone is the familiarity, the easy banter.

Unease unravels as we convene in the living room, hot beverage in hand.

Erick cuts through the tension first. "I can't believe my dad would go that far. No matter how hard I think about it, I just can't fathom why. The rigid but just man I've always known has vanished before my eyes like a sick, twisted magic trick. The only thing left is that...animal run by its hunger." His lips close into a thin line. The sadness in his eyes is evident. He really doesn't know what happened to his father.

"I'm so sorry, Erick," Finn answers. "I can't imagine how you must feel right—"

"Disgusted," Erick cuts in, "horrified, shocked. But mostly just angry at myself for not seeing any of it. For not really believing from the start that he would do something like this."

I get it. I truly do. Betrayal hits the hardest when it comes from the ones you depend on, the ones you never ever thought would let you down. For some twisted reason, even though you are the one being cheated, it always feels like you are the one who failed. Like you knew that person so well, you should have been able to guess something was wrong. But it's all hogwash, as Diane would say. It's the curse of the martyrs to take on others' wrongdoings, and I have a feeling that Erick carries on his back the sins of his father to try to atone for them.

I set down my cup of coffee and stare at him for a moment, trying to figure out how to best make him understand that his initial reasoning was sound. All the steps he has taken have been, in my opinion, the most logical ones. "You couldn't have known," I try. "Not for sure, anyway. I gave you shit for not putting the blame on the Berserker from the start, but you were right to do so. The threat could have come from any number of sources."

Erick's mouth twists in a ghost of a smile, but it's still a smile, nonetheless. "Can you say that again?" he says, a hint of humor in his tone.

I don't even think about barking back, which is a testament to how shaken I am by the whole situation. "I said you were right. Happy?"

"I wouldn't say happy, no."

Finn places his forearms on his knees, his sandy hair falling slightly into his face. "I need to know something before we dive into crisis management galore," Finn says. His body tenses ever so slightly, his head bending downward. "If you're not able to move against your father for any reason," he informs Erick with a solemn tone, "you have to tell us now. I know you were ready to stop him yesterday, even at the cost of your own freedom. However, now that the shock has passed, you might have changed your mind. I won't hold it against you, but we need to plan among allies. The gravity of the situation demands strong cohesion between our small numbers to optimize the resulting actions.

"Victor needs to be neutralized, and the witches need to be freed. The human police won't be any help in this. Victor would only kill every last one of them easily and flee. Also, I maintain that the Sennex shouldn't be involved."

"We may have to come to that, though," Erick chimes in. "If it does, don't hesitate. Call your parents."

Shock runs through my bones. "Wait, your parents are *currently* sitting on the Sennex's council of thirteen?"

"My mother, yes," Finn answers, unfazed.

Now I get why Erick was alluding to a trust fund. The leaders of our government are handsomely rewarded for their service. "But how is it that you are here and not there? I mean, you could be next in line for a seat down the road. A shot at making a difference."

Finn snorts and cozies himself back onto the couch, his arms draped along the back. The relaxed position is at odds with his usual uptightness. "Politics. It's not everything it's cracked up to be." His deep green eyes shine with sarcasm. "And it's a story for another time anyway. For now, all that is important is that I have had no contact or link whatsoever with my family and the Sennex for the past three years. They know where I am, but they don't bother keeping tabs on me since my older brother is the prodigal son. So, unless we raise suspicions by not being discreet enough or we purposefully call on them, they shouldn't get involved."

This does nothing to ease the pins and needles making their way into my stomach. Maybe I shouldn't have eaten before a discussion like this one.

Finn nails Erick with a hard stare. The small reprieve of humor he displayed just a moment ago is nowhere to be seen. "You haven't answered me. Will you, in good conscience, be able to work with us to plot against Victor?"

Erick stares back at him, his own features unyielding. The resemblance to his father in that instant makes me shudder in dread. But I remind myself that, unlike his father, Erick is the one that led our escape yesterday to make sure we wouldn't be in the line of fire if we were caught. It was also he who insisted on checking us over for injuries as soon as we got to the vehicle. He may have Victor's eyes, but I don't believe for a second he has the making of a beast. What we saw in that warehouse was nurtured by years of groomed resentment, of sharpened rage.

"Yes," Erick finally answers. "He may be my own flesh and blood, but I won't ever be able to look myself in the mirror if I don't do something."

Finn nods his head in acknowledgment, his shoulders relaxing ever so slightly. "Very well, then. Let's cover what we know." He raises his hand to tick each finger as he goes. "First, Victor needs a powerful necromancer. If we are to believe Erick's impressions, you"—he points his chin at me—"are a powerful necromancer even if you don't use that part of your magic. Second, as we witnessed yesterday, Victor's becoming more and more reckless and unhinged. My guess is that the powers he absorbed and retained are slowly driving him to madness and decay. I would very much like to delve more deeply into this illness to see if I can discover the cure my readings alluded to or if we'll need to find another way to deal with Victor."

He pauses, trying to gauge Erick's reaction to this last statement. But Erick only motions for him to go on, which he does. "Finally, Victor can syphon life force. You saw where his mind is at. Do you think he could be a danger to you, his own son?"

Erick shakes his head no. "It may be foolish of me to think so, but even though he has been a hard-ass in the last couple of years, he never felt like a threat to my safety. But, hey, what do I know? I didn't even see this coming."

Finn doesn't bother acknowledging the pity party. "I trust you'll tell us the minute it starts to feel unsafe." Erick raises an eyebrow, incredulous, but Finn carries on, "You know what I mean. I know your lifestyle is not a safe one, but if he gets edgier with you, just get out, okay?"

"Mm-hmm," Erick answers.

"Now, for the questions we need to answer before moving forward with a solid action plan. Why does Victor need a necromancer, and does he know that Riley is one? Is it safe to leave Riley alone at this point?"

"I agree with what Erick was saying yesterday," I pitch in. "If his father knew about me, he would have made a move already. I think it would look more suspicious for me to change my routines or hide. Even more so if Victor has increased the number of goons prowling the streets in search of his prize. Odd behaviors may attract unwanted attention."

After speaking with my best friend yesterday, I have yet another concern to add to my growing list. "I'm worried about Evie." My voice wavers on her name. "There's no way she'll stay out of this. She told me so last night. I don't want her, or any of my coworkers, getting caught in the crossfire if any of this goes south."

Erick drains the rest of his cup, puts it on the coffee table, and laces his fingers together on his lap. I know he doesn't want to involve anyone else in this mess, but I won't leave my best friend undefended.

"I can fortify the protection spell on her condo." This from Finn. "I could also see if I can upgrade her physical systems."

Seeing that Finn is on board with the idea, Erick settles. "And you can bring her to training until we decide on a course of action." The half-hearted invitation makes me smile. Grumpypants, as always.

"That sounds good," I agree. "I'll ask if it's okay with her. Thanks."

"And I can put an escape door of sorts in your apartment, Riley." Finn proposes. "I used to install those in my room when I was younger so I could get out unnoticed. Unlike full portals, they are single-use, and they're also a lot less complicated to cast. Portals are next level difficult and—" Finn stops what would have surely been a long-winded explanation about portals when he sees our long faces. "Anyway, the main advantage is that once you get through, nobody can follow you. I can make it lead wherever you want. But when I'm done upgrading Erick's bunker's security, I think it would be best to make your escape door lead to his place since it has a panic room and everything."

I'm not the safety and security expert, so I agree to it. It cannot hurt to take more precautions anyway. Erick doesn't even bark at the comment on upgrading his installations, which makes me believe they've already talked about it while I was getting ready this morning.

"We'll not only need to investigate why Victor needs a necromancer specifically," Finn says, "but we'll also need to research more about the syphon's powers. We need to know things like, how does the life-syphoning work? And does it prolong the void witch's life, and how? If it does, how old could Victor even be? I mean, we can no longer assume that Victor is, in fact, his true identity. Your father could be one hundred years old and have stolen his current identity or built a new one so that no one suspects that he is kind of immortal. But I digress...."

Finn hesitates to say his next idea, but since none of us takes the lead, he goes for it. "It would be really helpful," he says carefully, "if we could test out a syphon's strength and weaknesses with the real thing. I know you said you've never syphoned powers from anything other than inanimate objects before, but we need to understand better what we're up against and how it might feel to be caught. We need to know if we have any means to shield or defend ourselves against being syphoned. Maybe we can, I don't know, displace our powers while in contact with a syphon. I'll have to look into all this, but real-life experience would be invaluable."

Erick seems troubled by the idea, a deep crease appearing between his brows. "I won't put anyone in danger by using them as a guinea pig and—"

"You wouldn't," Finn interrupts. "I have already gathered old teaching volumes and can find more. Your ancestors used certain training methods for their young, so I would imagine they are as safe as can be."

Erick doesn't look convinced. He rubs his day-old stubble, pondering the implications. "Fine. I'll do it. But as soon as it gets even a smidge dangerous, we stop."

Well, that's more than I thought he would agree to.

But Finn isn't done yet. He turns to face me on the couch. "Riley, would you be open to doing the same? It might help us understand why Victor needs a necromancer if we know more about what you can do."

I instinctively wince at the suggestion. My head shakes no of its own accord before I can even process the request. "I can't. I... My teacher only showed me the basics to be able to stretch the muscles of it from time to time, but that's all."

How can I explain to them that every time I tried to go deeper into this side of my powers, I felt like darkness would swallow me whole? The pain of the dead is nothing like feeling empathy toward a living person; it pushes into you and drowns you until you become nothing.

My throat tightens as I try to make them understand. "My kind of necromancy is far from basic necromancy skills that allow the practitioner to do inoffensive stuff like talking to the ones that linger through talking boards or scrying for answers. There's a reason Diane warned me never to use this side of my powers other than for small, harmless increments at a time. It's not just fear of being shunned for the magic I possess. I can't control that side of myself. It controls me. It's dangerous. *I'm* dangerous. It... It's dark and twisted, and no. No. I won't risk it. I'm sorry. I can't." My face is streaked with tears that I have failed to contain. I know I should want to help. I do want to help, but I can't help that way.

Finn puts a hand on my knee. "Hey, hey, that's okay."

My head falls with shame. I immediately feel fingers under my chin, forcing me to lift it back up. Finn catches the droplets of salted water with his thumb. "You have nothing to feel sorry for. Your powers, your decision," he says as he brings his hands back in his lap. The cold air is abrasive on my inflamed face.

"Can I ask you one last thing?"

"Go ahead." I sniffle.

"Would it be okay for you to show us what you use your necromancy for at the moment? The safer way you deal with it?"

The thought of anybody witnessing me use that part of my magic is so alien to me, but there is no reason for me to refuse this.

It's safe, as far as I know, and I do want to put all the chances on our side.

"That would be fine." I'm surprised to hear my voice so steady.

Finn takes a deep breath, gets up, and starts to pace. I think we all feel the restlessness at this point. It's the inner warrior that needs to act, to fight for survival. He stops just in front of the bookshelves.

"Since we decided to go about our lives as usual to not raise any red flags, I suggest we go on with the book fair. Bree already finished the planning anyway, so we only need to be there the day of."

"It's a good idea," Erick adds. "Obviously, we'll continue combat training while we figure out a plan. But it would be even better to work on basic spellcasting in protection and offensive magic. Finn, that's your specialty, so you'll teach."

"Of course, sir, yes sir," Finn mocks, to which Erick narrows his eyes.

We all stay silent for a moment.

"How can we work fast enough to avoid more kidnappings or deaths and successfully free the prisoners in one piece?" I ask, trying to remain hopeful.

"How indeed?" comes Finn's answer.

Chapter 27

ERICK

I LOATHE BEING USELESS, but it seems life has its own way of consistently putting me in that position. It was Finn who installed the magical trap door in one of Riley's unused cupboards two days ago. I couldn't be there. I'm supposed to only know her as a potion master, nothing more, so I have to play my part inconspicuously, which means no direct contact with her in public. I hatc that hc has access to part of her life that I don't, and he can be there for her in ways that I can't. But it's safer that way for both of them.

To add insult to injury, it's also he, now, who is finishing the installation of all the security upgrades in my own place with *his* skills in spellcasting and *his* money.

I thought I had it all together before, but the new tech Finn chose is even more precise and customizable, run by artificial intelligence. I can't fathom where he got hold of this material. It looks like something even governments don't yet have access to. All of this is to say that the whole thing is expensive as fuck.

I protested that I found all the extra security a little excessive. To which he only retorted that if we were to use this bunker as a failsafe and a place to train, he would never forgive himself for not securing it to the best of his abilities. That way, if something was to happen, he would know he did the best he could. I couldn't fault his reasoning, so I dropped the subject after that.

Although, I still made him promise to remove the equipment and take it back when all of this was over. I'm not to be indebted to anyone.

I, at least, was able to be of use in finding out if my hideout had been compromised or not, which it hadn't, so that's good. I already knew nobody was posted outside since I have discreet cameras with facial recognition software that includes pictures of every goon my father ever had. At least all the ones I am aware of. What's more, if it recognizes a face more than once, the program brings it to my attention.

No, what I had to really watch out for were the different routes I usually take to get here. I am always careful, but I wanted to make sure my father didn't have me tailed. With his comment about my behavior the last time he came to the shop, that would be his style to put surveillance on me. I had Eleanor help me with this. Her eagerness at the possibility of trapping a stalker was a little disturbing. In any case, after many attempts, I was satisfied and declared everything clear.

Riley insisted on being here today while Finn programmed everything. She watched him work like a hawk all morning, her dark, inquisitive eyes following his every movement.

It's almost time for her to go to work when Finn steps outside to finalize the exterior installations of the building. He brought an electrician's uniform from a well-known electrical company—baseball cap included—which allows him to work outside without raising any suspicions. I've always loved how his mind works, thinking of every possible outcome. Playing chess with him is never boring.

Riley decides to sit on the couch right beside me. This closeness is new. She typically keeps a good six feet between us most of the time. Her usual abrasiveness toward me is also nowhere to be seen today. This only shows how unsettled we've all been in the last few days. We're working nonstop, but it's not moving forward as fast as we'd like. The good thing is that no other kidnapping has happened, as far as we know, and no bodies have been found either.

I will start syphon training after the book fair this weekend. If the reading material Finn gave me is to be believed, it's going to be far from a stroll in the park. I dread it, but my power doesn't. My power quietly anticipates the moment it'll be able to stretch itself and be afforded a longer leash. That frightens me above all. I've never experienced the depth of my void, and frankly, I am worried to look.

I don't store any energy inside me. I never did. I have always kept magic close to me, ready to use, but never in my body. I am empty. Not the way a human is devoid of magic but the way a black hole devours all the light. It is not a passive emptiness—it is a hungry hollowness.

The type of depth ruled by insatiable cravings.

The type of depth that is aware of itself.

The type of depth that looks back.

The possibility of becoming like my father haunts my nights. I share his DNA and his power, after all. Will I become a monster, too? Is this the fate that I must look forward to?

The couch dips as Riley moves forward to pick up the remote. She clicks on the TV and selects the last movie played. She surprises me when she moves back onto the couch and leans her head on my shoulder, a small kindness meant to comfort me. *I* should be the one comforting her. She's the key to my father's scheme, after all. I, on the other hand, am but a cog in his well-oiled machine.

Riley takes my hand, and I allow myself to rest my cheek on top of her head. The smell of her shampoo soothes me—citrus and some sort of faint flower aroma. It's then, in the midst of chaos, and only for a brief instant, that my mind rests. It's been years since I've felt that way.

Unburdened.

She begins to play with my fingers, crossing and uncrossing them. The ebbs and flows of her powers are less overwhelming now that I have felt it a couple of times already. The strength of her abilities allows me to believe in my own. For that, I am deeply grateful.

I lift my head to tell her exactly that, but she looks up at me, and it takes me aback. Her gaze is open, unguarded. I can see the concern shining there. We're so close that my hair is grazing her forehead. I don't know what she sees in my eyes, but her brows knot together in puzzlement. Seconds later, her features clear, and she moves ever so slightly closer, her breath mingling with mine. I can't help but do the same, which brings our lips dangerously close together.

I know I should pull back. I have no business feeding false fantasies. Because that's all that this is. I can't allow either of them to get close to me, even though I want them to.

Gods, I want them to.

I'm about to pull back when Finn enters the room. Riley and I were so wrapped up in the moment that we didn't even hear the bunker door. Instead of jumping back as I expect her to, Riley stays planted right where she is, her hands holding mine in place. She takes a deep breath before turning to Finn.

"Come sit down with us before I leave," Riley says. Her invitation is without expectations, as if she only wants Finn to gather a piece of comfort for himself.

He approaches hesitantly. Hope and pain are at odds with each other on his beautiful face as he finally removes his cap and sits on my other side.

Riley resumes her position on my shoulder, and Finn mirrors her. I grab Finn's hand in mine and squeeze it gently. His answering pressure is immediate. As I lay my head on his, my eyelids burn with unshed tears.

We stay still, the rise and fall of our breathing becoming one. The rightness of the moment takes root in my chest and wraps its thorns around my core.

Oh, how life is a cruel handler. Giving me but a taste of what could be, only to remind me that I can never have it.

My spirit will break from the anguish of it all before the end.

Chapter 28

RILEY

THE DISPLAY TABLE WEIGHS a ton. My muscles strain to carry it. My left arm cramps, which causes me to drop said table unceremoniously before the sale rep that asked for it.

"Sorry." I wince.

Authors and book vendors are already setting up their booths in the huge rectangular room, even though there are more than two hours left before the official opening of the book fair. Fortunately, the heat of the summer is starting to fade with the arrival of September, so the air conditioning of the venue is able to keep up with the growing crowd.

For the first time in weeks, I get to do something normal that doesn't require me to train or lose sleep. We all agreed that we need to stay on track and act normal, but now, I just feel silly indulging in this with everything that's going on.

Well, it's too late to go back out now, isn't it?

Albert graciously gave me the weekend off, which I will put to good use. I want to hit Finn's library later tonight. I think I might have found an old volume that has the key to unspell those horrible cages, but the writing is so old the ink is faded in places. I will have to transcribe it entirely before Finn can work on tailoring it to our cause. At least it's something.

In the meantime, I stress-brewed. I have outdone myself preparing gigantic batches of healing elixir, numbing pomade, and other useful concoctions. We'll need it if we're to get those witches out. We can't carry them all. They'll have to be in good enough shape to move themselves. The fact that they are still in there, hurting, while I am free, shatters my heart. Not that I want to be drained of my powers for Victor's goal, whatever it is, but they are innocents, only suffering because he is searching for someone like me.

Although, what he needs someone like me for may end up hurting a lot of people, too. It's hard to say. The jury is still out on that.

I walk up to Arcane's kiosk just as Finn arrives, perilously balancing a tower of hardcovers.

"Can you even see where you're going with that?"

He sets them down gracefully, not even making a pleat on the fancy sweater he bought for the occasion. The cords of muscles dancing under the ink of his forearms are the only indication he was carrying a heavy weight.

"Don't do that at home, kid. I have years of practice," he teases. I make a face but still help him to arrange everything on the different displays.

Evie is here somewhere. I couldn't get my best friend to stay home for all the gold in the world. She's been glued to my side since our discovery a week ago. I would normally be happy to have her with me, but I am afraid she might get caught in this twisted poison ivy of a situation. I love Evie like a sister; I don't want to taint her by association.

I shoot her a quick text to make sure she's okay, and the answering message contains only four words.

With Bree. Love you.

I chuckle, and Finn looks at me, amused.

"What's so funny?" he asks.

"Evie's with Bree. I think those two hit it off pretty hard. Did you see how they looked at each other when they thought the other one wasn't looking?" I put my two hands on my cheeks and bat my lashes wildly. "Adorable."

"Adorable," he agrees with a high-pitched princess voice.

Once I stop laughing long enough to be able to speak, I ask him, "You want to go for coffee before it gets crazy in here?"

His smile is wide, crinkling the corner of his eyes. "Sure. Lead the way."

I get halfway down the deserted staff corridor leading to the venue's coffee shop when I remember that I left my wallet behind. I whip around too fast, and since Finn is following me closely, the collision is inevitable. His warm hands fly to my waist to steady me while my own land flat on his chest.

I lift my head to profess a string of apologies, but the shiver racking my body leaves me silent. Finn doesn't move, doesn't say anything. His hold on me is loose. I could walk away if I wanted to. But do I want to?

I can feel the heat of his body through my own clothes. I told myself that the cuddling that happened earlier this week was the result of us being under stress and needing to connect to someone that understood. The fleeting moment of solace felt fragile and intimate, and it cannot repeat itself. *It can't.* But the more I use those words, the less they make sense.

Whatever is blooming between us refuses to be squashed. And it scares me to death.

I tentatively move my hands to untie his hair and bury my fingers in his thick mane. I've wanted to do that more times than I can count. Finn's breath hitches, his eyes closing. The small space left between us shrinks to barely anything as he takes a final step toward me. He lightly caresses my lower back, making lazy circles, and heat slowly floods my core.

"Please tell me I can kiss you," he whispers. The polite request is so like him.

Even though I know it's going to be messy. Even though there is a buried history between him and Erick that I only had a glimpse of. Even though I don't know if there is a remote possibility of either of us working as a pair and even less as a throuple. Even though I have been let down by my fair share of partners before. And even though I am afraid, there is only one word that slips from my lips.

"Yes."

Chapter 29

FINN

THE FAINT WORD SENDS a jolt of surprise through me, and I dare to crack open my eyes even though I am afraid to find that this is nothing but a dream. Except she's still here when I do. Riley is not dissolving into a cloud of neglected desires in the early morning light.

I trail my fingers on her skin, from her lower back to her arms, creating a path of goosebumps until they rest on each side of her neck, mimicking how I found her and Erick in my library. Even though we're alone now, I can't seem to escape his presence.

"Erick," I breathe, not knowing how to express the mess of jumbled emotions raging inside.

"I know," she answers without hesitation. "I understand."

Her evident disappointment twists my insides. Riley pushes my wrists away and turns to leave, but I can't let her go. I'm not strong enough. Not anymore. I pull her body flush with mine. Her lips part on a sharp exhale, and that's the last straw.

I collide with her in a tangle of tongue and teeth. My practiced restraint breaks as the taste of her invades every part of my soul. The kiss is much more intense than I intended, but for each hard stroke of my mouth on hers, she answers in kind. A small whimper escapes her as I cage her body with mine to the wall beside us. My mouth is hungry for more, and I bite her lower lip before roaming down her throat.

She growls softly and pulls at my hair. The sharp pain only heightens the wave of pleasure stirring in my core.

"Utility room, hurry," she says, taking my hand and dragging me to a door a little farther down the hallway.

As soon as we get inside, I kick it closed and descend on her once more. Riley hooks her legs around my hips, and I instinctively grab her ass, kneading it. We both laugh when I press her against a wall, and a cacophony of brooms and mops fall at our feet.

She grinds her heat against my rigid length, seeking friction, and I groan into her mouth. I can feel the prick of her nails through the material of my shirt.

She doesn't know what she's doing to me. If she continues, I might come in my pants like a novice. Gods know, it happened to me more times than I care to admit back in the day. The thought brings memories of the person responsible for those shameful orgasms. It takes a superhuman effort for me to slowly stop kissing Riley and delicately put her back on solid ground. Our shared breathing is ragged when I lay my forehead against hers.

"Fuck, I want to worship every inch of your skin," I whisper.

She shivers at my admission. "Then don't stop," she pleads, but her heart is not in it. Is it possible she feels the missing piece, too?

"Maybe I am misguided and give meaning to occurrences that are not meant to have one but... Do you...? Are you...*interested* in—"

"Him?" she cuts in. She looks at me then, adrift in her own mind. "To be honest, I don't know what I feel anymore. I thought I knew where I stood regarding both of you, but it's getting harder and harder to believe my own reasoning."

"Ah. It seems we have that in common." I gather her in my arms, and she lets me, sighing softly.

I'm afraid to ask, but at the end of the day, I need to know. "What do you want to do then?"

"I don't know."

I am distracted, not really listening to the customer in front of me. My mind wanders back to the utility closet, to the admissions, to the possibilities they unlock.

"Sure, sure," Bree says, taking me out of my reveries. "You just have to write down your name here, and I'll call you about the book club as soon as it starts in January. You know what they say, new year, new book buying budget."

She looks at me, murder in her eyes, as she sends the man on his merry way. "What's your problem, Finn? Did something happen that you haven't told me about?"

I don't want to talk about what happened. I want to cherish the moment for myself a little longer, but I know feigning ignorance will only spur on her line of inquiries. So, I do the next best thing.

I tell a truth. "I'm just concerned that we won't be able to get to them in time."

She understands. I know she does. She's afraid of something similar for her own family—not finding a solution in time to save them. She rocks back and forth on the balls of her feet. The momentum makes her long linen skirt swoosh around in time with her unbound hair.

"I know," she says after a moment. "I still have a couple of resources to go through. Maybe we'll be lucky this time."

There's a lull in foot traffic, and Riley and her best friend are chatting with the owner of an antique books restoration business that has the booth beside us.

Bree elbows my side to get my attention. "By the way, I'm sure she doesn't remember, but I promised Riley she could choose any ten books from here, and the store would pick up the tab. You know, to get her on board with the fair."

"Why are you telling me this only now?"

She giggles at my annoyance. "Relax. I just forgot, that's all. I say a lot of things in a day."

When Bree leaves my side to go behind the kiosk's table, my attention drifts back to Riley. She's still at the booth next door, but her demeanor has changed drastically. She's tense, and from my vantage point, she looks like she's not breathing, either. Her head is bowed down, and she lets Evie talk with the new customer that stopped by. He looks like a soldier on duty. His cropped brown hair and straight posture say as much. The man is all smiles as he politely bids his farewell to them to go to the next row of kiosks.

I'm about to go over, but Riley abruptly turns around and speed-walks to me. Her dark gaze is frantic, shifting from me to where the stranger disappeared through the crowd and back to me. She looks like she's about to bolt.

Something is very wrong.

I go to her and lead her behind our banner where the overstock is and sit her down on a pile of boxes. "What is it?" I ask as I kneel in front of her.

It takes Riley two tries before producing a sound. "The man," she whispers, agitation coloring her tone. "I know that man. Clarence, his name is, I think. He was at Erick's shop, his illegal one. He works for the Berserker."

Maybe it's only a coincidence. "You're sure it was him?"

Her face falls, and she hits my shoulder. "Yes!" she angrily whispers at me. That's when Evie appears on the other side of the pile of boxes. I don't know her well, but she looks at me like she would kill me if I hurt her friend. I like her already.

"Okay, stay here." I don't wait for their response before I spring into action.

Bree startles when I emerge from behind the banner. She asks me something, but I don't hear what. I'm on a mission.

If they found out about Riley, we're out of time. The buzzing sound of the crowd recedes to the back of my mind as I train my gaze over the space. I spent so much time in front of security cameras that my senses are attuned to any discrepancies or patterns. The endless rows of vendors and the sheer quantity of people offer endless possibilities for spying.

One by one, I spot them. They smile politely, act according to their environment, and demonstrate an interest in all the right things. To anyone else, they would look like regular customers. Although trained to blend in, they betray themselves with small things—observing the people they meet rather than looking at the products themselves, even following some people from stand to stand. They are hunting.

I don't know what information they hope to gather in a crowded space like this in broad daylight. They must be desperate.

One of them, a woman, has been talking to an author of young adult horror novels for the last minute. I know the author. He is a witch, but even though there are necromancers in his books, I'm certain he is not one. I read his novels, as I do for most of the books that enter my shop, and there are inaccuracies in his descriptions. I would be surprised if he did that on purpose. He's about to leave with her when another customer interrupts them. She waits a little longer on the sidelines but then walks away from her potential prey.

I need to warn him about her, but generally speaking, when a total stranger tells you you're in grave danger, it doesn't go over well. So, I opt for the next best thing and use the concerned event organizer card. I tell him there is a thief in our midst, and I'm helping the venue's security team to track her down. I give him the description of the woman he was talking to earlier and tell him to shout for security if he sees her again.

From there, I walk around for five more minutes but can't spot any other suspicious activity. I counted six goons in total. Most of them have left by now since closing time is in thirty minutes.

When I finally get back to Arcane's booth, Bree is chewing on her lip from worry. "What the heck? What happened?" she says, crossing her arms. "I turned around for two seconds, and when I looked back, you were leaving without a word, and the girls were huddled in the back."

"I'm sorry. I'll explain everything later, I promise. In the meantime, can you close the booth with Evie while I get Riley out? If anyone asks, Riley ate something bad."

"Finn, you're scaring me. What—"

I take hold of her shoulders. "Please, just do this. Okay?"

"Okay, okay. Fine. Jeez. Just...whatever it is, be safe, okay?"

"Always."

I walk to the back, where Riley sits with Evie, talking quietly. The worry in their eyes only deepens when they see me.

"There were six that I could spot." My words hit them like a blow. Evie's hand tightens on Riley's knee. "The good news is that I don't think they were here for you specifically."

"And how can you be sure about that?" Evie asks with barely restrained fury. "I thought you and the other guy were supposed to help her, not put her in harm's way. If anything happens to her because of you lot, I will—" Her voice is starting to get that crystalline quality that begs to be listened to.

"Enough, Evie. That's enough," Riley says. The steel in her tone begs no argument, and her friend huffs her discontent.

Riley pinches the bridge of her nose. "Okay, what do you propose we do about it?"

I take my glasses off and trace my forehead with my thumb to release the pressure of my building headache. "We should get you home. I'm not sure it's a good idea for you to come back here this weekend. We'll need to talk it over with Erick and see what's happening on his end. Although, I'm not sure it's a good idea to meet him in person if activity has picked up." I growl in frustration. "Evie, would it be too much to ask you to stay to help Bree?"

Evie jumps up and gets in my face at the suggestion. "You think I'll leave my best friend alone now? Are you—"

"It's fine, Evie. I'll be fine," Riley cuts in once more. "You can stay if you want to help. You should stay."

Evie narrows her striking hazel eyes at me. "If anything happens to her...anything...." She doesn't finish her sentence before walking out on us to allegedly help Bree.

I turn back to Riley. Her amusement at what is surely a dumbfounded expression on my face breaks the tension a bit. "Evie has quite the temper," I admit.

She takes the hand I extend to her and gets up. "That's one of my favorite things about her. Once you're family, she's with you all the way."

Riley doesn't let go of my hand when we start walking stealthily to the staff exit. She only weaves our fingers together like it's the most natural thing in the world. We both need the reassurance.

As we near the back exit, what Bree told me earlier pops into my thoughts. "I'm sorry, you probably won't get to choose your ten books."

Riley laughs and pushes the door open. "Of all the things you could say. I had completely forgotten about that."

Chapter 30

ERICK

IT FEELS GOOD TO spar. That's one of the things I miss from my time on the Faroe Islands. I always had someone that needed a practice partner. My instructors were strict with me, but I was worse. It paid off, though. The older I got, the fewer bruises and cuts I received until not one of my classmates could touch me.

I've lost some of it over the years, even though I'm in the best shape of my life. Technique and strength are two very different aptitudes. Finn, on the other hand, is better than I remember.

I dive for his legs, but he avoids the pass easily. "Check your balance," I instruct him while bouncing on the balls of my feet. "You're better fending off an attack, using a little more energy, and staying solid than evading it at the cost of your balance. I could have simply rolled into you, and you would have been on the ground."

Finn keeps his guard up even when he wipes the sweat from his forehead. Good Boy. "You're so cute when you use your instructor voice," he answers, his white smile spreading.

My temper is close to the surface today. I haven't slept well all weekend, trying to get answers as to why my father's men were at the book fair and if they swarmed other places too.

"Stop playing," I say as I take off my shirt. It's a real steam room in the bunker today. "You won't find it funny when you're trapped by an opponent on the ground, their weapon against your throat. I still can't believe you waited a whole four hours before telling me what happened this weekend. I could've—"

"What? You could've what?" he answers, following my lead and taking off his own shirt. "That's right. You could've done absolutely nothing without blowing your cover. For the hundredth time, I assessed the situation and made a decision. Afterward, I stayed at her home with her and drank tea until her best friend arrived. She was completely fine when I left."

We take back our positions on the mat, shuffling our feet and circling each other, looking for a weakness in the other one's guard. I crack my neck and grunt. "She should be better than fine. It's my father that put her in this position, which means I'm the one that painted a target on her back. I would understand if she wanted to be as far away from me as she could."

Finn growls at me and tries to hit me with a jab to the ribs, but I'm too fast. "Stop being so dramatic," he replies, breathless. "You are not your father, and you are not responsible for your father's actions. No more than I am responsible for my own parents' deeds." The sorrow written on his features clashes with his words of reassurance.

I don't want to hear what he's about to say next. "Please, let's not talk about that. What's done is done, and, like you said, that wasn't your fault."

"For once in your life, let me finish!"

His reaction surprises me. I'm not used to this new version of Finn yet. The one where he sticks it to me every chance he gets. I deserve it, though. I deserve every ounce of his pain. It belongs to me. It always did.

"I'm sorry," Finn carries on. "I didn't know what the council and my parents were planning back then, I swear. I've always loathed their political scheming, so I stayed as far away as possible from it, which cost you big in the end."

I don't know when we stopped moving, but we did. "You weren't to blame. Those bastards at the Sennex and my own mother—" I can't even finish the thought. "They're the ones to blame. I know I spat it back into your face when you found me three years ago, but truly, I never thought you had anything to do with the events of that night."

It's as if Finn takes a real breath for the first time in forever. It eats me alive to see how he carried my hateful words with him all this time. When he walked through the door of The Underground Castle three years ago after seven years apart, all I wanted to do was take him in my arms, but I couldn't. I had to make him leave somehow. I wasn't the same person he fell in love with anymore. I wasn't good for him anymore.

I knew that if I attempted to explain my situation with my father and all the illegal shit, noble Finn would only try to rescue me, but I was already far past rescuing at that point. I told myself the only option I had left was to hurt him so bad that he would go back from whence he came. Now, I'm not sure about it anymore. The ploy didn't even work, after all. He did get out of my life, but not out of my city and away from the dangers lurking on my side of the law.

Finn's eyes are as dark as an evergreen forest in winter. The sadness radiating from them is twin to the hole in the middle of my chest. I think we've both been hemorrhaging memories of lost love for a long time now, and the renewed proximity is only killing us by degrees.

"I don't know if you care about any of this," Finn says, "but I didn't have the chance to tell you when I came to you three years ago." I wince at the admission, but he goes on. "The last time I was on the Sennex's premises, your mother was alive and what you could call well. She is kept as a captive, a lure for your father."

A sharp sound escapes me, something between a laugh and a sneer. "Why would my father care what happens to her? He's convinced she's the one who betrayed him in the first place. The Sennex's logic is as flawed as their methods."

"For what it's worth, I don't think they believe you are a syphon. Your mother assured them that you were a mediocre caster, like every caster from her side of the family. And you didn't show any sign otherwise. You even fooled me when we were kids."

I want to say something, anything. An apology doesn't feel like enough for the damage my secrets made, but Finn continues before I can utter a word. "Since the void is an inconsistent gift through the generations, I'm pretty sure they bought it. Anything to not admit the possibility of a second syphon in the world, a second failure of their intel department. Pride is their downfall, and maintaining appearances is paramount in their eyes. You know, they didn't even tell anybody what your father is? The surviving guards that were there that night mysteriously turned up dead shortly after your escape. The Sennex's games sicken me. The only way I know any of this is because my eighteen-year-old self was good at sneaking around. That's when I decided to leave."

"But you didn't leave then." That wasn't a question, simply a statement.

Finn's shoulders drop ever so slightly. "Wanting to leave and being able to are two very different things."

I grow restless and start moving again. Finn follows suit. We circle each other, giving experimental feints and hits to test the opponent. To find an opening.

"My father's men are closing in, and we still don't know squat about what this whole thing is about. I hate being in the dark, and it feels like all my connections are tight-lipped right now. I know she said she didn't want to, but Riley would be better off knowing how to use her necromancy for offense sooner rather than later. If they catch her before we're ready"—I shudder at the thought—"she needs to be able to defend herself with more than her fists and potions. She has the resources to be among the great. I've heard of powerful necromancers being able to kill someone with one touch."

"You're one to talk," Finn says while lunging sideways to dodge my hit. "You're still refusing to syphon power from any of us for practice even though you agreed to it in the first place. You're refusing to get out of your comfort zone. Don't pretend it's for our safety. It's for yours."

I know he's pushing this because he wants to understand more, to be better prepared, and I get that. But what if syphoning power from a witch changes me for the worst? It's a lot more potent than power imbued in an object, according to the texts I've read. What if I become like my father?

"I read every fucking book you threw my way about syphons. Yes, they tell me how to do it, but I still have yet to find one that tells me what the long-term effects would be on the syphoned witch or what they would feel while I do it. Did you see what those prisoners looked like? I don't want either of you to suffer." I know my answer is nothing but pretty excuses at best.

Finn swishes his right hand to the side, using his magic to prompt one of the training mats to slide from under my feet. I just have time to gather my wits and avoid the fall, but not without uttering a string of curses.

"How many times will I have to repeat it?" he says as if to an unruly kid. "We are power-born witches. We are like batteries. When we use a spell, it doesn't hurt us, and we replenish our energy with time and rest. Why would you think syphoning a spell would be any different than us using one? In one case, we push the magic out, and in the other, you draw it out, but it's the same amount of energy expended. My guess is that your father drains those witches too much at once and obviously doesn't leave them time or a safe space to replenish." His smile grows taunting. "Are you afraid you'll put your straw in me and suck me dry?"

I know he's only trying to goad me into reacting and using my void, which I won't do. With practiced movement, I feint to gather his attention on a hit while I take one card from my pocket without him seeing it. Misdirection is my favorite tactic.

I throw the playing card into the air. It's about to glow blue and give me a minute of peace when Finn blows on it. The vessel and the spell it contains catch fire like flash paper. One second it was there. The next, there's hardly any residue left. This feels more and more like bringing a knife to a gunfight. Finn is one of the best and most powerful casters I've ever known. I'm so far out of his league it's laughable. I know he's right, and I should learn how to fight with my power as well as he knows how to fight with his.

We keep at it for a while longer, me landing a couple of blows and him hitting me with small spells not meant to injure but mostly to annoy.

Then Finn goes in for the kill. “I kissed her.” He says it with so much nonchalance that it takes my brain a moment to register the meaning of the words. Finn takes advantage of the distraction he just created to send his palms forward, producing a wall of air that throws me to the ground. He’s on me instantly, but it will take a lot more for him to win. We tumble together in a mass of limbs and grunts.

“It’s none of my business what you do with each other,” I hiss. “You’re not my problem.”

Finn holds me down, and I let him. I need a minute to recuperate from the physical exhaustion as well as nurse the inner scab he just scratched at.

When he sees that I don’t fight him anymore, not really, he leans forward and speaks directly into my ear. “Do you want to know how her skin tasted or how her body felt plastered between mine and the wall?”

The jealousy is suffocating. I envy the path of her hands on his body. I resent him for knowing the feeling of her lips under his. The image of them together angers me as much as it mesmerizes me. The thoughts become all-consuming.

“Do you want to know,” Finn whispers, “how each stroke of our tongues brought up thoughts of you?” His words are like the most delicious alcohol. They burn as they go down, but the heat spreads into my belly like wildfire. Finn’s admissions, his body straddling mine, the electricity of his power. It sets me aflame.

All I want to do is pin him to the floor and drink the taste of her from his mouth. I buck my hips and turn his hold against him, but I don’t know where to go from here. The hard ridge of his erection presses against mine, and I freeze. I want him so much my entire body hurts with the strength of my restraint.

I'm so caught up in the moment that I see Finn's combat spell too late. His hand is already glowing with a white ball of light. I don't have time to reach for a protection spell card. And, judging by the energy gathered like lightning just under the surface of his skin, even if I dodge the hit, it will seriously damage the installations around us. He knows this. The bastard leaves me no choice.

And so, for the first time in my twenty-eight years of life, I let go and consume magical energy from another witch. To my relief, Finn doesn't start to scream in agony. The energy syphoned from inanimate objects can be powerful but somewhat stagnant. Finn's spell, however, feels very much alive. It grows and moves as it enters my body.

Finn's hand barely dims, but he doesn't seem able to launch the charm. The amount of power he feeds the spell is gigantic. It feels unending. As I draw it through my pores, I start to feel lightheaded, but I don't have a receptacle to channel any of it out. I feel a second spell, his protection spell, trying to push me away, but I squash it at the source until his hand is completely normal again.

Then, and only then, do I stop. Finn's breathing is harsh to my ears. Each of my senses is heightened. I can smell him all around me—in me—rich, warm spices and something that is unapologetically him. All the colors seem richer somehow, brighter. My skin is hyper-sensitized. I am acutely aware of every point of contact with Finn. It's like I've drunk thirty energy drinks. I don't know what to do with it all. I need to ground the magic somewhere before I can't hold it in anymore and release the blow.

Finn seems to think about this at the same time I do. He reaches into his pocket to produce a brass disk, no bigger than a quarter, with symbols carved on it.

"It can hold enough," he says. I take it and close my fist around it, releasing the spells into the small talisman. As soon as the powerful magic leaves me, I feel grounded again.

Finn opens my hand, takes hold of the talisman, and turns it over between his fingers. "Fascinating," he breathes while trying to get out from under me.

Now that the danger has passed, my anger rises like the tide at the full moon. "Fascinating? Fascinating!" I press my palms to his chest and push him back down. I get into his face. "What's wrong with you? I could have hurt you or worse. I don't know if I should hit you or kiss you right now."

I only meant to think the last part.

I start to get up and off him. "Shit. I'm sorry. I—"

He takes hold of the back of my neck and wrenches me down to his lips, effectively shutting me up. I have no excuses. I know I should pull away. I should be able to control my impulses for their sakes.

But I'm only able to hold still for all of two seconds before I start kissing him back. The feel of him is different and familiar at the same time. It's been so long. I want more.

I push my tongue through his lips, and we both groan at the invasion. His mouth is soft and pliable against mine. The feel of his touch down my back makes me shiver despite the heat. When Finn moves his hips under me, seeking friction, I think I might die. It's all too much and not enough at the same time.

I leave his mouth to take hold of his wrists and pin them down over his head. "Is this what you wanted, Little Prince?" The old pet name flows out of me as if I never stopped using it. "You wanted to fill me up with your power so I can fill you up with my body, is that it?"

The bunker alarm chooses this time to ring. We're both flushed and aroused, and neither of us moves right away. I rake my gaze over his face. "This is *not* over. We'll talk about all of this later." Without another glance, I get up and leave him panting on the floor.

Chapter 31

FINN

I look at Erick's form disappearing through the door that leads to the control room. I touch my swollen lips in disbelief. Then I rub at each of my wrists in turn, still feeling his firm grip there. Now that my bones have been reminded of the weight of his body on mine, it'll be hard to try to forget it all over again when the connection growing between the three of us surely goes down in flames.

In my experience, life is not as kind as to bring hope and joy without taking something in return. Maybe the situation we find ourselves in is enough to balance the equation. Maybe I'll be able to keep them, and they'll want to keep me.

Maybe we'll be able to build something of our own without destiny plotting our destruction. I'm too far gone to care about my heart's ruin at this point, anyway.

"What is she doing here?" Erick says from the other side of the wall.

I peel myself off the ground and put my shirt back on before following the sound of his voice. Bree is in the antechamber. Her curly hair, long summer dress, and big eyes make her look like a porcelain doll on the camera feed.

She's so far from one.

Erick turns in my direction with a questioning look on his face. "You gave a security clearance for the antechamber entrance to your employee?" His tone betrays nothing. I cannot tell if he's displeased or not by my initiative.

She's so much more than my employee, though. "Yes. She's been helping us a ton, and she's as part of my family as Eleanor is part of yours. If she's here, it's because she found something interesting or something bad happened. Please, buzz her in."

His gaze lingers on my face a little longer before he turns back to the computer and grants her entry to the bunker. Bree walks into the space, all smiles and mischief. She watches Erick as he picks up one of his T-shirts lying on the ground and throws it on.

"Am I interrupting something?" she says suggestively.

Erick and I look at each other, not knowing how to answer that question. What has she interrupted? He shrugs and picks up a bottle of water from the fridge, leaving me to fend for myself with Bree.

I clear my throat. "No, you're fine." I motion for her to sit on the couch. "Did something happen?"

Her face falls as if she hadn't considered her arrival could alarm me. "By the gods, no. I'm sorry. I didn't mean to worry you by coming here. I just... I tried to call you and text you, but you didn't answer. Then I tried to open your computer to send a message through the board I always see you use, but the stupid machine refused to work."

My mouth twitches with the effort not to smile. "Okay. Why did you come here then?"

Instead of telling me, Bree shows me. She gets out three large tomes from her backpack and cracks them open at the pages she bookmarked, indicating for me to read.

I can feel my eyebrows reach my hairline as the words start to form a clear picture of her findings. "Are you sure about this?" I ask her in disbelief.

Her answering smile says it all.

"This could be tremendously helpful. Well done. But are you sure you want to move forward with this?"

Bree's features sober, and she straightens in her seat. In this moment, I take in the wisdom her age commands, the cunning she so often buries under an air of innocence. "I wouldn't have come here if I didn't want to at least attempt it and see if it works," she says fiercely.

I bow my head to her, a small show of the respect she deserves. Erick watches the exchange silently from his perch on the surveillance table.

Bree takes hold of the elastic around her wrist and pulls her hair up in a ponytail. As she rises from her seat, Erick moves toward us in astonishment.

"*Álfar,*" he breathes, eyes wide. He stops right in front of her with his gaze glued to her pointed ears. He turns to me then. "How is this possible? The last Taurus infraction was almost twenty-five hundred years ago, and the next one is months away. I thought it was the only time beings could travel between realms. That would mean that...." he trails off.

Bree cocks her head to the side, analyzing his reaction. "Your deduction would be correct for a god. As for me, I'm only a lowly elf. Some of us have means of transportation between realms that require less"—she searches for the right word for a moment—"artifices, although the vast majority of my kind doesn't bother leaving our homeland—*Alfheim,* I mean."

I've never seen him this baffled. It's almost funny. "So," he says, "you're not twenty-five hundred years old then?"

Bree huffs and waves her hand in the air in annoyance. "It's really rude to ask for someone's age. Do I look like I'm twenty-five hundred years old?"

"I suppose not?"

"Of course not. I'm only one-thousand five-hundred and forty-three, I'll have you know," Bree says with fake indignation. She looks so proud of herself, making poor Erick almost go into cardiac arrest at the statement.

"No, you're not. You're shitting me."

"First of all, I am not 'shitting you.'" She makes air quotes around the words. "Second of all, I would like to pursue this conversation"—she turns to me and rolls her eyes before turning back to him—"but I have a life to live, and discussing my personal history is not why I came here."

Erick looks like he wants to argue but wisely keeps his mouth shut. I know how he feels. When Bree told me her age, I had the exact same reaction—millions of questions, but mostly awe and disbelief. Having the privilege of knowing an elf is not something that I take for granted. Moving between realms is a hard feat to achieve. She never told me how she pulled it off, but I'm sure it took a good amount of resourcefulness and abilities. Elves are plant talkers as well as great healers. Their strength and speed are legendary. Not many have visited our world, but their impact is still felt long after their departure.

"I think Bree might have found a big missing piece of our syphon puzzle," I say to Erick, capturing his attention. "If these grimoires are to be believed, and the three say the same thing, a syphon can only syphon magic and life from its opposite. Obviously, humans don't have any magic to take. But here, it states clearly that void witches cannot syphon life from a human since they are not power-born."

I let this information sync in. Erick looks at me, puzzled, but then his features clear, and he throws his hands in the air. "No."

I get up and walk to him. I place my hands on his shoulders and look him straight in the eyes. "Think, Erick. Elf magic is born from elementals—fire, air, water, earth, and starlight. It makes sense. We need to know if you can syphon magic from a being of another realm. Because if you can't, then your father can't."

Erick takes a step into my hold, getting into my face. "Yes, but he still can use the magic he already syphoned. Do you really want to put another friend in the line of fire?"

I didn't even hear Bree approach. Erick and I both startle when she seemingly appears between us. "I can take care of myself," she hisses.

She's but a blur as she goes to the couch and lifts it effortlessly into the air. "Finn is my friend, and if I'm needed, I want to help," she carries on while putting the piece of furniture back down.

I know better than to try to tell her what to do. If Bree wants to help, she will. Once she has something in mind, she is relentless. My friend is fierce, and her heart is true. I am grateful every day that she imposed herself in my life all those years ago.

She blurs back to us and takes hold of Erick's arm. When nothing happens, she shakes it as if it was a radio refusing to play. "Okay, how does it work? Why isn't he syphoning?" she asks me. But she turns back to Erick before I can answer. "Why aren't you syphoning? Or are you? I cannot feel anything."

Erick delicately, respectfully, lifts one of her fingers at a time from his arm. It's comical to see him so careful. I don't know if he's afraid of insulting her or if he really can't lift more than one finger at a time because of her strength.

"I just tried to syphon from a living being for the first time not even an hour ago and—"

"Oh, *that's* what I was interrupting," Bree chips in.

"Sure," Erick continues, turning toward me. "What I was saying is that I don't even know if I hurt Finn or if I can safely do it again."

I take the brass receptacle and look at it closely. "It still can hold a little more," I answer. "You would only have to syphon a drop of magic to see if it works or not. And it didn't hurt at all. It felt like you were simply redirecting the energy I was already feeding the spell. I'm a little tired, but no more than if I had released the spell itself. I mean, it might be different if you had syphoned power directly from my core without me already expanding it. We'll have to try that, too, I suppose."

Erick gasps. "Woah, what?"

"Don't worry about that now," I rush to say. "We just have to do this small test for now. Please?"

He looks skyward and laces his fingers behind his head, thinking. Then he lets his arms down and steps in front of Bree. "Okay. I'll try. But if you feel anything wrong or painful, throw me across the room, okay? I believe you can do that easily."

She winks at him. "Sure, big guy," she mocks.

He takes her hand in his and frowns. "It's strange. I thought I didn't feel anything when she grabbed my arm because I was getting better at controlling my abilities. But I feel nothing. It's like I'm touching a table or something."

"Hey!" Bree says, offended.

"Sorry." He winces. "I didn't mean it like that. It's just disconcerting, knowing the amount of elemental magic your people can wield. Okay, ready?"

Bree nods her ascent. Erick's forehead wrinkles in concentration. After a couple of seconds, neither of them has moved nor made a sound yet.

"So?" I ask.

Erick guffaws, his features lighting up with glee. "Well, Little Prince, it seems you and Bree were right."

Chapter 32

RILEY

My hands are covered in paint, and I don't think my brushes will survive my energetic brushstrokes. Their bristles are all bent and split already. I'll see what they look like after a good wash. Either way, it's worth it. The old wooden table left in my apartment looks more and more intricate, with all the plant designs brought forward with hues of gold and green. It feels so good to be alone with my thoughts. I needed it.

My wine glass is long gone, but I can't seem to find it in me to get up and pour myself another one. I'm entranced by the swirls of my brush. I'm far from an artist, but I am enjoying this.

I was supposed to be with the boys for training today, but the events of the weekend shook me more than I thought. I decided to sit this one out since I'm not even sure what I should do anymore. I didn't want to make life-changing decisions on a whim just because I felt threatened or pushed. I am the one that is supposed to be in control of my life, right?

Diane would say I am like a fly to a pile of horseshit, drawn to make bad choices for myself. Colorful language for a colorful lady. I was so angry at her for saying that at the time, but she was kind of right. I cannot choose my circumstances, but I can consciously choose how I react to them, not just have a knee-jerk reaction which is usually my *modus operandi*.

I wish I could speak with her right now. The small bell hooked at the top of her staff reflects the light of the lamp beside it. I know I could try to contact her with it, but I'm as afraid to discover she is still here, a revenant not at peace, as I am to find she left me to fend for myself. I miss her so much it hurts.

I should have been able to heal her. Even with all my strength and all her tricks, the illness took my teacher in less than a day. It didn't respond to any treatment, be it physical or magical. She had her first symptoms at dawn, I found her lying on her kitchen floor just before lunch, and by the first light of the full moon, she was gone.

The autopsy the coroner did revealed nothing. By all accounts, she was in perfect health. It was as if her body just refused to live any longer, which I don't believe for an instant. She was so stubborn I always thought she would have the willpower to refuse death itself. I'm afraid her passing will remain a mystery. The only things I get to keep from her now are her staff and my sorrow.

My thoughts are murky. I'm not sure of anything anymore. I felt so helpless this weekend. If they had tried to take me, what would I have done? I mean, I practiced Finn's beginner combat spells, but I can only get them to work half the time if that. I am not a caster.

I am a healer and a potion master, but throwing glass bottles at people's heads won't help me get away.

Even if I know necromancy can be a potent battle art, Diane warned me of the dangers of using it, but as events unfold, I might not have a choice. She, herself, was a powerful healer and, I suspect, an even more powerful necromancer. It was luck that brought me into her path. My adoptive parents—very human, may the gods bless their kind souls—not knowing what to do with me at the first signs of my magical abilities, decided to bring me to the village healer, *la ramancheuse* as they called her.

Diane always told me to beware of my own darkness. It is so vast, she said, that even she couldn't see the edge of it. It is imperative that I always remain in control.

Sometimes, I would wake up in the middle of a moonless night, the ones so dark that you cannot even see the shape of your own hand before your eyes, and I would have a panic attack—rocking back and forth on my bed, thinking that my shadows had swallowed the entire world.

Erick doesn't know how spot-on he is with his pet name for me.

Speaking of the men, they are another matter altogether. I've known my fair share of grief, loss, and betrayal. I don't intend to experience more if I can avoid it. But it appears that my heart doesn't learn from its mistakes. It still beats, asking for more.

The feel of Finn's body against mine. Erick's fingers caressing my face. Their way of wanting the best for the people around them, even if it makes them do stupid deeds from time to time. I'm still not sure if I can trust either of them fully, but I do feel that their hearts are true.

It's something, I guess.

Although the decision is way past making at this point. The moment to stop all this emotional mess was a long time ago. Now that the feelings have been allowed to blossom, all that's left to do is let it play out and see.

Here, done. The paint job is good enough, I suppose.

Once the paint dries, I'll be able to varnish it. The intricate patterns are way more detailed than they appeared at first glance. I hope I'll be able to find a way to get the table out of here and bring it with me when I leave. No, I won't leave this time, I remind myself. I will do everything I can to keep this table, this new home I'm building. That's all I have left now, and I'll fight for it.

I gather all my painting material and go to the sink to rinse everything off before making my way to the bathroom to run myself a hot bath.

Erick and Finn have their own baggage to deal with, too, and I think it will do them good to have time to work on that on their own today if they so choose. As I undress and then let myself relax in the warm water, I'm wondering what they're doing right now.

The images my brain conjures bring heat to my core, and I chastise myself, trying to reel my thoughts back from the roaming hands and sweaty friction I imagine.

I fail miserably.

My body feels more and more like a coiled spring with each passing day. The tension of the dire situation, along with the growing pull toward both of them that screams to be acknowledged, acted upon in some way, is hard to keep up with without losing sleep. My body keeps replaying every shred of sensation they've given me in the last couple of days, and the more I try to push all of it down, the worse it gets.

What happened with Finn this weekend creeps up from the depths of my mind. Only this time, my imagination conjures Erick there with us, too. He's the one to close the door of the utility closet. It's his hard body behind me instead of the wall. It's his hands caressing my breasts, his lips grazing my throat as Finn kisses me. I imagine myself taking hold of each of their necks to pull them together into a searing kiss over my shoulder.

The warm water laps at my erect nipples, and I can't help but pinch them, imagining Erick's hands there instead of mine. My fingers trail down my body. In my mind's eye, Finn has taken off my pants and is kneeling at my feet while Erick keeps me upright.

It's Finn's hooded gaze disappearing between my legs that I see as my own hand rubs at the apex of my thighs under the water.

I'm still so aroused from the original events that it takes only a moment to build the waves of pleasure to an almost painful tightness. I'm so immersed in my own pretenses that I can feel Erick's erection grinding against my ass and Finn's tongue circling my most private part as if they were really here with me. When everything shatters around me, it's both of their names that I cry out in delightful agony.

Chapter 33

RILEY

I've never seen so many people in the bunker at once. If I ignore the training gear and long faces, it could be a regular friend gathering. Erick made good on his promise and asked me to bring Evie for this session. When I arrived, I was surprised to find Eleanor and Bree there as well.

Bree jumped up and down, throwing her arms around me as she always does when she gets excited to see someone. Her blue eyes got even bigger when she saw Evie step aside from behind me. They both looked at each other, not knowing how to act. My best friend, who is normally all smiles and easy banter, was toying with the hem of her workout shirt nervously under Bree's scrutiny.

I went and took a seat beside Finn on the couch while Erick poured everybody a copious amount of coffee in camping cups. None of us are early risers—apart from Finn, maybe—but six in the morning was the only hour we were all available at the same time, so we made do. The girls huddle around in the various seats of the makeshift living room.

"Do you have any almond milk?" Bree asks Erick. "I'm vegan," she explains with a bright smile.

Erick yawns. "I don't have milk. Period."

"Aren't you a delight in the morning," Bree fires back.

With a cup in one hand, Erick stands at the back of the couch behind Finn and me, his other hand resting between us, slightly touching each of our shoulders. I don't know why, but the small gesture feels huge and full of meaning, like a declaration of belonging. My attention converges on the tiny point of contact, and I wonder if Finn feels the same. If he, too, wants to reach back to put his own hand on Erick's.

When Erick speaks, his voice is gruff from sleep. "Finn and I called all of you here because we understand that, even though it shouldn't be your fight, you all want to help and participate, which we are grateful for." He looks at Eleanor, Bree, and Evie in turn, then sighs. "Although I would prefer everyone to stay out of this and hide in this bunker until it blows over...." Everyone except Eleanor laughs at Erick's admission, but he plows on, "At this point, you need to know what we know so you can keep yourself safe if need be."

"Each of you has specific abilities," he carries on, "and if we're to be a unit, we need to be aware of each other's strengths and weaknesses."

Finn scoots forward to open the small box sitting on the coffee table in front of us. Inside is a small piece of smoky quartz. He picks it up and gives it to me, letting his fingers graze mine just a little longer than necessary. I turn it over in my hands, examining it closely.

"I spelled the gem to act as a temporary alarm of sorts," Finn says. "It will glow as soon as someone with ill intent toward you gets close. Once the alert is triggered, the charm is spent."

When Finn resumes his position beside me, one of his hands goes to rest on my knee, squeezing it lightly to get my attention. "Can you give your smoky quartz to Erick, please?" he asks quietly before looking back at Erick looming over us.

Without taking my gaze off Finn's upturned face, I bring my fist up, and Erick takes the translucent gray stone from me. Finn's eyes stay riveted on his as Erick rounds the couch and crouches in front of me. Erick threads his fingers around the pendant hanging at my neck. I think he's going to take it off me, but he simply stays right where he is, resting his hand on the hollow of my throat. I swallow loudly, trying to keep my breathing even to avoid showing the effect that Erick's feathery touch has on my body. When I finally find it in me to turn to the rest of the room, Evie's smile is full of dirty meaning, and I scowl at her. Finn sees the exchange and laughs quietly.

"I'll go first with demonstrating abilities," Erick says. Gasps of awe and surprise echo through the space as our friends witness Erick's power transferring Finn's spell from the gem to my pendant.

"He also successfully syphoned power from me," Finn adds while Erick finishes his work.

I tense up at the statement. I have no right to the jealousy rising in me at the thought they got to experience that first together, as I suspect they have already experienced many other firsts with each other, but here we are.

Erick feels my reaction and smirks. "Don't worry, Darkness," he drawls, "you'll get to experience it, too."

I swat his hand away and huff in indignation. Erick simply unfolds from his position and motions for Bree to join him. While he pushes the table out of the way, Bree rises from her chair with a mischievous smile that makes me fear the worst.

"We also discovered," Finn continues, "that humans and beings born of different magic sources, like elemental magic, cannot be syphoned."

Evie snorts at that. "And how, pray tell, can you be sure about it? I mean, how can we know for certain that your old, musty books tell the truth?" The disbelief in her tone reflects my own incredulity. But when Bree pushes her hair behind her ears, my jaw falls to the floor.

"*Álfar,*" I mouth in astonishment.

"You're an elf?" Evie squeaks, just as baffled.

Bree winks before bowing in an exaggerated curtsy. "Brennandi Einn, at your service. And before you ask rudely," she says, giving a pointed look at Erick, "I am not *that* old. Some elves have means of traveling between worlds without waiting for a Taurus infraction."

"One-thousand five-hundred forty-three," Erick coughs under his hand.

Bree glares at him, her small fists going to her hips.

"No," Evie breathes, "you can't be."

Bree seems to vanish before our eyes and reappears just beside Evie, who shrieks and jumps back. Then, as Bree returns, she goes a little slower so we can see her running through the space. She steps in front of Erick and lifts him clean off the ground as a groom would do his bride.

Eleanor has been quiet the entire meeting until now, but no more. She jumps into action, her blond locks floating behind her.

In one fell swoop, she wrenches Erick from Bree's grip and pins Bree to the bunker's wall beside the couch. Eleanor's face is impassive, no anger to be seen. For all I know, she could be watching TV right now.

"Eleanor, stop!" Erick barks, walking over to the girls. "We discussed this. It's training. None of them will really hurt me." He puts a hand on her forearm and pulls at it with all he's got. She doesn't budge an inch.

Bree doesn't even seem bothered by the hold, but when she goes to pull free from Eleanor's grip, she has to wrestle her a little. Deep lines appear between her brows. "What are you?" Bree asks, genuinely curious.

"I am a creation," Eleanor answers as she sits again.

"No, you're not," Erick says to her intently. Then to the rest of us, he says, "Well, yes, at the beginning, but not anymore."

Finn has moved to the edge of his seat, studying Eleanor. "Fascinating," he says before he stands and walks to the training room.

He returns seconds later with a knife and goes to Eleanor's side. "May I?" he asks her, waving the weapon in the air. She only extends her hand to him. Finn looks at Erick, who shrugs as if to say it's her choice.

"Wait!" I shriek as I jump from the couch. I try to take the knife from Finn's grip. "What are you doing? You'll hurt her." Finn only raises the knife over his head, out of my reach.

"No, he won't," Eleanor assures me. "I won't feel a thing, and it's going to heal right away. I cannot be hurt. At least, not like that."

Before I have time to protest further, Finn brings the weapon down and slashes her hand open. A strangled scream escapes Evie's throat. But the gash doesn't even bleed. Instead, it reveals some kind of brown substance that I scarcely have time to see before her skin stitches back together in seconds. She holds her hand in front of herself to show everyone she's not hurt, and the tension in the room falls.

"See? I'm fine," Eleanor insists. "I'm a great practice dummy."

"Don't say stuff like that. You're the only family I have left now," Erick answers, sadness coloring his words. Eleanor looks puzzled at the admission, but she doesn't comment further.

Bree takes a step forward, rubbing at the muscles of her arms. "Care to enlighten us?" she says as she nods toward Erick.

Erick looks at Eleanor, who motions for him to go ahead. "Eleanor was created by my father seven years ago," Erick starts as we all take our places again, except for him. He sits on the floor between Finn's legs and my own, lying back against the couch. "When my father passed the shop—well, shops, really—to me, he wanted to make sure I would stay safe and had help. So, he 'gifted' me a protector." His look of disgust gives away what he thinks of the wrongness of the words.

"I'm a golem," Eleanor goes on. "I was created from clay to be Erick's protector. We've been working on ridding me of the urge to defend him, and I've made good progress. But as you just saw, I'm not totally immune to my instincts." She winces and looks at Bree. "Sorry about that."

Bree waves her apology away. "No need. I'm just excited I'll have a sparring partner my own size to train with." She winks at Eleanor.

"All the literature on golems that I've read say they are bound to their maker and cannot escape their purpose," Finn says, perplexed. "Nor can they have feelings or goals of their own. *Obviously*, the literature is wrong."

Eleanor doesn't seem insulted by the inquiry. "Well, I'm not a witch, so you'll have to figure that out yourself. But I can tell you I have hobbies. My crochet doilies are particularly beautiful. Also,

Erick is my friend, and I love him very much. You, on the other hand, I'm not sure yet."

Finn guffaws. "Your honesty is appreciated," he replies.

Erick lays his head back on the seat of the couch to look at Finn. "Only powerful witches can bring inert matter to life. Most of those powerful witches are highly placed close to the Sennex or directly on the council of thirteen. I would wager they are too full of themselves to even imagine that, with time, their creation would grow into themselves. Most of the accounts I read myself were about golems that were alive for a very short period of time. Given more time, they would probably have learned and developed as a child would after birth. Those powerful witches are not creating a *thing* to be used. They are giving life to a sentient being, and they would be able to see it and write about it adequately if they would get their heads out of their asses." Erick vibrates in indignation with each syllable.

"I'm tired of talking about this," Eleanor says plainly. "Can we do something else? I'm getting bored."

Erick smiles broadly at her. "Sure, Lenny." The nickname suits her well.

"I think you all know what I can do," Finn says as he waves his hand at the coffee table, which moves several inches to the right. "What about you, Evie? I've heard tales about the great bard of The Drunken Sailor. Care to give us a performance?"

Evie's mouth quirks into a feline smirk. "Of course," she drawls as she gets up. But she doesn't sing, only hums between words. "Come here, Finn," she commands him. Her voice drips with power. The ripples of it move through the room even though her words were targeted at Finn only. He wasn't prepared for it, so with a dreamy smile, he walks hazily toward her.

Evie glances at the knife Finn left on the coffee table before saying, "Good. Now, Finn, take back the knife and cut off your fingers."

Erick jumps up from the floor at her command, trying to get to the weapon before Finn does to stop him from hurting himself. However, Erick doesn't even have time to reach the knife before Evie says calmly, "Erick, stop. You will sit back down and watch silently." Erick struggles against the hold her words have on him, but it's no use. He finally sits back down, his spine straight as a bar.

I, on the other hand, am not alarmed. I know my best friend; she would never hurt anybody unless they deserved it. Finn picks up the knife, his haze fading a bit. He frowns as he looks at the weapon in his grip.

"Go on, Finn," Evie pushes. Finn puts his left hand on the ground, but before he can move the knife toward a finger, Evie releases him. "Finn, you may stop now."

As soon as she stops humming, Finn shakes his head and drops the knife. "What the heck?" he exclaims.

She sits back down. "I see you've never met a good bard before," Evie says, looking at her long black nails. "Well, now you have. Riley, my love, come over here," she says to me in her sing-song voice, but I was prepared for it. I knew she wouldn't be done that quickly.

My walls are up and strong. She repeats the command, but I still don't move an inch.

"Fascinating," Finn repeats for the second time today. "Can you show us how to shield from you?"

Evie winks at him. "Only because you asked nicely."

The boys turn to me expectantly. "There's only you left, Riley," Finn says.

Those are the words I've dreaded to hear ever since I decided to learn more about my necromancy. But, for now, I choose to start with something more familiar. I breathe deeply and roll my neck. I spotted the shallow cut over Finn's brow as soon as I arrived earlier. A result of his combat training, no doubt. "Healing works on the living, be it plants, animals, or people," I teach as I feather my fingers over Finn's injury. His eyes close at the contact. A greenish-white glow moves between our skin as it passes from me to him. When the healing takes hold, I pull back, and everyone can see the cut closing slowly until only a red mark is left.

"There will be no trace left in a couple of minutes," I say with certainty. "For bigger ailments, I prefer working with healing mixtures so the patient can continue the treatment at home without me. That way, the healing is more gradual and likely to be durable." I turn to the rest of the room. "Most of you must know this, but those curative compounds are made from plants infused with healing magic so that life brings life. You can try and infuse healing in an inanimate object, and it may work, but it'll be a lot less potent, and you'll have to recharge it over and over again."

Finn brings his hand to his forehead, rubbing it to see how it feels. "Thank you," he says. His gaze moves from me to Diane's staff that I left by the entrance. "Have you thought about working on the other part of your powers, your necromancy?"

Cold spreads through me just thinking about it, but I want to at least try. "I don't know to what extent I'm willing to go, but I'll start and see. First, I'll show you what I do use necromancy for. It'll look like healing, but I guarantee you, it isn't."

With that, I grab the small plant I picked up from one of the pub's windows. Its wiry leaves are brown and dry, breaking at the softest touch. I need to print out a watering and plant food schedule for Albert to follow. If he's going to have plants for decor, he's got to take care of them properly. "It's almost dead, but not quite. An imprint of life is still there. Most people would throw a plant like this away."

Bree emits a small squeak of pity, bringing her hands to her mouth, and I am reminded of the way her people see nature and its inhabitants as sacred.

"Don't worry," I hurry to tell her. "This little guy will be back in shape when I'm done with him."

As I'm sitting back down, I have an idea. Maybe it could help them understand how dangerous this power is. "Do you want to feel how it works?" I ask Erick.

His surprise is evident, but I plow on. "Just put your hands over mine on the earth."

He does as instructed and nods at me once he's ready. The entire room is holding its collective breath. With my fingers hooked in the dirt, I close my eyes and reach for the tiny spark of life remaining in the spider plant in front of me. I circle the fragile flicker of essence with tendrils of dark power, holding it on this side of existence just a little longer while I send healing energy to its roots. I see light dancing on the other side of my closed eyelids as life and death play a game of tug of war to see which side will win the final battle.

Then I hear Erick's sharp intake of breath at the exact moment life takes back its hold, and I can feel the plant reacting to the healing. His fingers finally relax over mine when my dark influence releases the plant's life force. I wait just a little longer, and once I'm sure the plant doesn't need life support anymore, I disconnect my magic from it.

Bree lets out a little squeal of excitement, but I keep my eyes closed until my senses go back to normal. Necromancy always has that effect on me, as if it takes more than it gives, which I suppose is true.

When I finally open them, Erick stares at me wide-eyed. I know he felt how wrong and unnatural that side of my magic is. Shame and disgust about myself rise from the depth of me as it usually does most of the time I use this wicked power of mine. The familiar emotions sour my mood instantly.

"I told you it was dangerous. Do you see now?" I whisper to him.

His forehead creases in confusion. "Dangerous? You just brought back a little life from the brink of death," he states matter-of-factly as if I didn't just defy death itself with my small act of compassion. As if it was completely natural to go against the most basic law of nature. You're born, you live, you die. That's how it's supposed to be. I know magic in itself defies certain principles of physics all the time, but necromancy brings all of it to a whole new level of messed up. He needs to understand how hazardous necromancy is. They all need to.

Frustrated, I give the now green and flowering plant to Bree, who immediately starts talking to it in a cajoling tone, and I drag Erick by the hand toward the entryway where I left my staff earlier.

"It *is* dangerous. Stop being so nonchalant about it," I snarl.

I take hold of the weapon and unhook the clapper from the bell hanging at its top, so it can ring. Then I wrap Erick's fingers around my forearm and, taking the staff with both hands, I hit the butt of it on the ground. The sound of the small bell reverberates through the ether. Immediately, I can feel the tendrils of smoke-like darkness rise inside of me, curling around every bone, squeezing my lungs, and filling my vision with shades of gray. I know what they all see right now. I know that the black of my eyes slowly extends beyond my irises until there is no white left.

The temperature in the room has dropped several degrees already. Then I thump the staff a second time. The energy around us starts to pulse, making the empty coffee cups rattle, their clinking sound twin to the echo of my bell. Even Evie, who knows what I can do, looks scared, and with good reason.

The dead are coming.

Pain seizes my throat as the power demands to be spoken aloud to amplify the call, which makes me grasp the gravity of what I am about to do. A third thump of my staff and it would summon the revenants that are close, summon those who need help to cross to the other realm. My breath is labored, and my eyes mist over with tears as I use all the strength that I have left to wrestle death back inside of myself before it takes over with darkness and agony.

I unglue my hands from the staff slowly. My fingers move as if they were thawing from being outside without mittens in the dead of winter. It takes an extraordinary amount of energy just to hook the bell clapper back into place. Then my legs crumble under me, and Erick follows my fall to the ground, slowing my descent. I don't have the courage to look at my friends. I am too afraid to see the abomination that I am reflected back at me in their gaze. So, I burrow my face in Erick's chest and mutter a string of apologies.

I feel arms and hands wrapping around me as I sniffle away.

"Shh, shh, shh," Finn croons from somewhere behind me. "You're fine."

"I'm not fine. I'm a freak," I hiss back, voice wobbling through the tears.

"Never that." Evie's voice floats closer as she walks over to where I am slumped on the floor.

Heavy footsteps follow. "Don't you get it?" Eleanor asks no one in particular. "We're all scared of some part of ourselves. This doesn't make us monsters or freaks—it only makes us alive."

Chapter 34

FINN

Erick didn't push Riley to try for more. After we got acquainted with each other's powers, Erick insisted on seeing how the newcomers fended for themselves with physical fighting. It was all over fairly quickly. As predicted, Bree was nimble on her feet, evading all the hits coming her way. Eleanor was a real tank. Once she had her target, she was unstoppable.

As for Evie, her skills were more in the realm of basic self-defense. She was pissed when Erick gave her exercises to do at home. Her reaction was the only thing that made Riley's lips quirk up in a ghost of a smile after what happened with her.

I'm not sure exactly what she was trying to do. Necromancers use bells for all sorts of workings, and I didn't have it in me to ask and thus take her back to the dark place she seems to go every time that side of her power is unearthed.

Once everyone left, I stayed behind to help Erick put everything back in its place. When I asked him about it, he said he could feel her powers building silently under her skin, pooling at the surface like slithering ink. He thought he heard muffled screams as if from the other side of a glass wall, but he wasn't sure. Everything happened so quickly. The only thing he was certain about was that he could not fathom the depth of her energy, even with the tempering spell she has on it.

If Victor were to get ahold of her and master her powers, we still don't know what he would be able to accomplish with it. That's why we're back at the drawing board today. Riley and Bree are reading side by side in Arcane's basement, talking in hushed voices as if it were a public library. Earlier, Riley asked Bree some questions about elves since she wasn't familiar with elf lore other than the stories she heard as a kid. She wanted to be sensitive and not just assume stuff, which I found incredibly sweet.

I've been through a dozen books on the subject of necromancy—the power itself, the difference between *draugr* (revenants) and peaceful dead, the most common uses of necromancy, the theories, and so on. So far, all I've read I already knew.

Necromancy is not more nor less dangerous than any other magical art. It gets a bad rap partly because it has to do with death, and most living beings are uncomfortable with the idea of mortality. The other part is that some necromancers in the past used their powers to bring back people against their will. From what I gather, it is an excruciatingly painful process for the conjurer as well as for the dead. Still, with enough willpower and strength, it can be done. Although, from what I read, it's not everlasting. After a while, the individual that was brought back starts to waste away in their own decaying body. That magic is expressly forbidden, of course, being deemed unethical.

The majority of necromancers only hear the whispers of the dead left behind. Scrying and seances are common tools. Riley's type of necromancy, though, seems to go deeper than this and be more similar to the death artificers from days past—the ones that could kill with one touch, had the willpower to commune with the dead, and transmute deathly energies without dying themselves, thus gaining power over death itself.

The book I am currently reading is a journal where a woman, Louise Dubois, describes her husband's research on her necromancy powers. The tome is old and tattered. I found it buried behind thick volumes about plant healing in the depths of my personal library. The words rattle me. She was clearly not a willing participant in this "research." Her husband was cruel and abusive, making her test all sorts of techniques that were more often than not very painful for her.

I found myself almost hoping she would kill him by the end. I know it's bad to think that way, but what he made that poor woman do is unforgivable.

As I approach the final pages of the journal, my gaze snags on one piece of information.

It's October, and we've spent the best part of today in this old cemetery. My frozen feet are still thawing and hurting while I write these words in front of the fire. He was willing to risk my life to test his theory. To see if I could bring back his parents and previous lover, all of whom were at peace on the other side of the veil. Oh, I already knew I could do it. I just refused to. He didn't need to know this, though. When misty forms started to solidify instead of corpses rising from their graves, Mathieu was confused.

But I've finally done it. He's gone. I never even dared to write about this before. I was too afraid he'd find it, and I would lose my only hope of escaping this nightmare.

I'm still shaking with the spent power it took me to help the willing dead become corporeal. It seems my theory was correct. Some draugr *are waiting for an opportunity to avenge their fate or redeem themselves. If you ask them with a pure heart and you have the power to back your query, a fair few of them are finding their salvation through helping those who suffer at the hands of cruel masters.*

Today my jailor is dead, and my deceased saviors have crossed over to the next life.

No, no, no, no! It cannot be. I can feel the blood drain from my face. I've never heard about this before. I wobble on my feet, and the book slides from my grip, making a heavy thud as it hits the ground.

Riley is instantly at my side, helping me to a chair. "What is it?" she asks, alarmed. "Finn, what is it?" Her insistence pulls me out of my stupor.

"I—I'm not sure. I still don't know why he does what he does, but I think I can guess at what the Berserker wants with your type of power."

I didn't hear Bree approach, and I startle when she picks up the book from the floor to peruse through it.

"Finn?" Riley says through gritted teeth, her hands braced on the chair's arms. Her gaze darts between Bree and me as she waits for whoever will give her the answer first.

I hope with all my heart that I am wrong, but either way, they need to know of my discovery. "I've never heard of this before"—goosebumps erupt on my arms as I talk—"but the woman who wrote this seems to have been able to make the dead corporeal."

Riley looks at me, puzzled. "You mean raise them from their graves? More than one?"

I shake my head no and take hold of her wrists. "No. I mean that, with enough power, she was able to make more than one revenant solid at once. If he gathers enough necromancy powers inside him, Victor may be able to materialize himself an army of angry *draugr*."

Chapter 35

RILEY

I'VE BEEN DISTRACTED ALL night, mixing up drink orders and dropping pints of ale left and right. Fortunately, Albert isn't here to see the mess I made of his bar.

After Finn's discovery this morning, we continued digging. We didn't have to search for long. There was a pocket at the back of Louise Dubois' journal where she stored her monster of a husband's most prominent theories and findings.

It turns out that even if the Berserker doesn't find revenants to help him willingly as she did, with enough power, he still can raise more than one corpse against their will. It would most likely cause an atrociously painful death for the syphoned necromancer, but I don't think Victor cares about anyone anymore. Louise's husband obviously didn't either, since he pushed her to try over and over again until she raised ten corpses at once at the cost of her health. That final day in the cemetery, he wanted her to double that number, not caring if she died in the process.

What Louise wrote was astounding. She described the two processes in detail. The first one, the better one, is where the roaming spirits of the dead, the ones that are not at rest on the other side, used her demand as an opportunity. With the help they provided, they finally could achieve what their soul's needed to cross over—whether it be revenge, honor, or self-forgiveness. She described the transfer of energy that allowed them to materialize as painless. It was as if a caster was to release a spell—tiring but not painful. She called it the good kind of advanced necromancy, if such a thing exists.

What her husband forced her to do, however, almost brought her to the brink of death, the corpses themselves screaming in agony alongside her. She wrote that she could feel the anguish and despair of the peaceful dead being dragged from the other side and forced into their putrefying body. She compared the process to trying to pull someone out of an acid bath. She said the physical pain was so bad it felt as if her flesh had been peeled from her bones. Her lungs could only take in the black slithering smoke of death. I can't even fathom how physically, mentally, and emotionally taxing it must have been on her.

I can't believe we're talking about actual zombies, either.

I decided to order a taxi to get home tonight instead of walking, and I'm still waiting. I shiver as a gust of cool wind carries a few colorful autumn leaves past me.

We don't yet know why Victor wants to raise an army of the dead, or even if it really is his purpose, but I cannot risk everybody's life, in addition to my own, by not being careful enough. Because if he succeeds, many more people than just me will be in grave danger. Hence the cab instead of walking alone at night.

I can't keep my head in the sand anymore. I need to train harder. I need to dive headfirst into the study of necromancy. Oh, I remain afraid of the darkness that comes with this gift, but I can't unlearn those discoveries, and they change everything. The depth of what's going on is even more vast and dark than any of us could've imagined at the start of all of this.

I check my phone for the tenth time. It's been twenty minutes since I called the taxi. The pub is dark, and with the streetlight's yellowish glow, I cannot make out the tables and chairs I know are on the other side of the glass. I only see my reflection in the windows. A pulsing red light draws my attention to my neck. My pendant glows on and off.

The alarm spell. *Shit!*

I spin around, looking for the source of the danger, but nothing stands out of the ordinary. The businesses have long been closed for the night, and no one is in sight. Still, my necklace won't stop its warning. I can't stay here, out in the open, like a sitting duck.

If the source of the menace can see me, they already know that I'm aware of them—the alarm spell is not subtle—so there's no need to react carefully. I start to walk-run in the direction of my apartment. If only I could reach the trap door Finn installed in my cupboard, I'll be safe at Erick's. I train my eyes on every patch of shadows and keep my ears alert to any small sound, but still nothing.

I know it's wishful thinking to believe that the alarm spell may be misfiring, but I need the comfort. Just as I'm about to take out my phone to call Finn, I hear rapid footsteps behind me. With all my training, I should have had the reflex to start running. I know the precious seconds it takes to turn around and look at the possible attacker can make the difference between life and death, but the surprise of the hard sound in the dead of night causes me to turn around anyway.

As soon as I see the stranger's predatory smile, I know he is here for me. The attack is not random. I recognize him as one of the Berserker's men I saw in the warehouse. Panic seizes me as a strong set of arms encircles my waist from behind, placing a rag over my mouth and nose. I instinctively know that if I take a breath, I'll fall asleep and wake up in one of those dreadful cages.

My hours of grappling with the guys finally kick in. Still holding my breath, I put both my hands on my assailant's forearm, the one holding the rag, and jump. I usc thc downward momentum to flip him over me. Chloroform guy falls directly in front of his colleague, that was running toward us, making him trip and fall.

With both of them on the ground, I seize my chance and run with all I've got, hoping they don't have guns or other long-range weapons. I am too stunned to shield properly. The small amount of chemical I couldn't escape inhaling makes it difficult to focus my energy, even more so on magic I struggle with in normal circumstances.

I can manage, however, to unlock both of my doors on the first try. I shut and lock them back up one after the other in a surprisingly fluid motion, not stopping to think before I'm somewhat safe in my entryway. I sag on the back of my apartment door for a second to catch my breath.

"Come on, darling!" one of the men shouts from outside as his colleague cackles. His voice turns into a mocking song. "We can't enter, but you can't stay hidden there forever, little necromancer!"

Finn's protection spell around my apartment would take them days to undo.

The roar of my pounding heart swallows everything around me.

I need to leave.

Now.

I can see my world crumbling around me at once. The life I wanted to build for myself here was but a dream I don't even know if I'll be able to come back to one day. Tears cloud my vision, but I swipe them away with angry fingers. Now is not the time to grieve a life that barely existed in the first place.

I pick up my staff and the emergency bag I purposely left under the entrance table. With one last look at my apartment, I step through the watery shimmer of the activated escape door.

Chapter 36

ERICK

I'M LYING IN BED, going over my notes, unable to sleep, when the portal shoots open. My mind goes immediately to the worst outcomes possible. The seconds it takes for Riley to appear are the longest of my existence.

The moment she steps through and sees me, her hands go slack, her belongings dropping to the floor as the portal closes behind her. Her face falls, and fat tears run down her cheeks.

I'm beside her in an instant, just in time to catch her as she crumbles in anguish to the ground. I hold her to my bare chest. Her body releases adrenaline in violent jolts that come in waves.

I rock back and forth to try to calm her down. "Darkness, talk to me. Are you hurt? What happened?"

My questions only spur on her tears, renewing her struggle to calm herself down once more.

"You're safe now. You're safe. Shh. Shh. Nobody can hurt you here...." I continue to croon my litany of reassuring words in her ear, but it feels completely inadequate. I'm utterly powerless in the face of her distress. If only I could syphon away the hurt.

I gather Riley into my arms and bring her into the control room. On my way to the couch, I pick up the new burner phone I bought yesterday. I sit down but don't dare let go of her as I shoot a text to Finn's phone.

Riley stirs on my lap. "They—" she attempts.

"Don't hold your breath. Try to inhale and exhale deeply."

She does as she's told. Once she regains a smidge of composure, she tries again. "They came for me. My taxi didn't arrive, and my pendant started to glow, and I couldn't see the danger, and they tried to put me to sleep with chloroform or something like—" Another round of sobs interrupts her tale. "I got away and ran as fast as I could, and they were taunting and shouting at me from outside my apartment because they couldn't get in, and they thought I was trapped in there, and all I could do was leave everything behind...." she trails off, exhausted.

My muscles lock up, ready to tear through the ones who dared attack her. *Mine*, my mind roars with all its might in time with the blood in my ears. All I can see now is retribution. All I can smell is vengeance. All I can taste are the ashes of her assailants. My power screams at me to hunt and bleed them dry, of their magic or of their blood, I don't know. Everything at once, I suppose.

Riley pushes from my chest and fixes her red-rimmed eyes on mine. "They were there especially for me, Erick. They were your father's men. I recognized them from the warehouse. They knew what I am."

Finn arrived within the hour, and Riley recapped her story for him, stopping here and there to recompose herself. By then, her shock had passed a little, and she was sipping on her whisky. I proposed chamomile tea instead, to which she replied with a string of curses, so I stuck with the whisky.

Finn and I are sitting on each side of her on the couch. Her vacant stare and his frown of worry eat at my insides. All I want is for them to be safe, to be happy. But I only succeed at putting them in more danger.

"Don't do that," Finn says sternly. Even though reading thoughts is not something you can accomplish through magic, Finn could always divine mine. His green eyes are darker than usual, and I can't be sure if it's because of the early morning or the absence of his glasses. His tousled hair is haphazardly put together in a messy bun on top of his head, exposing the strong column of his neck.

"I'm not doing anything," I reply halfheartedly.

He huffs in derision. "Don't play dumb, either. I can see you're blaming yourself for this."

"He's right, you know," Riley agrees. "Your father's wrongdoings are not for you to shoulder."

I don't know how to respond to that kind of generosity and understanding. The emotion blossoming in my chest is foreign and uncomfortable. I pick up Riley's glass to refill it, thinking that the short walk from here to the cabinet will help me relieve some of those feelings, but she doesn't let me.

Instead, she puts the glass on the coffee table and lays her head on Finn's shoulder. Then she picks up my hand to fuss anxiously with my fingers. I know she's still wound up from the events of the night. Even though she might feel tired, her body won't be able to sleep for quite some time. It's still on high alert.

Finn extends his arm along the back of the couch so she can be more comfortable. His hand lands on the back of my neck and plays with the strands of my hair.

Those two small points of contact are all that's needed for the feel of their powers to reach me, and I let it envelop me. The familiarity of it warms my core. I shouldn't let myself indulge, even in something this small, but it becomes more and more difficult with every passing day to ignore my urges. I'm at a point where I need to feel them under my touch, and my body won't ever stop reminding me.

When I sigh in contentment, Riley looks at me intently. Then, she unfolds from Finn's side and kneels on the couch cushion to lay a gentle kiss on my closed lips. I'm too stunned to react. She does the same with Finn before she sits back down, taking each of our hands in hers.

"I'm ready to explore this if you are," she whispers, looking at our joined hands.

Her intent is clear, although I cannot guess if her decision is due to tonight's event or if it comes from deeper inside her. But my resolve is melting away fast. At this point, I will take whatever she wants to give me. Whatever they both want to give me if I am so lucky.

The tempest raging inside of me at the prospect is mirrored in Finn's questioning look. I don't have to wait long for his answer. We move at the same time, meeting directly in front of Riley in a rough kiss. Finn becomes pliant under my ministration and lets my tongue roam inside his mouth, tasting every corner of him as if it were the last time, and it may very well be. I drink him in with everything I've got.

A small whimper brings our awareness back into the room, and we stop kissing. Finn's lips are swollen, and all I want to do is bite them. But before I can make good on my desire, he takes one of my hands and puts it on Riley's cheek, bringing my attention back to her. Her eyes are ablaze with desire, her harsh breathing echoing our own.

I have the small thought that I've never done this before, sharing intimacy with more than one person. Although, I can't imagine things any differently now. It feels like my soul knows theirs the same way an artist knows their muse.

The moment my lips touch hers, I am reborn. Black tendrils of power mixed with soft healing in a kaleidoscope of color greet me, and the thread of restraint I had left breaks. I revere her tongue with mine as Finn bends down to graze my neck with suckles and kisses. His electric magic meets my senses, and I think I might die of the feel of them.

Riley's hands roam over my naked chest, following the path my scars create down my abdomen. I reach behind her and burrow my fingers in her thick raven hair, pulling slightly to bare her throat to me. I bite her jaw and lick down the column of her neck and kiss the hollow between her collarbones until she is nothing but liquid and loose under my touch.

I've lost track of whose hands are where when Finn's strong grasp takes hold of my erection through my sweatpants, wrenching a growl out of me.

We're all drunk with lust, but I find it in myself to voice my concern. "Is this really what you want?" I ask no one in particular. My forehead rocks from side to side on Riley's shoulder as I speak. "I know we've all been under a lot of—"

"Yes," Riley interrupts as Finn wrenches my head back to plant a brief but violent kiss on my mouth. Well, that's settled, I guess.

Finn grazes his fingers along the bottom of Riley's shirt and then lifts it slowly over her head. We both groan at the sight of her soft, porcelain skin. Her plump breasts are wrapped in red lace.

More.

I roughly pull Finn's T-shirt off him and kiss the rune tattooed in the middle of his chest, the one he got for me. The one that started his path as a rune master.

"Not enough space," Riley growls in frustration at the tight quarters of the couch, which currently limit her reach.

My need to take charge is close to the surface. The soft command passes my lips before I can think better of it. "Kneel for me, Little Prince."

Finn falls graciously to his knees on the floor. There is no trace of hesitation as he looks at me expectantly for the following direction. All traces of nervousness or worry on his perfect face vanish with the position, and I am struck by the trust he still places in me.

Even back then, barely adults, we knew we had different needs, but it was never a struggle because we had each other to rely on. We started with small things at first, defining with each other's bodies the ebbs and flows of our desires. Finn, ever the scholar, read on the topic of power play and everything he wanted us to try, but we were young men then. Lovers without the baggage of life. It was nothing but a game. But now...

"What's your safe word?" I demand.

"Arcane," he answers. The familiar word makes me smile. When I learned he chose this specific name for his bookshop three years ago, it was almost enough to send me groveling, begging him to come back and be mine.

"Of course, it is," Riley cuts in, rolling her eyes.

I'm suddenly deeply aware I don't know what she thinks about this kind of dynamic. But it seems that she, like Finn, has developed the ability to read my thoughts.

"It's a first for me." Her gaze goes from me to Finn and back. "Although I'm not a total stranger to power play, everything I've done so far is pretty soft, but I'm open to trying. I just want you both as you are, and I'll see where I fall in all of this if it's okay with you."

I cradle her cheeks in my hands as my gaze roams over her face. Her features are open. I can see the truth of her statement in the set of her jaw.

"What *is* your safe word then, Darkness?"

Her answering smile is bright, crinkling the corner of her eyes. "Castle."

I huff a laugh at the mention of part of my shop's name. "Castle, it is. If at any point you feel like you want to stop, you only have to say it, and everything will stop immediately. You have both our words on this. Do you understand?" I ask her.

She nods yes.

"Use your words," I order.

"Yes."

I take a deep breath, my nostril flaring. "Get up for me then." She answers by getting to her feet.

"Take her jeans off," I tell Finn. He gets to work with an enthusiasm that betrays his impatience to see more of her. I can't fault him for that. He reveals the feminine curves of her body inch by inch until she stands before us in nothing but her bra and panties.

She lowers her gaze, but I put a finger under her chin to bring her head back up. "You are a vision. Keep your head up and let Finn look at you."

Riley's little squirm reveals her discomfort, but she manages to keep her head high as Finn roams his gaze over her. While he does, I arrange myself on the couch, sitting behind her, and I let my eyes wander, too. My fingers hook in the red lace of her panties. Her fists open and close, resisting the urge to hold on to the small piece of clothing. When I draw the red lace down slowly, I hear Finn's breathing quicken, but he's not novice enough to let his instinct to touch her take over. He knows that by doing so without my permission, he would be denied pleasure for the rest of the night. It would kill me, but I'd do it.

At this moment, they both belong to me to do as I please. The hunter in me slowly stretches from its slumber. The urge to master and control is intimately tied to the nature of my void.

"You're so beautiful, both of you," I compliment them with awe. She shivers when my fingers push her hair over her shoulder to get to the hooks of her bra, but she still doesn't move. Finn groans as the last piece of her clothing falls to the floor.

I trail my index finger down her spine to bring her attention to me. Once her eyes are firmly on mine, I let all the pride I can muster shine with my next words. "Good girl." I wait for her retort to my praise, but it doesn't come. Instead, she blushes and averts her eyes, still keeping her head up like I asked. My cock jerks at the submissive gesture, to which she responds by wetting her lips. Fuck, I don't know if I'll survive this.

I let my finger run down to her hip. "Now, sit on my lap facing Finn."

She turns completely to me then. "But you're both still dressed," she argues. I raise an eyebrow at her in silent question. *And?*

"Okay, okay," she breathes. She's clearly not used to being looked at, but I intend for her to be thoroughly worshipped tonight.

I close my legs together, which leaves her to straddle my thighs. Then I band my arms around her tight stomach. At once, I pull her to my chest and open my legs, which effectively bares her completely to Finn. In this position, the most private part of her is indecently exposed.

I can't see her cunt from my vantage point, but I am rewarded with the sight of Finn's tented linen pants. His eyes are hooded with need while his entire focus is on her.

"Take those off. I want to see you," I tell Finn.

He doesn't need to be told twice. The last time I laid eyes on his naked body feels like a lifetime ago. I wasn't prepared for the sight of him. His rigid length bobs free as soon as he pushes his pants down. Gods, he wasn't wearing any briefs all that time. I guess waking him up in the middle of the night has its perks for me. He folds the material neatly before going back to his knees between our legs.

Riley wiggles slightly on my lap, rubbing against my erection, and I pinch one of her erect nipples for her offense. Although her soft gasp reveals that she took it more as a reward than a punishment.

"Our Darkness is so impatient, Finn. What does she look like? Is she dripping for us?"

He licks his lips and swallows audibly. "Yes, she's swollen and...so wet. Erick, please."

Waves of heat go straight to my groin at his plea. "Use your words, Little Prince. What do you want?"

"Everything, anything," he groans.

"Well then, help yourself to a taste. And Finn, you're not allowed to stop until she comes, do you hear me?"

His face is the picture of ecstasy as he braces his hands on my thighs. I scarcely have time to see his tongue dart out before his head disappears between her legs. I know the exact moment he makes contact. Her moan of pleasure vibrates down my spine, and it takes everything I have not to thrust up into her. I can feel pre-cum making a mess in my pants already.

"Don't move," I whisper in her ear. "If you want Finn to continue what he is doing, you need to stay still for me."

I take hold of her wrists and box her arms behind my neck. Her breasts jut forward, and I play with the furled tips, rolling and pinching them between my fingers. My teeth gently worry her earlobe. Her soft moans become more heated with every passing moment, her thighs trembling lightly. She's getting closer.

"You may use your hands now, Finn."

His fingers graze my balls through my pants as he plays with her folds and prods her entrance. She arches back before visibly remembering that she was asked not to move. She returns to her initial position immediately.

"Good girl," I praise. I reward her with more wet kisses down the column of her neck. My tongue swirls on her skin the way it would if it were between her legs.

I let Finn work her for a little longer.

"How many fingers does he have in your tight little pussy, Darkness?" I tease.

It takes her two tries to get the words out. "One." A gasp. "No, two now."

"Has he found your G-spot yet?" On cue, Finn follows my words and hooks his fingers inside of her. The desperate sound coming from her tells me as much.

"Stop teasing, Little Prince, and make our Darkness come for me. Now."

The suction noises coming from him doubling down on her clit and the wet sounds of her pussy as he fingers her create the most delicious symphony. Her pleasure is skyrocketing in time with her sensual cries of bliss.

"You can move now," I croon to Riley as I thread one hand through Finn's hair and push his face down on her.

"Yes. Right there. Yes, don't stop!" She cries as she rocks her hips to him once, twice, and then she's coming. Her orgasm is so beautiful I want to burn it in my memory.

I release Finn to roam my hands on her, and he continues his movements until she's completely spent. Once her body is fully relaxed, I lower her arms down to her sides, and I lay her gently down beside me. Then I turn my attention to Finn and his glistening mouth. I take his face in both my hands and kiss the taste of her from his lips. The heady combination is divine. He grabs my wrists, and I pull him with me onto the couch.

As we both come up for air, he hooks his fingers in the waistband of my sweatpants. "Please," he whispers against my lips. "I need to see you."

The desperation in his words goes straight to my dick, and I give him what he so beautifully begged for. I rise from the couch and let him pull my bottoms down. His gaze roams over my body, drinking me in. In that moment, with Riley content to look at both of us from her spot on the couch, with Finn and I threadbare in front of each other, I allow myself to think of a future. A future where I get to come home and have them like this every night.

"Finn is going to pick you up to carry you into the bedroom," I tell Riley, and she sighs in satisfaction. She's still too drunk on pleasure for me to trust her legs. Finn's gaze lingers on me, the longing in his eyes plain to see.

Not yet. I want to draw out this pocket of time for as long as possible.

I get the opportunity to look at him more closely when he goes to pick up Riley. There is a lot of new ink on him. His whole upper body is covered in tattoos. No color, only thick black lines forming intricate rune patterns that move over his muscles as he lifts her in his arms. I want to memorize them, etch those tattoos in my mind so I can follow their path in my dreams forever.

The walk to the bed feels like a procession, like walking to an altar to offer a sacrifice to the gods.

Finn lays Riley carefully on the bed and turns to me. At this moment, I allow myself to indulge in him without restraint. I grab the back of his neck and pull him to me. It's like we're young men again, discovering each other anew. We fumble, not being able to choose where we want to touch and squeeze and bite and suck first. Our cocks are firmly pinned between us, spreading copious amounts of pre-cum over our stomachs. With every movement, every contraction of abs, my erection rubs against the velvet of his. We are both rutting against each other, desperate for more.

When I glance at Riley, she's circling her clit with her fingers, hunger written all over her body.

"On your back on the bed, hands behind your head," I tell Finn. Riley scoots over to let him lie down on the narrow surface. I wish I could give them more—a fluffy, luxurious bed comes to mind, but this is all I have.

I walk over to the bedside table to retrieve a condom. I bought the box on a whim after my last training session with Finn, hoping beyond all hopes.

I give the foil packet to Riley. "Go on, Darkness. Our Little Prince has done such a good job thus far. He deserves a reward. Look at his cock, all red and angry, weeping for your cunt." She shivers at my lewd words and gets to work, rolling the condom down over his length. He hisses at the contact of her fingers, which brings a smile to my lips.

She leans back on me when I take hold of her hips from behind, and I kiss the top of her head. I move her body over his. Once she's where I want her, I guide him to her entrance. With agonizing slowness, I bring her down on his thick cock until he is buried to the hilt in her heat. They moan in tandem when I move her hips in a rolling motion, which massages his dick on the tender spot inside her and rubs her clit on his pubic bone.

When I release her, Riley puts her hands on Finn's chest and resumes the movement on her own, languid rolling waves that have him fighting for restraint. I lay down on my side next to them, my head resting on my hand, and watch them fuck. I like to watch, and what a mighty sight it is. Their bodies rock ardently against each other, her long black hair falling like a waterfall down her back as she throws her head back with a moan.

I lean forward to gently bite Riley's nipples in turn, then suck them in my mouth as I go, which prompts her to increase her pace on Finn. Once her chest is peppered with the imprint of my teeth, I do the same with Finn. They are both panting wildly now. Every breath, every slide of their sweaty skin brings them higher.

I kiss her, then him. Then I bring my lips to his ear. "Let go."

He looks at me with wide eyes, making sure he heard right. I nod my head yes. Finn's hands fly to Riley's hips, and he flips her under him, never losing rhythm. His thrusts are hard and powerful, making her slide up on the bed. Riley is a wild thing in his arms, scratching at his back and biting at his neck. Her hand reaches for mine, squeezing it for dear life as she comes a second time.

"Yes, Erick. Oh, Finn," she cries over and over like a prayer. Finn grunts, and his thrusts become disorganized as the walls of her pussy contract over his length. He lets his weight fall on her and buries his head in the crook of her neck, roaring his release. It takes everything I have not to come myself.

After the last of his aftershocks, Finn rolls off her with a look of amazement on his beautiful face. While they take a moment to catch their breath, I walk over to the shower and make sure the water is hot before taking them both in, one after the other, to wash and take care of them. The stall being too small for all of us to fit into at once.

I start with a sleepy Riley. I hold her to me while I go through the motion of lathering soap on her body and rinsing her hair. She makes small sounds here and there—little mewls of satisfaction that tug at my heart.

Once she's dried, hydrated, fed an energy bar, and tucked in, I do the same with Finn. We get under the spray, but he doesn't let me wash him right away. Instead, he steps back and frowns at my still-hard cock.

"You didn't come," he states as if it were a crime.

"I had plenty of fun," I tell him. I hope he hears the truth in my words. The gift they gave me tonight is more than I could ever have wished for. They're both exhausted, and I don't want to take more from them.

He reaches over to put his palm flat on my heart. "I know that, but let me do this for you. I missed you so much," he whispers. "I mean, not only your body but your heart, your mind, the way your left eyebrow always rises a little more than the right when you're surprised..."

I know very well what he means. I missed every little habit of his, too.

"Please," Finn says as he drops to his knees in front of me once more, his head bowing down.

A supplicant.

And so, I let him worship me with his mouth and hands until my whole world shatters to then be put back together in such a way that I know they'll be a part of me forever.

Chapter 37

RILEY

I WAKE UP BETWEEN two warm bodies in what I think should be deemed the smallest bed in the world. Finn faces me, his head pillowed on his arm, still deep in slumber. My heart jumps when I notice his big hand grips one of mine as if he is not ready to let go yet.

I can feel Erick's strong frame at my back, holding me in the cradle of his body. His own hand is resting on Finn's hip on the other side of me.

We're...connected.

Dammit! Don't feel it, don't feel it, don't feel it...too late.

What we shared last night... I think I have never felt alive before meeting them. And what I thought to be simple infatuation is morphing quickly into emotions I'm afraid I can't control anymore. I know it's crazy, but in this moment, I want to learn to wield death to make sure they are safe. I want to feel them both inside of me so our bodies may commune in the physical world the same way our spirits have already begun in the ether.

But another part of me is terrified that I will lose them, as I've lost so many before. The people important to me all end up leaving in some way or another. And, just like that, my mind shifts gears. The weight of Erick's arm on my waist is suddenly too much, and Finn's peaceful face sends alarm bells blaring through my skull. I can't breathe.

"It's alright, Darkness," Erick whispers in my ear. "Deep breaths in and out."

I try to get a grip on my spiraling mind, so when Finn opens his eyes, I latch onto the forest I see in them. Finn's gaze moves from my face to behind me, no doubt sending a questioning look to Erick.

When his attention returns to me, I don't dare put into words the emotion I see written all over him.

"What is it?" Finn asks.

It takes me a minute to find my footing. In the meantime, neither of them moves, their hold anchoring me to the bed.

"I don't know," I confess. "It's all going too fast. I… I'm afraid this is all a mistake, and we'll end up getting hurt or hurting each other, or—or you'll leave with a part of me I never intended to give."

Finn smiles softly at my words while Erick peppers gentle kisses down the side of my neck.

"It won't come to that," Erick says from behind me.

"You can't know that," I reply.

"But even if it does," Finn carries on, his tone solemn, "we'll suffer the most rewarding kind of pain because it will mean that what we had was real. And we'll look after the part of you that you leave with us and carry it within ourselves like the most precious gem, as you will do with ours, I'm sure."

"It's all too much," I whisper, closing my eyes.

"We're not getting hand-fasted tomorrow," Erick argues. "This is not a binding contract. I don't expect any of you to move on with this if you don't have it in your heart to do so. And if any of you want to back out now, it changes nothing for me. I'll still help you. I'll still do my best to be there for both of you. But if you want to try. If you want to see where this relationship leads, then—"

"I want to see where the path leads," Finn says. "I've already lost my way by letting circumstances have the upper hand. No more."

I open my eyes at Finn's words. His statement ignites something within me, a small flame of hope that refuses to be extinguished. A kernel of pure truth that bolsters my courage. I turn in Erick's arms so I can lay on my back and take each of their hands in mine as the men hold on to each other's.

Again. Connected.

I sigh deeply, coming to a decision. "Okay. But no expectations. I—"

I'm interrupted by the ringtone of my phone. With everything that's happened, I need to see who it is, just in case. I bring the bedsheet with me as I get up to fish the cell phone from my bag, leaving the men without. When I turn around to show them Evie's caller ID, I see they are still entirely naked, and I can feel the blush creeping up my neck. When Erick smirks, I huff at him.

"Put her on speaker so we can all give her the information we have," Erick says as Finn hops out of bed to pick up something from his book bag.

"Hey, Evie," I answer. "You won't believe what happened to me after work."

Finn stops abruptly in his tracks at the voice that slithers from the other side of the phone. One of a woman, but not Evie.

"See how easy it is to get to the people you love? Behave, little mouse, and follow the breadcrumbs."

The line goes dead.

Thirty minutes later, we're all dressed and still arguing about the best course of action.

"It's a trap, Riley," Erick says. "Don't fall for it. Finn sent Bree to check on her. Evie has the reinforced protection Finn put on her place, remember?"

I know he just wants to shake me right now, but the only thing I can think about is my best friend trapped in one of those horrible cages.

"Believe me," he continues, "it's really easy to steal a phone. Plus, Evie is so extroverted she has a million people who would notice her disappearance, which would alert the local police and eventually the Sennex itself. It wouldn't make sense."

"Oh, I think your father is way past making sense at this point," I hiss at him just when the bunker alarm detonates. My gaze darts to the screens on the wall, and I see my confused best friend in posh loungewear waiting in the antechamber with Bree.

I spring from my seat and run to the door that Erick unlocks from his perch at the console table. I wrench it open.

"Riley, what—"

I squeeze Evie so hard in my arms that she has no other choice but to hug me back.

"Were you followed?" comes Erick's voice from behind me.

"No," Bree says. "I have my ways... Anyway, your father's men are so bad at trailing discreetly that I would have had time to walk them in a circle and be the one to trail them." I can hear the laughter in her voice, and it helps loosen the knot of anxiety inside of me.

"Too tight. Need air," my best friend wheezes.

I release her but keep my hands on her shoulders, giving her a cursory look to make sure she's not hurt.

Her hazel eyes pin me with their inquisitive look. "I lost my phone last night, and the next thing I know, I am dragged from REM sleep—you know, 'cause it's only nine a.m.—to haul my ass here. What. The. Fuck?"

Finn is the one to bring us all life-giving coffee this morning, and the mundane gesture helps me ground myself as I recap last night's events for Bree and Evie. Well, minus the sex.

Looking around the room, I see that everyone has taken back the places they held the last time they were here. Even Eleanor's seat remains empty, as if it is hers. It feels like we're holding council.

"If my father is asking them to do stunts like that phone call," Erick pitches in, "it's because they don't know where we are or who's working with Riley—which means that my cover is still intact. He wants to draw Riley out. I know how he operates..." His voice trails off, and his attention drifts away for a moment, no doubt seeing old memories we're not privy to.

He shakes his head. "Even before his descent into this power craze, he couldn't tolerate not being in control. He needs to know and master everything. My guess is that his goons will be asked to do even more crazy stuff to find her. He might even do the tracking himself. We'll have to be extraordinarily careful. I don't think we can maintain this level of stealth for long. We're bound to make a mistake at some point." Erick looks around the room before sighing heavily. "We need to act, and fast," he says.

"My priority is to keep everyone as safe as possible," I tell him before I turn to Evie. "I think you should stay here until this blows over."

Her delicate eyebrows lower. "How much time?" she asks.

"We'll need to move within the week," Erick answers. Finn nods, agreeing with him.

Evie's face is one of resolve. "Okay, I'll call the job to let Albert know I have a family emergency for the next week."

"As for me," I say, putting my mug down on the coffee table, "I think it's pretty clear I need to lay low. I'll stay here with Evie." At that, Erick seems to start to breathe again, his shoulders relaxing a little. "Also, I'll call Albert and tell him I'm going out of town for a few days. If they come sniffing at The Drunken Sailor, I don't want to implicate my boss in this."

Erick lets out a sharp laugh. "Even my father is not unhinged enough to risk attacking Albert. He's neutral ground. Hurting him would mean war with more people than just the few of us."

I open my mouth to ask Erick what that means, but I'm distracted by Finn taking my hand in his. Bree zeroes in on the gesture, but she doesn't say anything. She only lifts a brow, but he doesn't see her. "I don't think Victor will mess with either Bree or me directly, knowing my personal connection to the Sennex," Finn says. "He doesn't know that I'm not on speaking terms with my family. He won't want to ring any bell that could reveal where he is. I think that's why he hasn't messed with me, even though my powers could be useful to him."

Erick slithers his arm behind me on the back of the couch and squeezes Finn's shoulder gently to get his attention. "I don't like that," Erick tells him. "I would prefer to have you with Riley and Evie in this bunker for the next week."

Finn gently pats Erick's hand on his shoulder. "Of course, you would," Finn patronizes. "If you thought we would go with it, you would have shipped us to Australia already and tried to deal with this alone."

I can't be sure, but if Finn's grunt is to be believed, Erick just squeezed his shoulder a little harder than necessary in warning.

"My father is not a threat to Eleanor or me. I'm sure of it." Erick grimaces in disgust. "We're both his creations, after all."

"Don't say that," I tell him fiercely.

The dynamic developing between me and the boys is starting to seep out into the world on its own and betrays our growing intimacy. Evie smiles knowingly as she stares at us in satisfaction.

I smile at her in return. "Okay," I ask, "do we have a plan then?"

Finn opens yet another one of his books. "With Riley's help, I succeeded at finding the right way to cancel the cages' spell without everything blowing up in our faces." His smile kicks up a notch with pride. "Once the prisoners are out of their confinement, it's a matter of getting them in good enough shape to move and get to safety.

"Bree also found a more detailed account of the cured syphon. The ancients found a way to make the void witch empty themselves of their power on their own. I'm still trying to decipher how. After that, it's pretty straightforward. Once the mind is free of the power lust the overflow of magic created, it's a question of rehabilitation. It's similar to what a recovering addict would go through."

He looks at Erick then. "I will work night and day to make sure I'm ready with a solution by the time we make our move," Finn promises him.

Erick is silent for a moment. I can't quite place the sentiment crossing his features—gratitude and something else. "It's settled then," Erick declares. "We'll iron out the rest of the details in the next few days. In the meantime, you all need to take care of yourselves and stay safe. We'll all get through this. Nobody stays behind."

Chapter 38

ERICK

"WHY ARE YOU TELLING me all this?" Eleanor asks me as she carries a new batch of amulets to the central display of the back room.

Her question catches me off guard. "What do you mean?" For the last half an hour, I've been detailing everything she needs to know to stay safe and be aware of our plan.

She drops the merchandise onto the glass top, and I go over to help her put the talismans in place.

Eleanor looks at me pointedly. "You know exactly what I mean," she huffs. "You're only telling me so I don't mess up your plans, not because I'm really part of the team. I know I'm only a creation, a disposable thing, and my existence doesn't really matter anyway, but no need to treat me like I'm a possible nuisance."

I stop everything I do at once. "Where is that coming from? Have I ever given you the impression that you weren't important to me?" A simmering anger grows in my belly at the way she thinks of herself. I tug her forearm to make her look me in the eye.

When she does, I put every ounce of certainty I can muster into my next words. "You are my friend. You are part of my family. I've *never* thought of you as a nuisance and even less as a 'disposable thing.' Your origins don't define you, just as I have begun to understand mine don't define me either. It bears repeating. You. Are. My. Friend. And like all my other friends, we'll work together to ensure *everybody* gets out of this alive and well. Do you understand?"

For the first time in the seven years she's been on this earth with me, a tear rolls down Eleanor's cheek. A real tear, made of salt water, which should be impossible for a golem to achieve. She doesn't seem to feel it, however, because she looks puzzled at my gasp of wonder.

"Your cheek" is all I can muster. She frees her arm from my grip and wipes at her face with her hand.

Her fingers come away wet. Pure joy illuminates Eleanor's features, and more of those precious droplets drip down her face. "I'm crying!" she exclaims. "I'm— What does it mean?"

"I don't know, Lenny," I answer, my voice thick with emotion. "I don't know, but you've been changing and evolving all your life. This might be the next step. We'll find out together, okay?"

She nods her head yes. "How do I stop them?" she asks, and I laugh.

"They'll stop on their own once you calm down. You'll see."

Eleanor's tears abated, but not her excitement. She talked my ears off about everywhere she thought she might be able to find answers concerning her "new water," as she called it. I assured her that Finn would be more than happy to help her dig through her findings. The scholar in him cannot resist a good search for knowledge.

The front door shuts behind Eleanor. I took it upon myself to do the close today, so I sent her home early. Not even a minute later, the doorbell rings once more.

"Did you forget something, Lenn—" I stop when I see who it is. "Dad?"

My father stands before me. Day-old stubble mars his normally clean-shaven jaw. His usually tidy suit has been replaced with jeans and a dress shirt rolled at the sleeves. His eyes are not totally focused on me, as if his mind is here but not here at the same time.

"Seen your new neighbor lately, son?" he says. He keeps his voice completely monotone. He often does this when he doesn't want me to get an inkling of his plans.

I decide to play dumb. "Which new neighbor? There have been a few move-ins lately."

He laughs. Instead of the deep, rich sound I'm used to hearing, this laugh is shaky, unhinged. A shiver rolls down my spine, and I hold my breath, waiting for his next words.

He strolls to the cash register and leans on the counter, putting his head in the cradle of his hands. The position makes him look childish, which is not an adjective I would have ever thought to use to describe him before this very instant.

"I finally saw your neighbor the other day," he says conversationally. "The potion I asked you for was remarkable but on par with other potion masters, which I found bizarre given the way she was the talk of the town...." he trails off, not finishing his explanation, but I don't dare ask for more so I don't blow my cover in the slight chance it is still intact.

Dread increases in steady waves in my gut.

"Has she already moved out?" he asks when his mind finally comes back into the room. "She doesn't seem to live there anymore."

I make a superhuman effort to keep my face blank. "How should I know?"

My dad looks peeved for a fleeting moment before a frightening smile appears on his face. "It took me a while to remember where I had seen that face before. You know, she looks remarkably like her mother at her age."

I startle at the comment. Riley's mother? He knows Riley's mother?

"Her family line is supposed to be extinct," he carries on, "like ours, I suppose. They are extremely powerful necromancers and healers. Two ends of the same stick, really. Do you know how rare it is to have those two in perfect balance as main powers? To be able to influence the cycle of life and death...." He loses himself in thoughts again for a few seconds before laughing to himself. "I don't know why she bothers with her parlor tricks of potions. Oh, well, everyone needs a hobby."

I know what comes next. The anticipation makes me sick to my stomach. Bile rises in my throat.

"I should very much like to add her talents to my team. When you see her next, you will bring her to me, or you will live to regret it. Do I make myself clear, son of my heart?" The threat is plain as day.

This monster is not my father anymore.

And the man standing before me now may be too far gone to save.

Chapter 39

RILEY

Erick looked frazzled when he came home earlier but didn't say anything. I have the feeling he wants to talk to me alone, but with Evie here, his bunker doesn't have that much space left to be alone in the first place.

He has been staying at his cover-up apartment—the one paid for by his father—every night since we slept together with Finn. He says it's so Evie and I won't feel cramped here, with the added bonus that it allows him to maintain appearances and stay above suspicion with his father.

But I feel like what we shared is already seeping away as if it only existed in a dream, a pocket out of time doomed to never repeat itself. I tell myself I'm being dramatic, and it's only because of the circumstances. Still, I can't shake the feeling of wrongness their absence provokes in me. Not that I can't take care of myself; it has nothing to do with that. It's just that, in the last few weeks, I've come to rely on either Finn or Erick or both being next to me.

I feel like I'm missing a limb.

We're all sitting around the coffee table having take-out in silence, and the continuous quiet is making me crazy. I drop my fried rice container onto the table. "Okay, I'm done with this shit. What is it?" I ask Erick, my tone brooking no argument. "I want an answer now."

His gaze fleets to Evie. "Maybe you would prefer to be alone for this," he says, confirming my earlier suspicions.

"Fine." I turn to my best friend. "Can you give us a minute?"

"Sure," she says, filling her arms with food containers.

Once the bedroom-slash-training room door closes behind her, I turn to Erick and take one of his hands in mine. "Go on, talk. You're making me nervous. I know I'm in your hair a lot. Is it— Did you change your mind about us trying? Because if—"

I'm interrupted by Erick's lips closing on mine, and relief washes over me. His fingers grip the hair at the nape of my neck, pulling gently, which makes me whimper. He angles my head to deepen the kiss, and I think I might melt on the spot if he doesn't stop soon.

He breaks off the kiss abruptly but doesn't release me. Instead, he lays his brow on mine. "No, not that, never that," he says.

And, in that moment, I believe him. The conviction behind his words is all I can hear. "What is it then?"

He gathers me on his lap on the couch. "My dad came by today," he says in an ominous tone.

"Okay…" I give an encouraging tug on his shirt.

"He asked me directly to bring you to him. Said he was interested in adding your talents to his team." I tense at that, and Erick starts rubbing slow circles at the small of my back to calm me down. "If you could have seen him, Riley, he looked... Well, he doesn't look like my father anymore. He's sick."

I can hear the distress in his voice. "And I think I know how he found out about your powers."

"What? How?"

His hesitation only ramps up my unease. "He said that he finally had a good look at you. He must have had you tailed and finally saw the photos or something. He didn't say. Anyway, he said that you look remarkably like your mother did at your age."

"My mother? I look nothing like my mo—" I stop as understanding hits me. "Oh, you mean my *birth* mother? How could he know that? I don't even know who my birth mother is. The process was handled anonymously by a private agency. Unless my adoptive parents lied to me, which I don't think they even knew how to lie—that's how honest they were. I don't see where he could have found that information or actual pictures of her, for that matter. Trust me, I dug into it when I came of age and couldn't find a single thing." Goosebumps erupt down my arms, waiting for his next words.

"That's what I was afraid of," he says. "My dad said your family line was supposed to be extinct. They were very powerful necromancers and healers. Both ends of the same stick, he said. Riley, I think my father knew your birth parents, and I think it's no accident you were placed for adoption. Either you were orphaned or, most likely, you were hidden."

I have absolutely nothing to say to that. Disbelief and fear twist together in my gut. I free myself from his embrace and start to pace the length of the control room.

"You think my parents were killed? Or that they hid me for some obscure reason? That doesn't make any sense. Other than being an untrained necromancer, I'm your run-of-the-mill witch."

Erick guffaws. "I beg to differ. You're very powerful, Riley. I've felt it."

"There's a lot of powerful witches that walk this earth. Finn, for example, is extremely powerful, too. I mean, it doesn't make sense to me."

"Yes, but Finn's family is part of the Sennex, which means they are protected as royalty. Their powers are also in service of the administration, so they are never a threat to the institution in place. I've seen what the Sennex is capable of when they think they have a traitor in their midst...." he trails off.

I take a deep breath and try to think about this logically. "Okay, one thing at a time. No matter how your dad found out, what is important now is that we deal with the most pressing problem at hand, which is the menace he presents and freeing those captives. We'll have ample time to figure out the rest later. If we succeed in curing him, Victor could even give us answers willingly."

Erick gets up and wraps me in his arms. "You're right. You're right. The good news is that I still don't think he suspects a thing about me, but he increased his surveillance of the city again. I had to jump through hoops to get here undetected today."

"Do we need to move up our timetable then?" I ask, my face firmly planted in his shirt, voice muffled.

I feel him nodding his head over me. "Yeah. I'm only waiting for Finn's go-ahead with the equipment and confirmation of our plan. He thinks he found out how to trap my father to push him to empty his magic."

"When?" I ask.

"Tomorrow. We move tomorrow."

Chapter 40

FINN

I SPENT LAST NIGHT finishing what I hope will be worthy of my forefathers. Not many bother to learn the ancient art of rune carving. Well, there are not many rune masters left in the world to learn from, either. With the discovery of new metals and gems that can sustain big amounts of energy by themselves, the discipline lost its appeal. Indeed, the carving is mainly used to imbue more magic into an object.

I thankfully have a friend who lets me borrow his forge outside business hours. It's been a long time since I had the chance to stretch those magical muscles. I was worried I'd lost my touch. However, the small disk that I was able to fashion was a resounding success. I know Erick was pissed that I forced his hand to syphon me that first time in training, but I needed to test my work. The engraved talisman, no bigger than a nickel, should not have been able to contain the amount of energy Erick transferred into it while remaining stable, meaning not disintegrating and releasing the spell. Nevertheless, the rune carvings made it so.

To be successful, the engraving of the runes must be precise. It requires special skills and equipment. In the case of a syphon's convergence disk, the delicate procedure's goal is to create a receptacle that can be carried easily while being able to contain huge amounts of magical energy, sorting it through the different rune's channels so that the syphon can use the magic threads together or separately at will.

Erick took to it like second nature and disposed of his preferred pack of cards in favor of the disk that now hangs at his waist. My gear is much heavier than it was the first time we were at the warehouse. I need a lot of items and ingredients for the confinement spell I devised to trap Victor. It's my first attempt to do one of this magnitude, and I pray to the gods it'll hold. We cannot know exactly how much energy Victor has stored in him and on his person.

Even though it's still the afternoon, the cloud cover is so dense that I can't even see the shape of the setting sun. The foreboding skies combined with nature preparing itself for winter in these last days of September only heightens my inquietude.

"Did you fix your neighbor problem?" Erick asks as we lay low behind a couple of bushes, waiting for Evie's signal. She's the lookout for the guards' rotation.

I know he's only trying to release some of the tension I hold. I'm happy to go with it. "I didn't. Bree did."

His forehead creases in amused surprise. "How did she manage that?"

"It's not funny," I angry-whisper. "One morning, Gavin just went to the city council on his own initiative to retract all his complaints. He even came in to apologize to me for his crappy behavior with a big bouquet of flowers. But all the while, I could see him glancing around nervously. It was obvious he was looking for Bree, but when I asked her about it, she refused to tell me anything. She just stood there looking mighty proud of herself."

Erick snickers at that, and I elbow him in the ribs before I turn back around and focus on the location where Bree, Eleanor, and Riley are also waiting for Evie's signal. I loathed letting her go without us, but we all agreed she needed to take a different entry to get to the prisoners sooner in order to administer to them the care needed so they would be able to get out on their own two feet. Bree should be able to help her with the healing bits, and, truthfully, Eleanor, together with Bree are a small army by themselves, which reassures me a little. I gave all the girls a skeleton key that will nullify the nasty charm of the cages. The three of them should be able to work fast enough so that when Erick and I get to them, neutralizing every guard we come across, they will already be set to exit the building.

Then, it's only a question of me working quickly to cast the confinement spell and get out as fast as I can from the perimeter with the anchor of the spell to make sure it's out of reach from Victor while Erick puts up small explosives to destroy the crates full of artifacts so that his father cannot syphon them and use their magic.

If my calculations are right, and I'm convinced they are, we'll have enough time to do all of this before Victor himself is alerted and shows up on the premises.

My heart hammers in my chest. So much of this plan rides on perfect timing and stealth.

So much can go wrong.

As the autumn days get shorter, night comes earlier, which helps us tremendously. The hoot of an owl floats on the wind in the pattern we were all waiting for. Erick moves first, and I follow. We walk stealthily to the same door we used when we were here last, but, this time around, I don't have to fiddle with anything.

The bugs I left last time, physical as well as magical, haven't been discovered. I only have to press my passkey to unlock all the warehouse's exterior entrances for the next ten seconds. By the time Erick makes the two steps required to get to the door handle, I already have all the cameras on loops. The magical wards let us through without any resistance or alarms, and we enter the installations.

That was the easy part, though.

Erick walks in front of me, making sure the corridor is clear, his gun held straight in front of him. The silencer on it makes it look more like a toy than the real thing. Erick gained muscle weight with all the training—we all did— and he looks especially good in his long-sleeve Henley. But I have no time to dwell on the fact. A bullet ricochets off the wall next to my head. By the time I pick up my own gun and get in position, Erick has already eliminated the threat silently—a young guard. I'd hoped we could do this without the loss of life, but I suppose it was wishful thinking on my part.

Without missing a beat, Erick takes hold of the dead man's radio and uses it to warn the other guards that there is a threat that has escaped the building with valuable items. If we're lucky, the majority of them will give pursuit to our imaginary threat.

Using the device tied to my wrist, I remotely disable all the valid codes that unlock the doors to the room with the cages, all except my code. This way, no guard will be able to check on the prisoners in the melee.

Erick and I have to duck and hide a couple of times in the scuffle as, like we hoped, most of the men run outside armed to the teeth.

It's total silence when we get to the ghost room door, and we're able to slip inside easily.

Relief floods my body when I see all the prisoners but one out of their cages. As I get closer, I notice that the person left in one of the cages wears a guard uniform and is no longer breathing. His hands are charred.

Following my line of sight, Eleanor walks over and answers my silent question. "I rendered him unconscious, but when he woke up a couple of minutes later, he thrashed against the bars. At that point, we had turned back the key, so the spell was working again, and it did that to him." Her voice is shaky, and her eyes well with unshed tears.

It takes a beat for my brain to catch up. Tears? It should be impossible in her condition. But it's not the best time to ponder this, so I file the information for later.

Erick has already begun sticking explosives to the different boxes while keeping an eye on both entrances to the room. I approach Riley, who is crouched on the ground, trying to bind a witch's leg as best she can after slathering it generously with pomade. The woman's face contorts in pain, but she grits her teeth and lifts a determined gaze when she notices me walking over.

"When will you be able to move them?" I ask.

Riley doesn't even look at me when I speak to her. "There are still two of them to patch up, but after that, everybody should be able to move," she answers while rummaging through her stuff for a potion to give to her patient.

Bree's movements are a blur as she distributes water and energy bars to the treated prisoners. Most of them are huddled close to the outside door already.

I find myself a discreet spot out of sight and get all my stuff out to cast the confinement spell. The anchor, a metal box welded shut, is heavy in my hands. All the charmed items needed are already trapped inside of it, including a ring belonging to Victor procured by Erick. All that's left to do is activate the spell and tie it to the perimeter of the outside gate. Then, I need to get the box out of the trap so that Victor cannot syphon the energy from it. I would have preferred not to need an anchor, but the spell I designed is too powerful to be held only by me.

If everything goes according to plan, we will all be able to get in and out of the magical enclosure at will, while Victor won't get so much as a hair outside the gate.

The sounds around me are drawn out as I concentrate on the litany of chant-like words I had to memorize for this spell. Silver threads of power slowly wrap around the metal box, creating a tight net. The container becomes warm as the items inside activate.

Out of nowhere, a huge explosion throws me to the ground, but I manage to keep my hold on the box and maintain my energy. Through the rubble and dust, I see a black head of hair sit up—Erick is okay. But my relief is short-lived. Victor enters the space, dragging the body of one of his men by the arm. The guard doesn't seem to be breathing; Victor has syphoned him completely—power and life. He takes three more steps before letting the limp corpse fall unceremoniously to the ground.

No, no, no. We were supposed to have more time than this.

Bile rises into my mouth as I contemplate my choices. Erick is furtively crawling around to reach Riley's side at the back of the room. I can't get to them without revealing my position and giving up the confinement spell, which would mean that everything we've done so far was for nothing.

"Well, well, well. What do we have here?" Victor's voice is devoid of any emotion. It sends a chill down my spine. His gaze stops on Riley, Bree, Eleanor, and the freed prisoners, who were thankfully out of reach of the detonation. Victor's cruel smile exposes a row of perfect white teeth.

"A special delivery? Just for me?" he mocks. "How gracious of you."

The building energy of my spell is starting to fade. I have to pick up where I left off quickly if I don't want it to fail. My words are no louder than a murmur as I hide behind one of the big pillars supporting the roof and resume my task. From my position, I still can keep an eye on the scene without being seen.

Erick is almost to Riley's side when his father sends a nasty petrifying spell her way. I don't know if Erick stored enough energy in his disk to make a shield big enough to protect everyone. It feels like everything goes in slow motion. Erick takes hold of his disk with one hand while lifting the other hand. Cloudy white energy sparks from his palm and into a giant dome. He falls to one knee as his shield takes the hit. The freed witches are crying and screaming in fear.

If I thought Victor's features were cold before, the look he gives Erick at that moment is made of sheer malevolence. Undiluted terror freezes my blood.

"You are no longer a son of mine," Victor spits through gritted teeth before launching toward them.

Without missing a beat, Eleanor wrenches Erick's gun from its holster and bolts from the group.

No. What is she doing?

Bree appears at Erick's side to prevent him from following Eleanor. The anguish on his face is almost too hard to look at. Eleanor raises the gun to Victor's head and empties the magazine.

All the bullets hover in the air in front of him for a moment before falling to the ground. Victor didn't even move a finger. He only did it with his mind. Holy fuck!

"Lenny, come back behind the shield!" Erick shouts to her, but it's useless. She goes to punch Victor, but he ducks easily. As he gets back up, he swipes her feet from under her. Then he crouches back down, bites his thumb, and traces a symbol on her forehead in blood.

The effect is immediate. Her skin turns a rich dirt-brown as she crumbles into dust, only leaving her clothes behind.

"No!" Erick bellows, the sound vibrating with sorrow. All the while, Riley kept on task, and everyone is now up and walking. Despite the tears running like waterfalls down her cheeks, she continues to help the prisoners to the door. At the same time, Bree wrestles Erick in the same direction. My heart bleeds at the sight, and my own eyes start to water.

It's then that I hear a familiar rumbling coming from the metal box I'm still holding. Next, a loud click announces the success of the activation of the confinement spell. However, it also announces my position, and Victor turns his stormy gray eyes on me. I scramble to hit the unlock button to the exterior door on my watch-like device and send the anchor flying toward Riley. The prisoners don't need prompting. They bolt out of here with speed they shouldn't have in their condition. Riley's mixtures worked wonders.

Since the anchor is powered by my energy, if Victor catches and syphons me, he kills the spell. Erick knows this, too. As I'm about to cast a protection spell as well as a speed charm for me to get out of harm's way, Erick frees himself from Bree's grip and calls to his father to get his attention.

"Stop! Dad! Stop!" he shouts to Victor as he walks slowly toward him, hands in the air in surrender.

Victor considers him for a moment. With each of Erick's steps, my heart jumps in my chest. I can't let him get close to his father. The combat spell I'm gathering usually manifests instantly, but I'm drained from my earlier workings, and part of my magic is tied to the anchor, feeding it.

Meanwhile, Erick is still trying to reason with his father, still thinking that he wouldn't hurt his own son. "Come on, Dad. This isn't you. It's all the power you keep inside that clouds your mind. I just want to help you."

No. No. Come on, Finn.

Victor's sharp laugh cuts through the space like a knife. "Help me? You think I need help?"

I'm too late.

As soon as Erick is in grabbing distance, Victor lunges for his throat. Erick is not fast enough to dodge the grab. With inhuman strength, Victor lifts his son from the ground. Erick thrashes against the hold, trying to kick his father to escape.

"Oh, son. Pathetic. You're not even trying to syphon my power from me. What a disappointment you've turned out to be. Well, if you're going to get in the way." That's all Victor says before throwing his son across the room. Erick hits the wall just over Riley's head. His inert body falls to the ground with a sickening thump.

No.

That's when my magic decides to launch.

Chapter 41

RILEY

THE SOUND COMING OUT of my throat at the sight of Erick flying through the room is more a cry from my soul than a scream of horror.

We almost had it. All the witches were out with Bree, but I couldn't leave Finn and Erick behind. I know I should bolt with the anchor. That's what we agreed to, but I can't.

As I crouch beside Erick's prone body to take his vitals, Finn's magic blasts Victor back into his crates of artifacts. As soon as Finn is sure Victor landed in the middle of the crates, he activates the explosives.

Half of the room goes up in flames, but I don't register the amplitude of it. My focus is entirely on Erick. He doesn't breathe, and I can't feel his heartbeat.

No, no, no... You won't die on me. Not now. Not ever.

My mind plays tricks on me, and for a split second, I see Diane lying there, dying, all over again.

A heavy hand lands on my shoulder, and I look up into desperate green eyes.

"Can you save him?" Finn asks as he maintains a protection field around us that, I now realize, protected all of us from the explosion.

I reach out with tendrils of dark powers. I can feel Erick's energy escaping through my fingers like sand, leaving his body on its way to the other side. But enough is still there. I have helped plants that were farther gone than this, but they were plants, not humans, not a lover.

My mind goes a hundred miles a minute. "I don't know. I'm untrained. I've never used my necromancy on a human before. What if it goes wrong?"

"Wrong is better than dead," Finn says. "I trust you. The decision is yours."

Every fiber of my body tells me this is a bad idea, but my heart disagrees strongly. I use the war raging in me to bring forth and merge both sides of my powers. Soft green healing energy rises through the black tendrils of death, creating a cradle in which I hold onto Erick's dim life force. At the same time, I work on repairing his broken body.

Pain rises steadily through my whole being. The more I attempt to take control of death, the worse the pain gets, but I can't let go. I am shaking violently with the strength it takes to stay upright.

Then, I feel something else in Erick, something aware and hungry, something empty. A second later, my magic starts to leave me in big bursts, as if Erick's void was drinking greedily from me. Colors quickly replace the ashen gray on Erick's face, but at this rate, I'm not sure how long I will be able to stay connected to him without passing out.

"Riley, release him!" Finn's voice is so far away. "His void is devoid of emotion or conscience. Its only priority is to survive. Let go, or it will syphon you dry!"

I shake my head vigorously, or at least I try to, unable to speak my truth. Erick's not strong enough yet. He needs more, and I can give him more. I know I can. Agony sings in my bones, and I welcome it. My body feels like it will rip in two, but I will myself to stay conscious.

A loud crashing sound comes from the rubble on the other side of the space at the same time as Erick springs into a sitting position. Finn looks back into the room while Erick's panicked gaze lands on me. He immediately scoots out of reach.

"No," Erick mouths. At first, I don't understand why he would have that reaction. I try to jump into his arms in celebratory relief, but all I achieve is almost face-planting on the cement floor. Finn catches me at the last minute.

I can't move. It feels like my body weighs a thousand tons. Every sound is muffled as if I were underwater.

"Erick, we need to leave." Finn hurries as he picks me up in his arms. "Now!"

When my head rests on Finn's shoulder, I get a glimpse of a form crawling from the wreckage of the explosion.

I cannot help, cannot do anything while Finn carries me, running to the edge of the property and through a big hole in the fence that was previously made for our escape. Erick follows closely on our heels, limping and carrying the anchor of the spell. All the others, including Evie, are still here instead of far away in the van we rented. I'm too exhausted to be angry.

Finn lays me down, facing what's left of the warehouse, and the carnage shakes me to my core. Victor's employees lay dead on the grounds of the property. It's evident to me they weren't killed by the explosion. Their bodies are not mutilated or missing limbs. No, this was the work of a syphon.

I find the strength to look up at Finn and Erick, who are both fixated on one of the only doors of the building left standing. "What did you see?" My tongue feels like it's made of plasticine.

I don't have to wait long for an answer. Victor appears through the opening and walks toward us. His clothes are in tatters, hanging in pieces from him. Half of his handsome face is bloodied beyond recognition but repairing itself rapidly. I guess that answers the question about the life force he syphoned. He's like a fucking cat with nine lives.

The mask has fallen. What's left of his features is unhinged. His strides look disconnected, abrupt.

"You will make an excellent battery, my dear," Victor shouts, his gaze trained on me. Coming up to the fence, he doesn't slow his pace. When he makes contact with the confinement spell, we hear a loud cracking noise, and Victor is thrown backward. That was the easy part, though. I pray to the gods that Finn's spell will sustain Victor's wrath.

Victor comes up to the barrier once more. He runs a hand over it, unable, as all void witches are, to syphon energy from thin air. His gaze roams the ground around us until it lands on the metal box Erick gave to Bree. She's still holding on to it like it is a comforting teddy bear.

His features become feral. "You dare try to imprison me?" Victor roars. "I will flay you all alive! You will learn what it means to trap a god!" With that, he takes a deep breath and, keeping both his palms flat against the energy of the barrier, stomps on the ground. The amount of energy he releases is meant to hotwire the confinement. The invisible barrier groans and ripples under the assault.

I turn to Evie and pull on her leggings to get her attention through the chaos. "Please leave and take everyone with you."

"What? No! I'm not—"

"Listen to her." This from Finn. "Even if I pride myself on my excellent research and execution, we need to get them all to a hospital."

Evie huffs, but she relents. She bends down and hugs me before gathering the others.

"Oh, leaving so soon?" Victor shouts with venom in his tone. "You don't want to wait for the party? Oh well, I will have to content myself with the necromancer then."

As soon as Evie gets to her, Bree raises a questioning gaze to Finn, who only nods his assent. Bree brings her fist to her heart and then moves the same palm toward Finn, who does the same thing. I've come to understand that this is the elven symbol for *I love you*.

Bree turns around and helps the wounded forward. The girls already have their orders. They know where to take the witches.

In the meantime, Victor doubles his efforts in attacking the wards. Finn's body is taut, ready to spring into action if the spell falters. The amount of magic in the atmosphere is raising the hairs on my body. But still, the spell holds.

Good. We need to make sure Victor empties himself as much as possible of all that power that clouds his thoughts. The best way to do that is for him to continue to struggle against the restraint.

Victor snarls in rage. He walks in a circle for a moment, a predator in a cage. Then he throws his might at the barrier once again. It looks like fire shooting from his hands, trying to melt the resistance of the wards. The energy of the barrier starts to become more and more fluid.

Finn jumps to the metal box that Bree left on the ground beside him. When he touches it, a thin film of ice forms on its surface, which, in turn, decreases the temperature of the barrier.

Victor cannot sustain this attack for very long. His stored magic finally sputters and dies. His breath is labored, and he falls to the ground. Erick takes an instinctive step forward to help his father, but he brings himself to order before going too far and across the barrier.

"Dad, I'm doing this to help," he says gently as if to a wounded animal.

Victor bursts out laughing. Then his full belly laugh turns into manic giggles. When, at last, he looks back at his son with bloodshot eyes, he is almost fully healed, but he looks to have aged a good decade.

"This word again. *Help*. I don't think you grasp the concept of help. Or loyalty, for that matter," he huffs. "You're so wrapped up in the stories you tell yourself. You don't take time to search for the truth."

"What truth?" Erick asks, throwing his hands in the air in exasperation.

Victor smiles like the cat that ate the canary. "There are things you don't know. Things you never suspected. Things I hid from you. You just put everyone in peril by trapping me. *Everyone*. Including your pets over there. If you free me, I'll explain everything."

"Nice try, crazy pants," I cough from my spot on the ground.

“Dad,” Erick pleads, “we’ll free you. I promise. Once you’re cured, we’ll free you.”

Victor doesn’t even bother giving a response. He only gets up, dusts himself off, and storms off the way he came, presumably in search of salvageable artifacts to drain.

Chapter 42

ERICK

CLARENCE IS ROUNDING UP the rest of my father's men in the city. After what my dad did to their colleagues and the fact that I was able to imprison him, they didn't need much convincing that I was now their new leader. I had to make an appearance at my father's main hideout and "perform" to lay claim to my new position. Lucky for me, I've been acting a made-up persona for most of my adult life, so they all bought it. The promise of money and increased status did the trick to secure me a pretty sizeable team.

Many were already turn-coats and part of my intel network anyway—Clarence included. Even if he played the hard ass when he became my father's right hand, he ended up trusting me more and more in the last few months until I eventually won him over, like many others. So today, with the stunt we pulled, he was one of the first to bend the knee, which helped my cause tremendously.

From the gang's point of view, it all just looked like a successful, well-planned coup that was months in the making. Although I don't feel very victorious right now. The important thing is that they now respect me for it. Well, most of them, anyway.

My father hasn't come out of his hiding yet. We couldn't stay there waiting indefinitely, so I placed my most trusted employees to stand guard on the perimeter of what was left of the warehouse with express instructions to contact me at any change in the situation. Anyway, my dad has no magic left and nothing to syphon from, so the dangerous part is behind us.

Now we wait to see what the emptiness of power does to his mental state.

We were lucky to have Paul and a couple other human moles on the police force. The explosion passed for a conveniently planned demolition job. The necessary paperwork was planted in the different computer systems they needed to be in. Paul also made sure that no one came looking our way for the foreseeable future, including curious neighbors, by deviating the traffic through another sector.

Riley sits down carefully on my lap while I finish my phone conversation with Clarence.

"Keep me informed of any new development." I hang up and toss the phone on the coffee table of Finn's living room. I'm still not used to employing this stern of a voice or this tight of instructions, but my "rule" only started a few hours ago. I need to secure my territory against a possible takeover from other groups and make sure everybody in my own hierarchy falls in line. The time for change and new politics will come later when the dust has settled.

Riley rubs her face in the crook of my neck like a cat. I still have the impulse to get away from her. She saved me. But it almost cost her her own life because my stupid void took over and wanted to live at all costs, not caring what or who it was draining. Thankfully, she has already regained most of her colors, and all that seems to remain from the ordeal is her exhaustion.

I knew she was powerful, but she practically brought me back to life with minimal training. It's as scary as it is amazing. I physically feel great. My injuries—a broken rib, internal bleeding, multiple lacerations and bruises, and a concussion, as Riley informed me—are all but a distant nightmare.

"Is everything okay?" she asks. "I don't like you having to do this."

I reach behind her to play with the ends of her raven hair. It's a miracle she's not afraid of me, of my touch, after what happened. "I know, Darkness, but it's the safest way to avoid a bloodbath in a struggle for power in the city. Once everything settles, I'll make other arrangements."

I have no intention of becoming my father. What I don't tell her, though, is that I haven't figured out yet any solution that won't require me to go into hiding and leave the city—leave them. Loss compounds on itself at the thought.

"I'm so sorry for Eleanor," she whispers.

I can't even utter her name. It still doesn't feel real that she's gone. I try to rub away the tightness in my chest, but it's useless. The person that has been my family for the last seven years is dead. Worse. She's dead because she wanted to protect me, to protect us. I never should have allowed her to come. I should have locked her ass in the panic room of the bunker and picked her up when everything was done. She would have been pissed at me, but angry is better than dead.

I. Killed. Her.

"Stop that," Finn says as he approaches us with tumblers of amber liquid that probably cost more than my monthly expenses. "Your thoughts are written all over your face. You're not responsible for Eleanor's demise. Your father is. We both know she would have never allowed you to go to the warehouse without her by your side." He drops the glasses on the table with a clunk and sits on his couch.

Again, I don't have an answer to that because I can't undo the damage created by the fact that, in the end, I wasn't smart enough to anticipate the situation and save her.

Finn pushes a glass of liquor into my hand and then clinks it with his own. After draining our glasses, he refills them and gives a third one to Riley. I don't know how long we've been sitting here—dirty, bloody, lost in thoughts—just looking at the bottom of our drinks when Finn's cell phone pings, making us all jump out of our skin.

Finn picks up his phone and reads the notification. "All the prisoners are okay and cared for." His words allow me to take a small breath of relief. "Bree and Evie are returning to the bunker to clean up and sleep safely. We'll devise something permanent tomorrow."

He walks to his bedroom and then comes back out after a minute. "I just checked the anchor, and everything is fine."

He left the metal box on one of his bedside tables. He placed an alarm charm on it, similar to the one he gave Riley. If the barrier falters, we'll know it.

Without a word, he takes my free hand and tugs Riley and me up. The usual sparks of magical energy coursing under his skin feel far away, and I hate it. He had and still has to use a lot of his inner resources to create and maintain that confinement spell. I hate that this situation has taken so much out of the most important people in my life.

"The only thing left to do is to take care of ourselves," Finn says while Riley enters the confines of his arms to snuggle.

They are so perfect it's almost too painful to look at. I can't help but take the remaining step to wrap my arms around them, my face in Finn's neck and my body flush with Riley's back. Our breathing synchronizes, and after a moment, I have trouble knowing where my body ends and theirs begin.

It's done. We actually pulled it off. Not without loss, no, but it's over. We can dare to dream of a future now.

Together.

The air thickens between us as exhaustion and grief slowly morph into comforting touches, then into need. Hands start to roam around, mouths start to kiss, and I finally allow myself to just be in the moment. Nothing else exists, no past, no future, just us. My lips glide down the side of Finn's neck as smoothly as the rogue tears escaping my eyes. We quickly become a tangle of salt water and staccato breaths.

"We should clean off first," Riley breathes, her body languid between us.

"Mm-hmm," Finn acquiesces while biting her jaw, making her whimper.

I take an experimental step to see if they will take my lead, and they do. Without missing a beat, I herd them toward the bedroom, tugging off pieces of clothing as we go. Finn growls in frustration at Riley's bra, not being able to unhook it. I simply take hold of it and rip it apart. Her small squeal of surprise is followed by a moan when I make up for my offense by taking one of her earlobes into my mouth, sucking and biting gently. Our now naked bodies are moving in unison against each other.

"Shower?" I ask.

"Yes," Riley answers.

The sound of the water running comes from the bathroom. Gods, I love Finn's powers—or technology. At this point, I am too wound up to decipher which one he used.

The prospect of shower sex only sends extra blood south. I need to feel them more, to be closer, so I pin them to the wall separating the bedroom and the bathroom, turning Riley to face me. As I press my erection to her belly, her behind rubs on Finn's dick, who can do nothing but take it since my arms cage them against the wall. We all groan in pleasure-filled agony, our movements becoming increasingly hurried.

At this rate, I don't even know if we'll make it to the shower.

Finn takes hold of my face to look straight into my eyes. The ink on his arms seems alive under his skin. "I need," he says before looking down at Riley, who is fixed on our mouths. "*We* need. Now."

The two of them are as lost to lust as I am. Witnessing Finn, the scholar, losing his ability to use complete sentences is beyond arousing.

"What my Little Prince wants, my Little Prince gets." My sentence finishes in a hiss as Riley palms my erection.

I move back out of reach, which makes her mewl in disappointment.

"Use your words, Darkness. What would you like?"

Her expression sobers a little before she steps forward and puts her arms around me. "I want you to let us take care of you," she says into my chest.

I feel the remainder of my heart fracture. After what happened today, she still thinks I deserve to be taken care of, even when I failed so many.

"I'm not used to being on the receiving end," I tell her honestly. "But if it's really what you want, I'll do my best." My genuine smile, although shaky, seems to be enough to satisfy her.

When I lift my gaze to Finn, he is fixed on Riley. His face is an open book, and the emotion written there is so potent that it breaks the last of my reluctance. I might as well face it. I will never free myself from the spell they weaved unknowingly around me, nor do I want to at this point. I can't control how I feel any more than they can. We are, for better or for worse, tied together by the spider web of our feelings and experiences.

I tried to rip love from my insides once with Finn, but all it got us was suffering for three years before ending up back together anyway. I am not one to believe in destiny, but what's happening now feels preordained, as if the universe is finally righting itself. As if the fog scrambling my thoughts has finally lifted, and now, I understand at last.

I understand the inevitability of the fall.

Riley takes my hand, then Finn's, and guides us toward the shower fit for a king. Finn's pet name doesn't come from nowhere. I've always seen him as royalty—the heir to one of the most powerful witch families tied to the Sennex. With his preppy outfits and pricy watches, he was to be our future political king. He won't say it, but I know he was and still is more powerful than his parents or his brother, and that's why they wanted him to enter the political playing field.

The only reason his family is not even trying to get him back right now is exactly because of his strength, not just magical but intellectual, too.

Riley, on the other hand, is all instinct and raw power. That's what captivated me at first. But then it changed, and her keen mind and unapologetic integrity cut their way into my heart as surely as the softness of her skin and the darkness of her eyes invaded my senses. She is both wrath and compassion, strength and gentleness, passion and perseverance, life and death… The dichotomy of her is intriguing.

As we enter the shower stall, it takes everything in my power to not take over, to let them decide. If that's what they need to feel better, I'll happily oblige—against my nature or not. Riley rises on her tiptoes to whisper in Finn's ear, her breasts brushing against his arm. All I can do is stare at them with my fingers curled into fists, restraining myself from touching them. Finn nods obediently at what she says and takes position facing the tiled wall, his palms flat against it, his head bent down. The water flowing in rivulets down his back mesmerizes me.

Riley's hips sway sensually as she backs up to the shower bench and sits down. She opens her legs for me. Her folds are swollen and glistening, inviting. But when I take a step toward her, she stops me.

"No, no, no," she tsks. "You'll have us both, don't fret, but I think Finn's been waiting a lot longer than me for this."

On cue, Finn shivers deliciously under the warm water. A pinch of pain and sadness squeezes my chest for a moment at the reminder of the time lost between us, and I give myself to it. I follow the thread of loneliness, despair, sadness, and guilt that have been directing so much of my life in recent years. I follow it to the memories of all those lonely nights touching myself with only the distant memory of his love. I follow it full circle to the present, where I now have the possibility, day in and day out, to do my best to heal all of this, to build something so strong between the three of us that it will never be destroyed, not even by death itself.

"Go on," Riley prompts. "You can play with Finn however you like. Take your pleasure." Her tone turns husky with her last words. I can't help the thrill coursing through my veins at her taking charge. Testing if she likes it or not. I can't promise I won't take back the lead from her, but I'll at least try to leave her in control as long as I can.

With my chest cracked open and my bloody heart out for everyone to see, I go to Finn. At this moment, I don't touch. I can't. All I can do is press my forehead to his back and breathe him in.

"I never thought," Riley says from her seat, "that I could feel this way. That I would find...you."

A small laugh escapes me, and I turn my head slightly to look at her while keeping contact with Finn. "Oh, I know. It feels powerful, strong, alive. It feels—"

"Sacred," Finn cuts in with his head remaining bent as if in prayer.

After that, the energy between us shifts again, as though that simple word changed the very molecular nature of the air around us.

Riley keeps her gaze on me while she trails her hand down her body languorously. Finn's skin heats in time with my quickening breath, his feet moving farther apart in invitation.

This time, I oblige. I take hold of his hair and bring his head to my shoulder so I can kiss him. His hands stay where they are as I roam my own over his chest, the V of his hips, stopping just short of his rigid cock.

"You're magnificent together," Riley breathes, still idly caressing her breasts and parting her folds for us to see.

"Look at our Darkness, Finn. She wants us to give her a show," I say as I take his jaw and turn his head so he can see her. The effect is immediate. His length gives a jump and sends a bead of pre-cum down the tip, which I lazily spread over his crown, making him shiny and ready for me. I crouch and sit down between him and the wall. My head is the perfect height to take him into my mouth.

I assume that when Riley said to take my pleasure, she probably meant using Finn's mouth and body to make myself come, but I have other plans to begin with. I know I'm pushing it and should ask for instructions instead of making decisions. She wanted to take care of me, after all. But neither of them protests my boldness, and I'm only a man made of flesh and blood, so I keep going.

My gaze locks with Finn as I take hold of his dick and give him a tentative pump before guiding him into my mouth. We both groan at the feeling.

"Shit," Finn hisses when I begin to roll my tongue around his length, teasing the tip. The velvet of his skin is glorious. I go slow, hollowing my cheeks as much as I can to draw out every little sound. I'm ravenous for him. For them.

His legs start to shake slightly, but I don't stop. Instead, I feel for the bottle of lube I spotted earlier among the shampoo bottles. Oh, how I love Finn's mind, indeed. Always thinking of every eventuality. I coat my fingers with lube and find his entrance, all the while keeping up the torturous movement of my mouth.

Once Finn's ready to my satisfaction, I push one finger in until I pass the ring of muscle there, which wrenches a strangled sound from his throat. Finn bites down on his lip hard enough to draw blood. The sight almost makes me release on the spot.

When I look sideways at Riley, she's wrapped up in the scene she witnesses. Her dark eyes are huge, and she's now kneeling on the shower floor, not far from us but still out of reach.

I release Finn's length from my mouth. "Come here, Darkness," I beckon.

She all but crawls the rest of the way to us and, fuck me if it's not the sexiest thing I've ever seen. Once she reaches us, I give her the bottle so she can coat her fingers in lube too.

"Go ahead, help me," I utter quietly, waiting to see if she'll go back to taking the lead or not.

In the end, she chooses to go with it. Good girl. She slowly enters one of her fingers beside mine. Finn's cock looks so hard it must hurt. Once he can breathe again, I start to move inside him, easily finding the spot that makes him moan. Riley follows my movements, and after a minute, Finn struggles to stay still.

"Are you okay, Little Prince?" I tease. "Will you come down my throat like a good boy?"

"Yes. Yes," he utters between sighs and moans.

"Another," I tell Riley. I know I'm taking charge and shouldn't in view of what they asked of me, but taking care of them is what I need to feel some semblance of okay again. If they really want to take care of me, that's how they'll achieve it.

Riley glides another finger in while I take Finn's length into my mouth again. My tongue follows the rhythm dictated by Riley's touch, and I relax my throat as much as possible to take him even deeper.

"I can't—" Finn starts. "I'm going to come." His voice is clipped, his breathing erratic, and through the chaos, I squeeze his thigh with my free hand to tell him he can let go.

His hips buck, which sends his dick to the back of my throat. One. Two. Three times, and then he spills inside my mouth. I try to memorize the ecstasy chiseling his features so I can replay it in my mind's eye later. I continue licking and sucking until his orgasm is spent—until I can't take it anymore. The taste of him, the smell of him. It's all too much and somehow not enough at the same time.

I get up and stand between his still-outstretched arms before taking hold of his neck and bringing him in for an aggressive kiss. When we come up for air, he looks completely lost in his aftershocks with a big smile on his face, and I can't help but smile back.

The hunger inside me demands more. With a couple of efficient maneuvers, I quickly have Riley back at her position on the bench and Finn on all fours in front of her.

"Do you have any condoms?" I ask Finn.

He looks back at me from his position on the floor. "Nightstand. But I'm clean. I'm fine without if you are." His admission makes Riley whimper adorably.

My pulse quickens with the thought of having him bare. "I've been tested recently," I tell him with a barely contained growl. "I'm clean."

We are all out of words at this point, and I guide Finn's face to Riley's mound. I don't need to look to know when he makes contact. She hasn't come yet, and she's hyper-sensitized. The sounds she makes are halfway between moans and cries as she bucks under his mouth, pulling on his unruly wet hair. She's already close.

I coat my cock in more lube and prop myself at Finn's entrance. When I start to push slowly inside, Riley's eyes are glued to the point our bodies meet. Once my crown passes the ring of his hole, a shudder that starts with me and ends with Riley passes through us. I stay there, caressing Finn's back, waiting for him to adjust, to relax. It doesn't take long before he starts pushing against me, and I follow his lead, meeting him halfway until I am buried inside him to the hilt.

My balls are so fucking tight I see stars. His heat clenching around me is almost too much pleasure to bear. The vision of Riley disheveled with her legs wide open to Finn's mouth doesn't help either. It's been a fucking long time coming—pun intended—and I have trouble controlling my need to drill into him like a beast right away.

Finn lifts his head and puts his forearms on the bench under each of Riley's thighs, allowing him to take hold of her while keeping his balance.

I give a tentative thrust and look at Riley, who looks at Finn, then back to me and nods. He just came, but he's already hard again. I don't know how long I'll be able to hold it together, so as I slowly pull out of him, I position my hips in a way that I know will rub against Finn's most intimate pleasure spot.

Then I slam back into him to the hilt, making his back bow in pleasure-pain. I'm sure Riley will have finger-shaped bruises from his death grip on her hips tomorrow.

"Do you want to use your safe word?" I ask him through gritted teeth.

"Fuck no," he answers.

The admission frees me, and I surrender completely, ramming inside him at a punishing pace. I don't recognize the sounds I'm making. More animal than man. Finn dives into Riley, doubling down on her clit. She hinges forward, and I meet her over Finn's back in a frantic kiss. The concert of slick sounds and moans creates an erotic symphony that only propels us higher. Riley is the first to come, but Finn doesn't relent, and he carries her orgasm to new heights until she screams her pleasure.

Once she slumps back onto the bench, spent, I seize Finn's shoulders and plaster his back to my chest, holding him in place with a hand on his throat. Then I take hold of his cock with my other hand, jerking him off the way I remember he likes it while I resume my almost violent thrusts.

"Yes, yes, yes...." Finn says like a prayer. When I feel his first jet of cum on my fingers, I allow myself to release deep inside him. My teeth dig into the crook of his neck as both our orgasms feel never-ending. *Mine. Mine. Mine.*

After I pull out of him, I stay there, mesmerized by the sight of my seed dripping from him. Something so small, but something that I thought I had lost forever. Riley sighs happily, bringing me out of my daze. Her hooded eyes peruse my body, and just like that, my cock already begins to stir back to life.

"Come on, Darkness, we'll wash up." For once, she doesn't argue. I gather us all under the water spray and scrub myself while they leisurely wash each other. The smell of Finn's shower gel surrounds us, connecting us.

"For the record, I never thought I would have this either," Finn finally says in a complete sentence.

Genuine laughter bursts out of me, but I sober up quickly when he turns around, visibly moved.

He puts his hand on my cheek. "Do that again," Finn says. "I want to hear you laugh again."

But I can't replicate my reaction. Not because I'm not grateful to be here with them but because the loss is too fresh for me to consciously want to laugh.

Riley seems to understand my hesitation. She drapes Finn's arm around her shoulders as she cuddles up to us. "I know it might take time to heal," she continues, "but we'll be there to help you through the grief. Okay?" The depth of her gaze tells me she knows a thing or two about grief herself.

"Thank you, both of you. I don't deserve—" Riley doesn't let me finish my spiel before she pulls us in for a messy three-way kiss.

"Yes, you do," she gasps as I squeeze one of her breasts before sealing my lips with hers once again.

"She's right," Finn mumbles while trailing his mouth on my jaw.

I grab Riley's ass, and she hops up to wrap her legs around my waist. Finn goes behind her to kiss down her neck, and we move as one to the bed, dripping water and all. She's grinding against my rigid cock eagerly, and I groan at the feeling of her slick pussy.

"Oh Darkness, you're so wet, you're dripping all over my cock."

"Please, tell me you're fucking my brains out now," she whines, prompting Finn to grunt.

I grin against her lips. "Since you asked so nicely."

I lay her down gently onto her back on top of the sheets while Finn takes a place at the head of the bed, where he pillows her head on his thighs.

When I move toward the nightstand for protection, Riley grabs my hand. "I'm under a birth control elixir, and I'm clean. I want to feel you. I mean, if it's okay with you."

She tugs me down gently, and I can't resist the pull of her eyes. I position myself between her legs. "You're sure this is what you want?" I ask as I brush her hair out of her face.

As a response, she slips her hand between our stomachs and guides my length to the heat of her cunt. Then she raises her arms over her head and takes hold of one of Finn's hands, wanting to be connected to both of us. Finn and I look at each other, taken aback by her small gesture.

Then my focus comes back to her face. I watch her every reaction as I enter her, inch by slow inch. Although she is more than ready for me, I want to make sure she has a good time. But after only a couple of seconds, I start to question my life choices as the slowness of my movements is pure pleasurable torture.

When I bottom out inside of her, we moan in unison. Finn uses his free hand to play with her nipples, to caress every inch of her skin he can reach. Then I start to move, and fuck me, she's tight.

The feeling of being inside her is insane. It's like dying and coming back to life at the same time. I take deep breaths as I pick up my pace and angle my hips to hit her G-spot.

"Oh gods," she moans, and Finn bends down to drink the sound from her lips. Seeing them kiss greedily is my undoing. I lift and hook her legs over my shoulders and pick up speed. I grunt and growl over them. Finn lifts his head from her, and his swollen lips reach mine while his thumb finds Riley's clit. She detonates, crying out our names.

I bring Finn down with me as I bare my weight on her, my thrusts becoming more and more uncoordinated. I leave Finn's mouth only to bury my teeth in her shoulder, marking her as mine too, while my orgasm barrels down my spine, and I pump her full of my cum. *Mine. Mine. Mine.* The word keeps replaying over and over in my head until it becomes absolute. I am distantly aware of Finn soothing Riley with kisses and hushed words, allowing us to leisurely come back to earth.

After quickly washing up again, Riley barely made it to the bed before she fell into slumber, exhausted. Finn and I followed suit not long after. It's completely out of habit for me to sleep this well, but the day's events have completely wiped me out.

I'm still deep into sleep when I feel hands shaking me. Then Riley's panicked voice reaches my dreams, and I startle awake.

"Erick! He's not here! Finn's not here!" she cries. Her dread becomes mine when I note the orange glow illuminating her face. The anchor is as bright as a lamp on the bedside table.

Chapter 43

RILEY

ALL I CAN PICTURE in my mind's eye is Finn's body mutilated among the rubble of the warehouse.

"Drive faster," I order Erick, who hasn't spoken a word to me since we left Finn's home. He, too, is imagining the worst.

Finn's car GPS puts him close to the warehouse still. It has been stationary since we looked it up. I try one last time to call him. No answer.

I don't even wait for the old beat-up taxi Erick borrowed to come to a complete stop before jumping out and hitting the ground running.

"Riley!" Erick shouts from behind me. "Riley, wait! It might be a trap. You don't know what we'll find!"

I know he's right, but at that moment, all I can think is to go faster because I might be too late to save Finn from his fate.

Erick catches up with me at the edge of the field surrounding his father's installations and grabs my arm. "Stop! Stop," he says firmly. "You won't be able to help anybody if you're dead. None of my men answered their radio. We don't know what we'll find. Please trust me. I want to get him back alive and well as much as you do."

He lets go of my arm and motions for me to stay silent and follow him. It takes all my strength to go along with his instructions, to subdue the panic, but I know he's right, so I do my best to calm my racing heart. He moves carefully forward, his gun raised before him, scanning the perimeter in the early twilight. None of Erick's employees are there. Where are they?

Unease crawls under my skin. Once Erick is satisfied that the outside of the fence is secure, we carefully cross what used to be the threshold of the confinement spell. There is no movement, not even a bird singing. The stillness is chilling as if the land itself does not dare to make a sound. Nausea rises steadily in me as we step over the corpses of the syphoned guards we couldn't get out of the enclosure of the spell yesterday. We had to wait for Victor to be somewhat sane again before risking crossing the ward to get them out of there for a proper funeral. So many vacant stares, the terror of their last moment preserved in their rigid, contorted bodies.

We walk into what's left of the building and search through the rubbles, but no one is there either. It's completely deserted. When we're about to turn around and go back outside to see if we haven't missed anything, Erick halts abruptly. I move around him to look closer at his findings and stop breathing altogether. There, on an intact piece of wall, is a message written in a dark substance. The metallic scent of fresh blood makes my stomach churn. My worst fear becomes a living thing inside of me as I read it over and over, hoping my eyes are deceiving me.

The necromancer for the boy...

The End

Thank you so much for reading the first part of Riley, Finn, and Erick's story! I hope you enjoyed it! If you did, please consider leaving a review.

Want to know what happens next for these three? The story continues with *Necromancer*, book two in the Fate Cycle series.

The Fate Cycle is a four-book series in the dark fantasy romance genre following our throuple, Finn, Riley, and Erick, through their epic journey.

Keep up with my latest projects and subscribe to my newsletter at *www.samfairburn.com*

ABOUT *the author*

Sam is a Canadian author of fantasy romance and dark romance with a healthy dose of spice. She loves daydreaming about new characters and can often be found staring into the abyss of the great nothingness, completely lost in thought. She also dislikes talking about herself in the third person. Hence, I'm going to stop this author bio here.

♥ I am deeply grateful for every reader who takes time out of their day to lay their eyeballs on one of my books. I couldn't be an author without you. ♥

ISBN 978-1-998204-00-7

9 781998 204007

Made in the USA
Columbia, SC
05 October 2024

43713137R00205